GABRIEL'S ANGEL

GABRIEL'S ANGEL

Mark A Radcliffe

Bluemoose

First published in 2010 by
Bluemoose Books Ltd
25 Sackville Street
Hebden Bridge
West Yorkshire
HX7 7DJ

www.bluemoosebooks.com

British Library Cataloguing-in-Publication data
A catalogue record for this book is available from the-British-Library

Hardback   ISBN 10: 0-9553367-7-5
ISBN 13: 978-0-9553367-7-5

Paperback ISBN 10: 0-9553367-8-3
ISBN 13: 978-0-9553367-8-2

Printed and bound in the UK by Short Run Press, Exeter

For Katie and Maia

Acknowledgement

Acknowledgements

I'd like to thank Bonnie Powell for her brilliant eyes and unwavering support and Gail Houghton, Tilly Bones, Paul Read, Gerry Holden, Penny Faith, Laetitia Zeeman and Matthew McGuchan for reading and commenting on early drafts and generally being kind when kindness helped. I'd also like to thank Kevin, Hetha, Lin and the family of Bluemoose for being so supportive, enthusiastic and energetic. And last but not least Katie for everything.

1

When Gabriel woke up nothing hurt, although as he opened his eyes he had the clear sense that something should. He turned his head from side to side and tentatively lifted himself up on to his elbows. He could move. There were no shooting pains, no absent or broken limbs, no pool of blood. A minute ago, unless he'd been dreaming, he had been walking through Shoreditch. He had gone to the bagel shop to buy bagels and a doughnut for Ellie. A moment ago he heard a car behind him, on the pavement. It had hit him—hard.

He was lying on a double bed in what appeared to be a motel room, complete with coffee and tea-making facilities and what looked like a trouser press. He was wearing the same clothes he remembered putting on that morning. The same clothes he had worn to what might laughingly be called the "job interview" at GirlsandGames.com.

He had no idea what he was doing here.

Slowly, he got up and walked across the room to the dressing table. As he stood he gently touched the back of his head, then prodded his back. No holes, no bumps, no stitches. He looked in the mirror. No cuts, no bandages, the right number of eyes pretty much where he had left them. In front of him, next to a box of scented tissues, was what looked like a business card.

He picked it up and read it: 'Welcome, Gabriel. You will be our guest for a while. Put your shoes on.'

'Fuck off,' he mumbled. He sat on the bed and tried to think. He remembered leaving the interview and walking to the bagel shop. He looked around for the salmon and cream cheese bagels. They were nowhere to be seen. Beside him were two more cards. He picked them up and read the first: 'We realise this is confusing. Try to relax.'

'Bollocks. Where are my bagels?'

He looked at the second card. 'You swear a lot,' it said, 'Forget about the bagels.'

Gabriel took out his mobile: 'No network coverage.' There was no phone in the room. 'Typical,' he said. 'No phone but they keep the bloody Bible.'

On the bed was another card; he didn't remember it being there before. He picked it up. 'Please try to be patient; in a few minutes someone will be along to explain things. Perhaps you'd like some herbal tea?'

'Oh for fuck's sake, I've been kidnapped by hippies,' he said loudly. It was possible, he thought, that this was a dream. He got up, walked to the wall, and banged his head against it. 'Ouch,' he winced. He rubbed his head. On the carpet in front of him, beside the skirting board, was another card. He picked it up:

'Don't do that!'

The night before the accident, Gabriel had had an argument with Ellie. Not a big argument, just a normal argument. The kind they had most days. Ellie had suggested, tentatively, that they might want to consider some kind of counselling in an attempt to cut down on the bickering. She wasn't convinced by the idea herself. She had suggested it mostly as a way of pointing out that they were bickering all the time and it was beginning to annoy her. She maybe hoped that mentioning it might have been enough but she wasn't really surprised by Gabriel's response. In fact, deep down she agreed with him. Which just annoyed her more.

'No,' said Gabriel. He had thought about investing this answer with all of the resentment he had collected that day but managed to restrain himself. He'd collected a lot of resentment, he gathered it the way those fat-lipped fish gather food from the bottom of the ocean floor. When Gabriel was having a bad day, he could scoop up ill-feeling from an empty room, and lately he felt that he had had more bad days than might be considered strictly fair.

'Why not?'

'Because they're fucking repulsive.'

'I can always count on you for the balanced view.' Ellie wasn't looking at him; she was sitting on the sofa, her feet on the coffee table, her long black skirt tucked tightly under her legs. She was sifting through a pile of letters. Gabriel hopped from foot to foot behind her. He closed his mouth long enough to pout. He had hoped for just a little attention.

'What are you doing?'

'Looking for a postcode,' she murmured.

'Are we having this conversation or not?'

'Not yet we're not, no.'

'Oh well, let me know when you're ready, won't you.' He overemphasised a sigh. Just in case it might have otherwise passed her by.

'Gabe, it was just an idea. That's all.'

'OK, thanks, but having given it some thought, and weighed up the pros and cons, I feel I would rather circumcise myself with a rusty tin opener.'

'That was plan B.'

Gabriel was a tall man, athletically built, and he was not used to going unseen in a room. When it happened, particularly at home, he didn't like it. There was, he knew, no point in looking exasperated if he was standing behind her, so he moved to the end of the sofa. They were in that place couples go to when they can't quite decide if they are going to start shouting or not. It was a place where they had spent most of last week and the week before that. They'd also visited it for much of the previous April and a fortnight in May. They'd gone on holiday in June, and holidays always made it better, but they couldn't keep away throughout a disappointing July.

'I know what! Fuck the counsellor—' snapped Gabriel.

'I think we'd have to pay extra.'

'Fuck the counsellor, let's go and see an aromatherapist instead—a couple of sniffs of lavender and some ylang ylang ought to swing it; or better still, why don't we go and see a mime artist?'

Ellie ignored him.

'I think that's a much better idea. Every time we have a row we could nip round to Marcel Marceau's house and see what he has to say. Well, obviously, he won't say anything, he'll probably pretend to be in an invisible box for about an hour, and then we'll come home, but I'm sure things will be better.'

She still wasn't looking at him. She hated mime even more than everyone else. She had told Gabriel once that whenever she saw a mute, white-faced performing-arts student in Covent Garden she wanted to punch him. She was sure that he was remembering this when he mentioned Marcel Marceau. He was bringing mime into this argument just to annoy her. The bastard.

'Why don't you start practising now, Gabe? And shut the fuck up.'

And he did. After a while he made her hot chocolate. She said thanks. He kissed her on the top of her head. They watched the news quietly and then they went to bed.

The day of Gabriel's accident had started the way most mornings did. He had brought the sleepy and hormonal Ellie a cup of tea, checked the teletext for any sports news that may have broken in the six hours he had slept fitfully, and subsequently smeared peanut butter on his trousers. Having established the rhythm of the day, he set off for the tube station and was rained on. Gabriel maintained that the advantage of living at the end of a tube line, like Walthamstow for example, or Upper Ongar, is that you always get a seat. The disadvantages are that you have to get on the bloody tube in the first place, and stay on it as the rest of London demonstrates its total lack of spatial awareness by standing on your feet or resting briefcases on your groin. You then have to wrestle past the unmoving, unhelpful, undead just to get off the train, and tramp round the decaying intestines of London Underground to find the bowels of hell that is the Northern Line.

Two more stops and Gabriel was in Camden, and at first it just seemed like an ordinary day.

The first hint that it wasn't came when he tried to log on, only to find the server was down. The next hint, and he really should have picked up on this before now, was that he was on his own apart from the two young administrative assistants, who were huddled in a corner.

'Server down,' said Gabriel matter-of-factly. They both looked at him sympathetically.

'Where is everybody?'

"Everybody" consisted of an editor, the IT guy, and Big Dave, the other writer.

'They're in there,' one of them said, pointing to the editor's office. 'They said to tell you to go in.'

Well, then why didn't you, thought Gabriel, who by now was a bit suspicious. As soon as he opened the door, everyone looked at him and Big Dave said, 'Hello mate, know of any good jobs?'

'Eh?'

'They've pulled the plug,' said the editor. 'I got a phone call late last night. No more website. We're all out of work.'

'Ah, fucking bollocks.'

'Quite,' said Dave.

'I'm going to fuck up the software,' said the IT guy. 'By the time I get through with this equipment, they'll be selling those computers off as hairdryers.'

'Yeah, that's a good way of ensuring you get redundancy pay,' said the editor.

'How much?' asked Gabriel.

'A month's salary for every full year you've been here, plus another month.'

I've been here five years thought Gabriel, that's six months' salary. 'That's not enough.'

Silence.

'Sports websites are not exactly booming at the moment,' said Big Dave.

'Apparently not.'

'Pub?' said the editor. 'First round's on me, then it's every man for himself.'

'Is the pub open?' asked Gabriel.

'I know one that will be,' said Big Dave.

In the pub—one of those large, open-plan affairs with TV screens and onion rings on the lunch menu—Gabriel sat next to Dave.

'What you going to do?'

'No fucking clue,' said Dave. 'All I know is, that it's not just us. Tellsport.com has laid off all its writers. It's just a betting site with a picture of a naked woman now. Worldsports.com closed two weeks ago. The only sites left are betting sites or fronts for TV companies. What are you going to do?'

'No bloody idea,' said Gabriel. 'But to start with, I may get drunk.'

'Sounds like a plan,' said Big Dave.

By lunchtime, workers from some of the companies that shared the building had heard of the redundancies and arrived to sympathise and buy drinks. These included Gabriel's mate Sam, who was Ellie's best friend's husband. Such was his friendship that he was buying them Scotch.

'Will you be able to get work?' asked Sam.

'I can't see it, no work on the websites, all the papers and magazines are full,' said Gabriel. 'Best I can hope for is some freelance, and that's not going to be easy. There are plenty of freelance journalists willing to write about football for next to nothing as long as they get a free ticket and a by-line. I'm a bit old to be competing with them. I need money.'

'What did Ellie say?'

'Haven't told her yet.'

'Right,' Sam said before adding, 'Why not?'

'Because I'd like to offer her a solution to the problem rather than just the problem. She's got enough to worry about at the moment, what with the IVF and the crap boyfriend. Feels like she's doing all the work. Appreciate it if you didn't say anything yet.'

Sam nodded.

'We need a money-making scheme, Gabe,' said Big Dave, who was tanked. 'Both of us—you for the kid you haven't got and me for the kids I never see.'

'Well, short of robbing a bank ...'

'Nobody robs banks any more.'

'Any ideas?'

'There's always GamesandGirls.com'

'Fuck off.'

'It's work.'

'So is drug dealing.'

'Not strictly speaking, it isn't.'

'What is "games and girls"?' asked Sam.

'It's a porn site,' said Gabriel.

'Well, they would describe themselves as a cross-interest website for men,' said Dave. 'Tabloid sports, top-shelf girlie pics, you can access chat with women and read all the latest gossip about football transfers. While you wank.'

'Are they hiring?'

'Not exactly,' said Dave. 'They virtually run themselves with freelancers. £120 a day, no benefits.'

'How do they keep people with money like that?' asked Sam.

Dave and Gabriel just looked at him.

'You thinking of going over to the dark side?' Gabriel said to Big Dave.

'I have child support to pay mate; I can't afford principles. Can you?'

'For fuck's sake.'

'I'm going to give them a call. Want me to mention you?'

Gabriel nodded. 'I'll get us both a drink.'

'I'll get them,' said Sam. 'Scotch?'

When Dave came back he was clearly not a happy man.

'How'd you get on?'

'Bastards.'

'No go?'

'Oh we can go, both of us: tonight at seven o'clock for an informal chat, put us through our paces. After that, any new freelancer is on £100 a day for the first two weeks, until they get to know the ropes. They knew who we were, both of us—said they'd read our work and whilst it might be appropriate for other sites, it might take a while for us to learn to produce material in their style. They fucking loved it.'

'£100 a day?' said Gabriel

'That's not so bad,' said Sam.

'After tax, and national insurance, you're looking at about £65 a day,' said Gabriel.

'Which is shit,' said Big Dave.

'But better than nothing.'

'Yeah—just. You up for it?'

'Not really,' said Gabriel. 'I'd rather eat my feet.' He paused and listened to himself. The bloke who was going to go home drunk and probably bicker again with the woman he loved. The woman who was, as he spoke, injecting herself in the arse with hormones—again—in order to give herself a one-in-four chance of getting pregnant with his child. And as of today, he couldn't even pay for the treatment, let alone—and this was the first time this had occurred to him—support them both if she did get pregnant.

'But if I did, I'd just fall over even more. So until something better comes along, GamesandGirls it is.' And he knocked back the whisky.

'Meet you there at five to seven,' said Dave. 'Leave your pride at home.'

Gabriel got home at 2 p.m. and fell asleep on the sofa. He woke with a start when Ellie came in, and with a headache. He was confused for a moment, and still drunk. And his mouth felt like someone else's trouser pocket.

'What are you doing home?' asked Ellie.

'Home early,' said Gabriel, an octave higher then he was expecting.

'Yes, and drunk.'

'No no, well a little, yes, I had to do this … thing …'

He looked at her. She was so beautiful, swaying about a bit, which was a surprise, but beautiful nonetheless. He looked at the wall because he couldn't lie to her and look at her at the same time, and the wall was swaying around a bit, too. He breathed deep, hated himself a little bit more, and said, 'I've got to work this evening.'

'What? You never have to work in the evenings. Not even during the football season.'

'I do sometimes,' said Gabriel, who found himself feeling quite defensive about the quality of his chosen lie.

'When?'

'Well, now,' he said irritably.

'We are doing this together, aren't we?' said Ellie, who was jammed full of hormones and feeling unusually tearful. Instantly she regretted it because she knew they *were* doing it together, and she didn't really mind that he had to work late; it was just that she wasn't really comfortable with the unexpected at the moment. She liked the routine they had established, it felt like balancing on a log, and if either one of them did anything that made them lose their balance then, well, maybe the drugs wouldn't work.

'Oh come on love, don't do that.'

'Well, what work exactly?'

'They are talking about making some changes—I don't know what that means—I am just watching my back and not making a fuss, pet.'

'Don't go losing your job, Gabe.' Which felt like she'd taken a kitchen blender to his liver.

'Well quite, which is why I think it's best I work late on the rare occasion I am asked.'

If Gabriel were the kind of man to be proud of his capacity to lie, this would constitute a double whammy. He had not only re-emphasised his commitment to keeping his job no matter what, but also put the prospect of his company being in a little trouble on the agenda, without worrying Ellie too much. However, lying well wasn't a major ambition and so he felt sick.

Later, after they'd eaten, washed up, and Gabriel had drunk two litres of water, he watched her as she folded clothes in the bedroom. She moved more carefully than she used to, more conscious of her body than before.

'How are you feeling?'

'Swollen,' she smiled.

'Nervous?'

'No, I don't think so, I expect I will be, I mean waiting for them to make the embryos, I'll be nervous. And then after that I will; won't you?'

Gabriel nodded.

'But at the moment, it's not nerves. At the moment I think I quite like the feeling of possibility, you know what I mean?' Ellie had tears in her eyes but was looking away.

'Yes, I know what you mean.'

'How do you feel?'

'It doesn't much matter.'

'Oh come on.'

'Sorry.' Gabriel paused. How did he feel? 'I don't ever want to let you down, Ellie.'

'I know, but how do you feel?'

'Drunk?'

'Looking for a bit more,' she said with a smile.

'Like the harder I try not to let you down, the more I do. I mean how much fun have I been to live with lately? I'm sorry.'

'Yeah, but how do you feel, Gabe?' Ellie laughed.

'Not worthy.' He laughed too.

'Yeah well, that's about right. How long are you going to be?'

'I don't know, I may be late; go to bed, I'll try not to wake you.'

'I'll see how tired I am. See you later.'

For Ellie, even though she loved him, the whole exchange had been automatic. She would not remember the words she had said an hour after he had gone, because she wasn't really in the world at the moment, she was in herself, preparing herself. Doing housework of the womb with the music turned up really loud so she couldn't notice the comings and goings of the rest of her life.

On the Tube to Old Street he thought about himself, Gabe the Liar. He had always been big on the truth, especially with Ellie. But, he reasoned now—the way people do when it suits them—that perhaps the truth can be the lazy option. Just throw the truth at people and leave them to deal with it. Mainly because your conscience won't let you keep it to yourself. Purging yourself of every minor activity in your life, without any thought for the impact your actions might have on those you love. He was right to lie. At the moment the only thing that mattered was Ellie's well-being. It was all well and good her saying that they were in this together, and of course they were, but whatever happened to them was really happening to

11

her. She needed—she deserved—protection from the nonsense of his stupid redundancy.

I only give her problems, he thought, with the self-dramatisation of a man with too many emotions in him. Followed by: I know, I'll send flowers!

When he got off the Tube, he phoned a florist and ordered a bouquet of carnations, roses, and freesias to be delivered to Ellie first thing in the morning.

'Any message, sir?'

'I love you more than life itself,' he said, before realising that he sounded worryingly like a James Blunt song. 'No, no, no, sorry. Just say, "Sorry for being a twat."'

'Twat?' asked the woman, more used to Mr Blunt et al. 'Is that with a big T?'

'Yeah ... no, no.' Stop apologising, thought Gabriel, that's so self-indulgent. 'I know' he said, without thinking, 'Say, "You're the sunrise."'

'"You're a sunrise?"'

'No, no. "You're THE sunrise." She'll get it.'

'OK,' said the flower lady, unconvinced. 'It's your message.'

He met Dave outside Shoreditch Church, and they walked without speaking down toward Brick Lane, like two men marching to a place that was going to cut their bollocks off. When you get past Shoreditch Church, the place stops being a road to somewhere else and begins to be what it has always been: a grey, impoverished mess. A buffer zone to the City. Just past the church, behind a taxi rank, the streets open up into rows of purpose-built flats, mainly occupied by Asian families. It is quiet there; the most striking thing about it is the complete lack of green. No trees, no grass, just unwashed buildings and one or two mildly anxious brown faces. There are only a few cars, all parked. One with no wheels, another with a broken windscreen. No noise, no life. This is a place used to being a shortcut to somewhere else. When you get past there, the road opens up again: one or two pubs, too many minicab offices, a strip joint, and the smell of Indian food from Brick Lane.

Still they didn't speak, until finally they arrived outside a converted warehouse. Cheap location.

'Here we are.' Dave pressed the intercom buzzer, and a voice said hello.

'Er, hello, Dave Gilbert and Gabriel Bell?'

Gabriel could have sworn he heard a smirk from the third floor, but the intercom was off. The door buzzed open. They walked up the stairs slowly, in part because Big Dave didn't really do stairs, but mostly because it felt as though they were about thirteen and going to see the headmaster for smoking behind the bike sheds.

On the third floor, they were told to sit and wait. Gabriel and Dave sat on a soft imitation-leather sofa in a corridor that passed for reception and watched a hard-faced secretary ignore them while she stared at a computer screen. After a few minutes, the smug bastard in charge popped his head round a door further down the corridor and shouted. 'Alright, come here; I haven't got long.'

Dave and Gabriel shuffled in. Smug Bastard shut the door behind them.

'Out of work?'

They both nodded.

'Didn't see it coming, eh?'

'Not really.'

'Doesn't that worry you?'

'What do you mean?'

'Doesn't it worry you that you didn't see that what you were doing wasn't any good?'

'Depends on what you mean by good,' said Dave.

'Yeah right, thanks professor. I am familiar with your writing. It's dull, but then maybe your editor told you to try to bore the bollocks off the reader. If you work here, you write to style, and you respect your audience, too many so-called journalists these days patronise their audience, preachy fuckers. That's why so many are out of work.'

Gabriel bit his lip so hard it almost bled. Smug Bastard looked at him.

'You think you can produce the kind of stuff we produce? If you think you are too good to give people what they want, you're both tossers.'

'What makes you think we can't write to style?' said Dave, diplomatically.

'Well, we'll see. Remember our readers don't want both sides of the story, they just want gossip they can borrow in the pub, and some tits to think about while they do their job. Transfer spec and links to the girls. You do not write more than 300 words on anything, and you never write about your own club.'

He looked at Gabriel.

'You. Who do you support?'

'Chelsea.'

'Tosser.'

'Fuck off.'

'Ha ha.'

To Dave: 'What about you?'

'Arsenal.'

'Fucking hate Arsenal.'

'Who do you support?' said Dave.

'Spurs.'

'Don't like football then.'

'Careful fat boy, no union here.'

Which was probably thrown in just in case they thought it was going to be OK.

'All right, hundred a day; start at 8:30. There will be some shifts, but we'll see how you go for a couple of weeks. See you tomorrow. Oh, and by the way, I won't necessarily want you both after I've seen what you can do.'

And with that he turned away.

Outside, Dave lit a cigarette and said. 'Well, that went better than I thought.'

'Let's get this straight: are we competing with each other for work?'

'Kind of looks a bit like that, or maybe we are competing with whoever he already has.'

'Feels bad, mate,' said Gabriel. 'I mean it was your idea. I can't, you know, be fighting with you over work, feels wrong.'

'I know, mate,' said Big Dave, exhaling a plume of smoke upward. 'But it's not like either of us has got much choice, is it? I mean gallantry and all that is a good thing, but fuck, you can no more afford not to show up for this than I can.'

They walked in silence toward Brick Lane, Dave puffing on his Marlboro, Gabriel wondering about what was likely to pay the most: freelance sportswriter for porno website, or paper boy?

'It's like Spartacus,' said Dave.

'Eh?'

'Kirk Douglas and Tony Curtis fighting it out at the end, you know, the loser gets stabbed by their mate, the winner gets crucified.'

'I'm Spartacus.'

'No, I'm Spartacus.'

'No, I'm Spartacus ...'

They wandered toward Brick Lane for some bagels. 'I reckon Ellie might like a cream-cheese-and-salmon bagel. May soften the blow.'

'I thought you weren't going to tell her.'

'I wasn't, but I have to. I mean for a week at least I've got some money coming in and this is as close to bringing home a solution as I'm likely to get. Anyway, lying to her makes me feel ill.'

'It will be more than a week. Most of those bozos are shite. If that smug bastard rated them, he wouldn't be hiring us would he?'

'Let's hope not.'

'See ya tomorrow, mate.'

Gabriel sighed. 'Guess so.' He headed back toward the Tube station. He felt OK. There was a part of him that knew he shouldn't, that he was going to work for an immoral lard-arse, writing crap for morons, and that wasn't exactly what he'd hoped for when he first went into journalism. But he had left the house with a problem, and was going home with a solution. That was as good as it got. That and the bagels, and a doughnut, and maybe when he got to the Tube he might splash out on a couple of cans of Lilt. It had, he reflected, been a funny old day.

Meanwhile, a blue rented Nissan had driven through Stoke Newington, Dalston, and into Shoreditch, each traffic light more annoyingly red than the last. Its driver, a pretty, if tired, art teacher who had travelled down from Norwich, was dying for a wee and listening to the one CD of Belle and sodding Sebastian for the third time. She wasn't exactly certain she could turn left straight after Shoreditch Church. But she did it anyway. The road was empty so she didn't slow down, she turned left and right quickly at the end. She was just beginning to realise that she didn't really know where she was when her phone went off again, she looked at her bag, and took a left into a quiet half-lit street at the same time as she saw a cat in the road and swerved. She saw a tall bloke too, ambling along the pavement, with a paper bag in his hand.

And then she was on the pavement too. He must have heard her, because he began to turn round. She tried to swerve but the man was too close and it was all happening too fast, and so she drove straight up Gabriel Bell's arse. Obviously, not actually into it. No car, no matter what the posters tell you, is that compact. But it was his arse she hit first, throwing him a good ten feet into the air. He had no chance and, as it turned out, neither did she.

She swung the car back on to the road and seemed to accelerate—hardly having the time to realise that under the circumstances this was an error—toward a block of flats on the other side of the road. The car didn't make it to the wall; instead it wrapped itself around one of those old fashioned lampposts that don't really bend no matter how hard you hit them. And she hit the lamppost hard. Not so hard that the airbags wouldn't have made a very significant difference to her chances of survival, had they been working, but they weren't. Dumb fucking luck, as the Americans say. If you believe in that sort of thing.

It was like a war scene, albeit a small one. People came from their homes to look. At first they didn't get too close. They didn't trust strangers, even unconscious ones. One man went over to the car and reached in to turn the engine off. Someone else put a blanket over Gabriel. Mostly they watched and waited for the ambulance.

There was a knock on the door of the strange room. Gabriel jumped up and opened it. What he saw was a tall, very thin man in his mid-to-late fifties wearing a flowing white cassock.

'Hippies, I knew it,' he mumbled.

The tall man smiled a welcoming smile: head tilted slightly to the side, warm, bright-eyed, he seemed careful not to show any teeth. Gabriel bit his bottom lip and stared at the stranger who held his smile. 'Hello,' Gabriel said. 'Where am I?'

The man pressed his hands together and said, 'My name is Christopher. If you would be so kind as to follow me, my colleague and I will explain what is happening to you.'

'I had an accident.'

'Yes, yes you did.'

'But I'm not injured.'

'It depends what you mean by "you."'

'Pardon?'

17

'The you that is here is not injured. Your essence, your spirit, your consciousness, your ... .'

'What about the other me? The one that got hit by the car?'

'The physical you. Yes, that you is rather badly injured. That you, I'm afraid, is lying in a hospital bed with all kinds of wires coming out of it. That you is, to use your words, pretty fucked up.'

Gabriel stared at the man, who was still smiling. 'Who are you?'

'I told you. My name is Christopher. I'm here to help you. I am, well ... I suppose you might call me an angel.'

'I don't think I would ...'

'I know this is difficult. If you just follow me, things will become clearer.'

'Am I dead?'

'No. I don't believe they use up hospital beds on dead people. But you're certainly not well. If you just follow me perhaps we can help you with that.'

Christopher turned slowly and smiled again, waiting for him to follow. As Gabriel stepped out into the passageway, he said, 'Is this a dream?'

'No,' Christopher said instantly.

'If it was, you wouldn't tell me.'

'Bang your head against the wall.'

'I already have.'

'I know.'

They walked down the white arching corridor, and Gabriel looked out of the windows. He could see that they were on the ground floor of a semi-circular two-storey building. Outside was parkland. No other buildings; no other people. The light was the light of early autumn, the sky was 4 p.m. blue, the land was flattish and, despite the lack of rain, the grass was green. Gabriel could see past the building he was in down to a calm grey lake. Beside the lake stood a thin line of trees; there was

18

little breeze, enough sometimes to make the leaves sound alive. It looked like a plush campus, an empty common, a flat corner of the Sussex Downs. It looked like England in September without the rain or the promise of autumn.

'Did the accident really happen?'

'Yes,' said Christopher, without turning round.

'How did I get here?'

Christopher ignored the question but said, 'I saw the accident; you weren't the only one hurt. You're going to meet the other casualty now. This is where we will be working.'

They stopped. Christopher opened a door and stood aside so Gabriel could enter the room. Inside were six chairs in a circle; three of them were already occupied. A chubby, vaguely orange man stood up as they entered. He introduced himself as Clemitius. He said: 'I used to be one of God's messengers but I got promoted. Now I'm a psychotherapist,' and he smiled a similar smile to Christopher's. Except that he showed his teeth, which were yellow and looked a little too big for his mouth.

Sitting on either side of Clemitius were two women who looked as confused as Gabriel felt. They didn't say anything. One of them was called Julie. The other was called Yvonne.

'Have a seat,' Clemitius said. 'We're just waiting for one more.'

2

Kevin Spine had never been a popular man. It wasn't just what he did for a living—he killed people for money—after all, not that many people actually knew that about him. Nor was it the way he looked: a small, lithe man of 57, he had powdery greyish skin with a thickly lined face, and he dressed a little bit like an undertaker, but without the big hat.

It had more to do with him being completely devoid of social skills. He wasn't rude, because that would imply some kind of insight and accompanying set of choices. He simply had absolutely no idea how to function around other people. He got nervous around strangers and that made him sweat, which made him self-conscious, and when he was self-conscious he said the first thing that came into his head.

He couldn't go into his local shop any more, following an incident where he found himself stuck at the counter while the plumpish girl on the till had to do a price check. He looked at her. She looked at him. He looked out the window. She looked at him. He began to sweat. She looked at him.

'Hot in here.'

She said nothing.

'Phew, very hot, I'm beginning to sweat,' he said, fanning himself theatrically. The girl stared. 'I'm sure you'd know about sweating,' he said.

This garnered a response, even if it was mainly blushing,

Kevin, immediately worried that he might have said something vaguely suggestive, tried to repair matters. 'I mean, you're a big girl, aren't you? Not tall; I mean big. Not that that's a bad thing, some men like that. Not me of course.' He sweated more but couldn't shut up. 'And not that you eat to please men, that is, assuming you're big because you eat and not because you have a gland problem or something.'

'Mr Nish!' the girl shouted. 'Mr Nish! We've got a nutter at Checkout Four.'

The only time Kevin relaxed in the presence of others was when he was killing them. Perhaps that is what drew him to the work. Or maybe it was because he was quite good at it. He spent nearly all of his time alone. It may be that if he had taken the time to get to know a few people, he might have found something to like just enough not to kill so many of the species. But he didn't have friends; what family he had, he hadn't seen for more than a day or two a year for twenty years, and whilst he had toyed with the idea of joining the chess club that met in the local library every Wednesday—he had a sense of chess as being a noble pastime for the modern warrior he sometimes imagined himself to be—he had finally decided against it because he worried that being with people might weaken him. And anyway, he was rubbish at chess.

So instead he killed people for money. Indeed, at the beginning of his career, he killed people for not very much money at all, reasoning quite sensibly that if you are to make a go of the contract-killer business you need a reputation as being reliable, elusive and effective. If he had to kill one or two people on the cheap to get a reputation, then so be it.

It ended up being three: a cheating husband, a business partner who was allegedly skimming money from a used-car dealership in Warwickshire, and a bloke who sold drugs to teenagers and made the mistake of selling some dodgy cocaine to the daughter of a retired gangster. Retired gangsters can be very touchy about 'a little rat's prick taking liberties.' Kevin slit the throat of said drug dealer and hung him from a tree in a quiet country road between Hatfield and Potters Bar. Far more flamboyant than he liked, but business was business. He did it for £1,000. Now he wouldn't get out of bed for less than £25,000.

Of course, some might consider the slaying and murder of a drug dealer to be less of an offence against humanity than, say, selling young people drugs. Indeed it might be tempting, for a moment, to get lost in the vigilante chic of righting wrongs and transcending the cumbersome justice system by striking down evil wherever it raised its spotty little head. But Kevin didn't moralise. He didn't think to himself, 'Oh good, a drug dealer; I'll sleep better tonight.' He didn't even think 'Well at least nobody will mourn this lowlife.' Apart from anything else, he had watched this particular lowlife for more than a week before killing him, and he knew very well that the man's aging mother, with whom he lived and who he pretty much looked after single-handedly, would definitely miss him.

No, Kevin Spine didn't think one damned thing. Drug dealer, naughty wife, annoying bloke down the pub, mechanic who didn't do a very good job on his client's Chrysler—it really made no difference. He wasn't interested in what people had done, although invariably his clients insisted on telling him, imagining that somehow the sheer outrageousness of a sloppy 30,00-mile service would make Kevin share their desire for justice and ensure he took his job seriously, maybe even agree to kill the bloke for nothing. Kevin turned off during the tales of wrongdoing, switching back on only for the important facts: address, place of work, any information about routine or habits. Then he gave bank details to his clients and told them that the wrongdoer would be dead within 72 hours of the money landing in that account. And they were.

This was his biggest job yet. In fact, he would go so far as to say this was his first corporate killing—a publishing executive who, for some ridiculous reason, was sabotaging her own company to the point where the share price was beginning to tumble like a space hopper down a really big hill. A reckless alcoholic about to cost her colleagues millions. £50,000 for offing a drunken executive. This was what all those early jobs were for; they were the building blocks. This was the big time.

It was also, in Kevin's opinion, indicative of the fact he was now killing a better class of victim that his brief had been simple. There had been no over-elaborate explanations, no sobbing or shouting, no long pathetic quest for vindication. He had been told his victim was 'bad for business'. It was unclear whether killing her was to prevent her doing whatever it was she was doing or to punish her for having already done it. Not that Kevin minded either way.

The only instruction was to kill her at home and make it look like a robbery. The problem, and Kevin considered it a minor one, was that he had never actually robbed anyone and thus wasn't exactly sure what a robbery looked like. He watched 'A Touch of Frost' and 'Cracker' for research purposes but both dealt with overly elaborate murder. Robbery, he decided, simply wasn't a prime-time crime any more.

His target lived in a large flat overlooking the River Thames near Canary Wharf. It was a rich part of town, so Kevin wore his best black Marks and Spencer's suit and a new grey shirt. He always travelled on public transport. Nobody noticed you on the Tube unless you were mad or busking, even if you were carrying a gun in your otherwise empty briefcase.

He wasn't a fretful killer. He would normally be quite happy to sit quietly and read the paper, but this afternoon he had a nagging thought that he had forgotten something. Gun? Check. Name and address of victim? Check. Bullets and silencer? Check. Travel card? Check. He even had a key to his victim's flat, which had been copied from the target by the people who were paying him. He was very happy to take it, and not only because it made his job easier. He knew that having a key would help him to confuse the police investigation before it had even started, and that was always a good thing. On first appearances the police would find a robbery—and Kevin would perhaps break a back window to help them hold on to that thought for a few moments. But, after due consideration, they would congratulate themselves on discovering that the killer did not come in through the window but wanted them to think he did. They would thus suspect a lover, friend, relative or neighbour. They might even suspect the caretaker, but they would not suspect a professional. Especially as he didn't plan to kill her with the gun.

But still there was something he'd forgotten. Kevin took his small black diary from his pocket and looked up the date: February 17th. His daughter's twenty-first birthday. Bollocks. He might not have seen her more than five times in seventeen years, but he never forgot her birthday. Well, he did, but never an important one: he'd remembered her eighteenth, for example, and had written to her to ask what she wanted for her twenty-first.

'A card would be nice,' she had emailed back a few days later, and he had decided then to push the boat out a little.

Satisfied, he sat back and read his horoscope in the free paper. 'You need to relax more,' it guessed. 'Don't keep over-reaching yourself; it's bad for you!'

How easy is it to come up with a few words that fit together loosely enough to suggest they spoke directly to around four million people in the UK? Well, it doesn't wash with me, thought Kevin, deciding that he and he alone had seen through the charade known as astrology. I never over-reach myself.

Silver Street was his stop, and he left the station at exactly the same pace as everyone else—the best way to blend in. It was just after 5 p.m., already dark, and it had been raining lightly. He walked steadily toward Cresswell Street; the further he got from the station, the fewer people there were walking with him. His mark's luxury flat, number 42A, turned out to be half of an imposing detached redbrick mansion.

The lights were not on. If this were any easier, he thought, he'd have to give them some money back. He began to whistle softly—'In the Ghetto,' from Elvis's sensitive period. It was a song he had never heard until after the King's death, and when he discovered it, he had found it terribly moving, mostly because he believed that Elvis was singing 'In the Gateau.' He imagined the King, approaching middle age with bigger trousers than he might have hoped, serenading forlornly the cake that was to play such a significant part in his downfall. Kevin often thought of this song when he was about to kill someone. Why, he didn't know.

He walked up to the door without looking around, without pausing unlocked it and walked straight in. There was, he knew, a small chance that he might bump into someone in the hall and that if he did, he might have to kill them. But it was a very small chance. His victim lived alone, she was— his reconnaissance had told him and the lack of lights in the flat confirmed —likely to be out, and the neighbour had left his house two days earlier with a large suitcase and some skis.

He walked straight to flat two, put the key in the lock, and entered what was a large, plush hallway painted in a rich golden yellow. To his right was the lounge, a big room with high ceilings dominated by large windows facing the river. In its centre was a long beige sofa with a matching armchair at a right angle. He walked round the edge of the room, taking in entry and exit points, and stopped at the windows. There was nowhere offering a view into the flat, but just to be on the safe side, he drew the curtains and sat in the armchair.

In front of him was a glass coffee table with a magazine without a picture on the front and some flowers, fresh white freesias. They smelt like summer and life. Beside them was a glass-brick ashtray. He took out a cigarette, a lighter, and his gun, screwed on its silencer quietly and slowly, then set them all on the table in front of him.

He put his feet up and smoked. Later he'd mess the place up a bit, later he'd find a present for his daughter, but now was a time for stillness, for quiet reflection and a B&H. Kevin never failed to be amazed at how easy killing someone was. Take all the fluffy moral baggage off the carousel of life, and all it took was a moment, a minimum of force, and the will. Drive down the high street and mount a pavement, walk up behind someone on an Underground platform and nudge them under a train, point a gun and squeeze a trigger—it was a doddle, and this was going to be no different.

What does a man think of when he's waiting to murder someone for money?

The money mostly, and in Kevin's case, his shoes. He looked at them on the coffee table. They were worn on the outside: must be the way he walked, it was the same with the other shoe. Maybe he should see an osteopath about that, or at least buy some new shoes. Nice shoes from Bond Street, nothing too extravagant, although looking a bit classy couldn't possibly be bad for business. Treat himself to something nice and Italian. He could afford it now.

He was still immersed in his shoe reverie when he heard the front door close. Not a problem, he was nothing if not professional—feet down, gun up and pointing straight at Yvonne Foster as she walked into the living room and turned the lights on.

She didn't freeze, she didn't scream and in fact, to her eternal credit, her first reaction was to reach toward a vase on the sideboard beside the door to use as a weapon. He's small and older than me, she thought, then quite absurdly, How dare you smoke in my home?

Kevin admired the fact that her instinct was to fight but he hissed, 'Be still or I'll kill you now.'

And still Yvonne was. She was a well-dressed woman, with immaculate blonde hair pushed back tidily from a handsome tanned face, a face that looked its age: late forties. She looked like a woman who was used to being in charge of her surroundings.

'Come in, that's it, toward me.' Kevin's mouth was dry. 'Stop. Stand still. Now I'm going to ask you a question. You answer correctly and I'll be out of here within four minutes. You don't, I'll stay, you'll get hurt, everything gets messy. Right?'

Yvonne nodded, thinking she could beat him in a fight, but then she stared at the gun.

'Where do you keep your jewellery?'

She breathed a sigh of relief. (Poor cow, thought Kevin.) 'Bedroom, in a box, everything. Take everything—I'm insured—take it all, except well ...'

'Except what?'

'There's a ring my son bought me: it's not worth anything, but I'd be really grateful if you just left that. It's blue, a glass stone; he got it in a market in India—it's just that ...'

'Shut up, I'll leave the ring for fuck's sake. Now turn round and face the door.'

'Why?'

'Just do it!'

Yvonne turned round. Did he want her to lead him to the bedroom? Not a pleasant thought, but it was unlikely he'd leave her here, she supposed. Why didn't he tell her to move? And what were those sounds?

What she heard, albeit briefly, was Kevin picking up the ashtray, which was even heavier than it looked, and walking up behind her. She didn't hear anything else. Not the shattering of her skull as Kevin brought the ashtray down on her head with all his weight. Only he heard the four other blows, delivered with equal ferocity to her broken head.

He threw the ashtray onto the sofa, picked up his own cigarette stubs, put them in his pocket, and walked quickly, without looking back, into Yvonne's bedroom. It was enormous. You'd never guess from the outside how big the rooms are in these places, he thought as he made his way to the oak dressing table. On the side, in front of a picture of what was presumably her grown son smiling boyishly from a boat, was a velvet jewellery box. Kevin opened it and tipped everything out onto the floor. His eye caught a silver bracelet with linked opals; he knew instantly that Christine would love it—or rather he would love it for her, because he didn't have the faintest idea what she might or might not like.

He had to take the rest as well, of course, or it wouldn't look like a robbery. He went back into the living room. My, Yvonne had bled. He stepped over the pool of thick dark blood oozing across the floor toward the sofa, retrieved his briefcase from beside the armchair, returned to the bedroom, and filled the briefcase with the baubles on the floor. He looked around and decided the room looked a bit tidy, so half-heartedly kicked a chair over. He felt somewhat foolish doing that. Strange, really— smashing a skull into bits came easy; pushing a chair over made him feel self-conscious. Still, he was a professional, so he opened up her wardrobe and pulled some dresses out, littering them across the floor.

Then he went back into the living room and, picking up Yvonne's handbag, emptied it on to the floor beside her body. Masterstroke, he thought, rummaging through the handbag as well; the police might think it was junkies. He picked up her purse, took out all the cash, put it in his pocket, and threw the purse into the puddle of blood on the floor. He went down the hallway and to the kitchen. This would, if he had been some kind of lowlife druggie thief, have been his only point of access. The back door was wired and would probably trigger an alarm at the local police station if broken, or at least it would if he broke the window from the outside. He picked up a tea towel, held it against the thick glass nearest the door handle, and elbowed it. It didn't break. Bloody hurt his elbow though. Beside the oven was a fire extinguisher. He grabbed it and smashed the base against the window. The window shattered and a surge of foam came spurting out of the fire extinguisher all over the kitchen floor.

Oh well, he thought. The place looks a mess; that's the main thing.

On his way back through the hallway, he stopped in front of an ornate mirror to make sure he looked OK and that there were no unsightly bits of skull in his hair. He nodded to himself, looked around, and grabbed his briefcase.

Kevin Spine left the building.

Outside the cool air tasted good. Grubby and polluted it might be, but it suited him quite nicely, thank you. He walked along the bank of the Thames. It was quiet here, exclusive he guessed, and the moon shone high in the sky. Kevin inhaled the dirty damp air, filling his chest the way men do after a job well done. He took a cigarette from his pocket, lit it, and smoked as he walked. Why hurry, he thought, and so he sat on a bench and looked at the distant lights of Vauxhall Bridge and, further along, the Millennium wheel.

I love London, he thought, it's so anonymous.

He finished his cigarette and walked on until he reached a break in the riverside wall where steps led down to a jetty. There was an old rusty gate stopping anyone from getting down, probably because it was considered unsafe, but if he could get past the gate, the first few steps would take him down behind the embankment wall and out of sight. He looked behind him—there was nobody around—and clambered down without catlike grace, less ninja assassin than middle-aged, 40-a-day, conscience-free killer. He stumbled, breathless, down the first flight of stone steps as far as a barbed wire fence. Behind the wire there were only five steps down to the wooden pier, which hadn't seen a boat in years. Kevin didn't need to go further than this: the black water lapped the side of the steps, and he knew the currents would drag whatever he threw in outwards and down. He opened his briefcase, put in his hand and picked out all the jewellery he could, tossing it underarm into the water, quickly repeating the action until the case was empty.

Only then did he remember the bracelet. He checked his jacket pockets, nothing. His trouser pockets? No.

'Fuck fuck fuck,' he hissed. He looked over the barbed wire fence. 'Jesus Christ, it's meant to be,' he said aloud, seeing the silver bracelet glistening on the edge of the jetty. The fence came just about up to his chest. He pressed the briefcase on to the wire, took off his coat and laid it across the case, then leant gingerly forward, reaching toward the twinkling bracelet.

Not far enough. He looked around. There were no handily placed sticks or other jewellery retrievers. Still, Kevin was not averse to improvising: he took off his shoe, leant over again, and this time was only about three inches short. He stood up, shifted the case down his stomach and gave a little jump so that he was higher on the fence. Nearly toppling over, he caught his foot on the wall behind him for balance and reached again—nearly there. He was by now balancing almost fully on the briefcase, seesawing, with his lower abdomen acting as a kind of fulcrum. Reaching forward he felt the wire beneath him sink a little, which actually helped, taking him closer to the ground. He could nearly touch the bracelet with the end of his shoe.

One more lunge should do it, he thought.

It didn't. He lurched forward, his body slipping across the case and over the fence. If it hadn't been for his genitals catching around the barbed wire, he might have fallen on the jetty and bumped his head.

'Nrgh!' was the noise he made. He could swear he could feel a piece of sharp metal embedded in the top of his penis. He couldn't move, not without cutting open his dick and impaled testicles and pouring their contents into the Thames. He was bent double at the groin over a barbed-wire fence, feet and hands off the ground, pretty much being supported by his bollocks.

He decided to try to manoeuvre backwards gently, very gently, reaching out his fingers to the ground in the hopes of easing himself back over the fence. Christ that hurt.

Plan B: he doubled up and tried to move the wire from beneath him. It was a good idea, but the wire wasn't so much beneath him now as in him. It had to leave the way it went in, which meant Kevin making the exact opposite movement that he had inadvertently made a few moments earlier. He had to go forwards over the wire, pushing the barbs downward and hopefully, dear God, outward as he went. He took some deep breaths: the initial agony was passing. I'll laugh about this in the morning, he lied to himself. He held the wire tightly in both hands, ignoring the trickle of blood rolling down his fingers. He pushed the wire down—'ouch ouch ouch'—but he could feel it leaving him; when it was out, and his testicles told his brain they were free, he would roll forward.

Unfortunately, and this is not the first time this has happened to a testicle, it went off a little too early. 'Clear!' it shouted at Kevin's brain, even though it wasn't. Kevin rolled forward, leaving a bollock attached to the barbed wire.

The pain started in the groin but charged up through his chest to his throat, no doubt intent on giving the idiot brain a good kicking. It didn't make it that far, tumbling out of his mouth in a piercing scream. He clutched at his bleeding groin, falling on to the jetty. Stillness might have helped but was quite simply impossible. Nobody sits still after they've left a testicle on a fence. He thought he was going to retch but didn't; shame really, it might have kept him awake. Instead, he rolled on to his side toward the water—any spatial awareness he may have been equipped with must have resided in his absent ball, because he didn't stop as he rolled toward the edge of the water, and he had no sense of impending sewage-laden doom.

What went through his mind as he hit the water? Was it, 'Shit, I can't swim?' Was it, 'I need to grab the jetty before I sink too deep?'

No, it was—quite unwisely under the circumstances—'I mustn't let go of the space where my ball used to be, in case the water is dirty and I get an infection.'

3

Anthony Foster was lying naked on a roof terrace in the small Spanish city of Almunecar with his equally naked girlfriend, practising—or at least pretending to practise—his Spanish.

Tash was lying on her stomach. Her long, tanned body and perfectly shaped bottom weren't helping Anthony's translation attempts. *'Estan listos para pedir?'*

'Oh I know that: *pedir* is to ask for ... "Are you ready to order?"' He reached out and stroked the top of her thigh. 'Can I just say, "*Si*, I am more than ready."'

Tash smiled. 'Yes you can say it, but only in Español, *por favor*. Try this: *'Tienen una reservacion?'*

Anthony rolled off his towel and onto Tash. 'I need a reservation now?'

'We won't learn this language by osmosis, you know.'

He kissed her on the end of the nose. The phone rang. 'How do you do that?' He smiled, kissed her again and moved to roll off her.

She smiled, lowered her hand to his cock, and said: *'Estoy ocupada.'* Anthony winced slightly but got up anyway, saying in a really poor Schwarzenegger voice, 'I'll be back.'

Something made Tash turn toward the open door that led into the flat. She saw Anthony slowly buckle downward, holding the phone to his ear. It was as if the bottom of his spine were melting as he folded onto the arm of the sofa and paled. The soft, tanned skin of his face shrank in the light. His thick hair, the hair of a young man, seemed to grow wiry and draw back from his face. She watched as the life left him and he became old. So old he could barely hold the phone. And then as whatever he was being told took hold, he became young again, childlike, crying without breathing, trying to speak, trying to shout, but nothing coming out. Like a little boy whose puppy had been run over. Like a child lost and alone in the woods. Like a young man being told that his mother had been murdered.

4

Kevin Spine stood beside the double bed. He stared at the wood-framed 'Van Gogh self-portrait' print above the bed and fingered the crisp, pale-blue duvet. He sighed, straightened his back, and looked into the full-length mirror on the wardrobe door. He was wearing the same black suit and white shirt that he had been wearing when he virtually castrated himself on the banks of the Thames. Still, he was dry and bloodstain free, and given the circumstances, remarkably pain free as well.

He was in what appeared to be a motel, with en-suite bathroom, a small television, and a saucer full of mints. He picked up the remote control and turned the TV on: it was showing an episode of 'Porridge'. He flicked through the channels: 'Friends', 'The Young Ones', 'Brideshead Revisited', another episode of 'Porridge', and finally 'The Tweenies'. There was no text button, no news, nothing to tell him the date.

He pulled back the patterned green curtain and looked outside. Wherever he was, it wasn't London. He was on the second floor of what appeared to be a white-walled, curving two-storey building that stretched for maybe 150 metres and formed a large, incomplete circle. Opposite his window, a path led down to a lake surrounded by trees. The sky was remarkably clear, the grass exceptionally green, and for a moment he thought he was dreaming. He began to wonder, among other things, who had brought him here and why. And where was 'here' and 'why doesn't my groin ache?' He glanced down at the bedside table and saw a small card with his name on it. He picked it up and turned it over. It read: 'This is a safe place.'

He walked to the door. Locked. How long had he been here? He looked at himself in the mirror; he was clean-shaven but that didn't necessarily mean anything. It was obvious that whoever had brought him here must have patched him up and dried his clothes. They might also have shaved him. If he was kept clean-shaven there would be no way of knowing how long he had been unconscious. That might be a way of disorienting a prisoner, he thought.

However, nobody ever heard of anyone trimming someone else's nose hair, and Kevin knew his own nose hair. He stood in front of the mirror, pushed his nose upwards, and stared into his nostrils. There were no untoward or overgrown nose hairs. There was, however, a card tucked behind the top of the mirror. He took it out.

'Don't do that; it's not nice.'

Kevin was not a man given to rumination; he believed himself to be a man of action, and he had the video collection to prove it. If he found himself at any time in his life requiring contact with the world, he watched a video. Something with Jean Claude Van Damme or Chuck Norris tended to do it for him. Single-minded men of few words and fewer thoughts. Lone men; armed men. Violent, inarticulate men. But given that there were no videos currently available to him, he was forced to ask himself what the bejesus was going on. He sat on the bed and saw another card on the pillow.

It said: 'Someone will be along shortly to help you understand. Try to relax, and know this: you are closer to God than you ever imagined you could be. Take comfort from that.'

'Comfort my arse,' he muttered and went into the bathroom. He pulled down his trousers and pants to examine his genitalia. Not only was it all there, it was all in the right place. There were no dressings or scars. Kevin began to get nervous. More nervous than any man discovering he still had genitals should. Had he been dreaming? Was he dreaming now? He stopped staring at his willy and glanced up at the basin. On its corner was another card. He hopped over and picked it up:

'You have some odd habits. Someone will be along shortly and everything will become clear. Now leave yourself alone, for goodness sake.'

There was a knock at the door. Kevin answered quickly. He even smiled and said, 'I've been expecting you.'

The man standing there looked like a kindly uncle. The kind of man who had worked in an office for thirty years and smiled at his own confusion as the mores, language, and habits of those around him caught up with him and passed him by. Had he been a man in an office, he would have been in charge of the tea-and-biscuit fund. He would be polite and dependable, recognised by those around him mostly for his height, or rather his usefulness in getting things from on top of other things. Not for his gentle decency, nor his innate tolerance, nor his capacity to take small pleasure in the small pleasures of others. He would have been the tall man who smelled just a tiny bit of lavender.

'Please, follow me,' Christopher said softly. 'You must be feeling a little confused. We're here to help you with that.'

'Why do you think I'm confused?' asked Kevin as they walked along the corridor.

'Because most people are when they come here. One moment you are going about your everyday business—in your case killing someone and castrating yourself as you fall into the Thames. The next minute you are here, seemingly healthy.'

'You shouldn't underestimate everyone,' said Kevin.

Christopher stopped and looked at him. 'Do you know where you are?'

Kevin looked out of the window. 'I might. I'm not telling you.'

'I don't think you do know, Kevin, actually.'

'I do.'

'You don't.'

'I do.'

'So tell me then.' Christopher could feel his serenity slipping.

'No.'

'Because you don't know.'

'I do know. This is not unlike something I saw on the *New Avengers* once.'

And Christopher—an angel who, had he been a man, would not have argued with other men—thought to himself, You're an angel. And a therapist. You have lived through the ages and watched with a bemused detachment as people have run and jumped and warred and fallen. You are old, uninvolved. Unflappable.

And then: This man killed people for money and we're not actually in the therapy room yet. Sometimes he knew that all the insight in the world didn't make a blind bit of difference.

'Right,' Christopher said to Kevin. 'So you know that you are dead and that this is a therapeutic community just beneath heaven where you will undergo group counselling with other dead or near-dead people in order to establish where you will spend eternity. You know that, do you? You worked that out by your close examination of your genitalia and nose hair, by watching a bit of 'Rising Damp' and from eating the complimentary mints, did you? Did you?'

Kevin stared at him. His hand slipped down toward his groin. The tall thin man in front of him was shaking.

'Dead?'

'Yes!' Christopher softened a little. 'I'm afraid so, but all is not lost. Please follow me.'

'I'm dead ... and there is a God?'

'Yes.'

'Fuck!'

'Yes.'

'But I'm not in hell?' Kevin thought he was going to be sick. He thought, This must be a dream. He pinched his thigh as hard as he could. It really hurt.

Christopher didn't reply; he just turned and walked toward the therapy room. Naturally, Kevin followed.

37

'You know what I do ... what I did for a living?'

'Yes.'

'And ...?'

Christopher stopped and inevitably Kevin stopped with him. They were standing in what amounted to a curved corridor. Outside the sun was shining; Kevin thought he could hear birdsong. The grass was very green, the trees very straight, and the walls of the corridor were spotless and white. And so was the floor. Christopher watched Kevin as he looked down. He thought, You have never seen such a spotless white floor in your life, Kevin.

'Look, those old commandments, the 'Thou shalt not kills' and 'Thou shalt not covets'—all that—they weren't doing the trick. God is interested in the inner you, your salvation in spite of what you do or did. God believes in resolving difficulties rather than punishing evil these days.'

Angels, by tradition, watch and sometimes guard. They have been known to deliver messages and to fight the soldiers of darkness when necessary, but theirs has, for all the excitement, been a fundamentally simple existence, their being characterised by a clarity around Good and Bad that other people can only dream about.

It was that sense of deep-felt confusion among people that played on the mind of God. And so he sent the ever-faithful Peter to set up a project that reflected the complexities of modern times. Pre-death therapy. A project that didn't judge but rather enquired as to what brings a person to wherever they are and offers them a chance, albeit a very slim chance, to do something about it. To make themselves better. Most importantly, and this is perhaps to what Peter clung, it was an endeavour that sought to heal.

Many of the angels who were called upon to make this experiment work had their doubts. They had worked for God for a very long time. They may have muttered things like,

'If it ain't broke ...' But Peter said that as people evolved, so should heaven. He might not have believed it, but he said it nonetheless, and that is what counts. He added that the choices people make are less clear morally than they once were, that while the commandments remain 'a useful if not fully comprehensive guide,' they don't always legislate for the many confusing influences people encounter.

God is gentle and God is good, Peter said. He's not going to get all Old Testament on the world just because it creates false gods and calls them celebrities or sometimes, quite bizarrely, role models. Peter said that his was not an angry God, nor a moping one. His was an inventive God, a responsive God—a God capable of trying things that might surprise even his most devout followers.

Peter interviewed all the angels, and those selected received training. Many received therapy of their own, up to three times a week in some cases.

Christopher found it very hard to know what to talk about. He thought of the process as a job interview. It didn't matter that he didn't particularly want the job. It only mattered that he did his best. So he was pleased when Peter told him he was 'a grounded and well-focussed angel, one who would benefit this enterprise,' although he wasn't terribly sure it was a compliment.

He was less moved when he was told that he retained an 'admirable moral clarity'. He was an angel. That was surely like saying he had wings.

Christopher opened the door to the therapy room and Kevin, who was now quite pale, stepped inside. There he saw four people, including Yvonne Foster who stared at him in horror.

'What the ...?' Slowly Yvonne stood up.

Kevin looked at her and his normally grey skin turned almost translucent. Colour didn't so much fade from him as evacuate. The fingers on both hands started to twitch, but the rest of him froze. His stillness was drawn not from the school of cold-blooded killers of which he had always liked to consider himself a graduate, but rather the fact that his brain had pretty much closed down. He was staring at one of his victims. Yvonne was wearing the same blue business suit she had had on when Kevin had bludgeoned her to death. The same white silk blouse. Her hair was impeccable. Blonde with a tinge of white at the sides, short, perfectly set. If he had ever imagined a Judgment Day it would probably have looked like this. But he hadn't. He had killed her. And she was staring at him. And standing up. And she looked really angry.

He pinched himself but didn't wake up. He raised his right fist and hit himself on the head hard. It really hurt.

'That man attacked me! He ... killed me?' said Yvonne, half accusing and half asking.

'Yes,' said a short, stout man with a round, slightly orange face, and thin sandy hair. 'So I understand.'

Yvonne took a step forward.

'Please sit down, Yvonne. I assure you, you are perfectly safe here.'

'Yes, but he isn't,' she said.

Clemitius raised his hand. However, he expected his actions to carry a weight his appearance couldn't quite carry off. What authority he had came from his old eyes with the large bags under them, and of course the fact that he was an angel in a cassock, a robe that did for angels what uniforms do for everyone. 'There can be no violence here,' he said. 'Violence is not tolerated, no matter what. It is forbidden. If you strike anyone here, you will be ritually removed. This will be a safe place. For everyone. Regardless of anything that went before. Do not doubt this rule.'

He paused and looked around the room. Everyone was looking at him. He drank in the moment then added, with something approaching a smile: 'Consider it God's law.'

Clemitius once said to Christopher, when they were first assigned to work together, that a therapeutic community is as close to heaven as a person can get without dying. As Christopher thought when he said it, that comment said more about him than it did about anything else. Christopher and Clemitius were a match made in heaven. Clemitius believed absolutely in what he had been charged to do; he relished the therapy he had been offered. It was probably the attention. He arrived early and devoured it. Waiting for a question, a reflection, an insight from the poor sap charged with his treatment, he talked and talked about whatever came into his head. When he wasn't being treated he read; he read everything he could about therapy. And he became a believer. Devout. He had been an angel for thousands of years. Nobody had ever asked him very much about himself before.

Christopher, on the other hand, had found it a bit embarrassing. Clemitius said Christopher was a born host. He said it with disdain, but Christopher took it as a compliment.

After Clemitius had handed down God's law, the group sat in silence for a few moments. Christopher was going to speak, to comfort. It was what he thought a host should do. He was going to say something about how surprised they must feel to be here, or perhaps even how sorry he was to see them all here, when he was pretty certain they would rather be somewhere else but—and it may have been that he could sense Christopher's need to offer something like comfort—Clemitius spoke first.

'Well, I'd like to welcome all of you here to what must seem a very confusing place. I'm sure that you would like to know exactly where you are and what you are doing here, and we will try to help you with that now. All of you are, technically speaking, either dead—sorry for your loss—or nearly dead, in which case we wish you a full recovery or an end to your pain, whatever seems most appropriate. You, Gabriel and Julie, your bodies are in a hospital in Central London, coincidentally quite close to each other I understand?'

He looked at Christopher, who nodded and said, 'Almost as close as you are to each other here.'

'Quite,' said Clemitius. 'Kevin, your body was discovered on the embankment by a woman out jogging early this morning.'

'I'm quite embarrassed to hear that,' stammered Kevin.

'Yes,' said Clemitius. 'Well, anyway, the important thing is you are all here. Yvonne, as you probably know, you were murdered earlier today by Kevin. Brutal and shocking as that undoubtedly was, you are here now and I hope that somehow you can find it within yourself to work with us toward a good place.'

'Don't be ridiculous,' Yvonne said. 'And where, exactly, is "here"?'

'This is the place where you find out where you are going to spend eternity.'

'So there is a hell?' said Kevin.

' Yes,' said Clemitius.

'Shit,' said Kevin quietly.

'Oh don't worry. You haven't blown your chances yet,' said Clemitius, lifting his fingers in the air and miming inverted commas. 'That's why you are all here. To use a modern colloquialism, the jury is still out on you.' He paused for dramatic effect.

Gabriel was staring out of the only window in the room, at the brilliant blue sky outside, which seemed to irritate Clemitius slightly. Looking directly at Gabriel, he said, 'This is a therapeutic group. You are here to work on yourselves, to look at those characteristics, neuroses, anxieties, or simple personal blockages that prevented you from leading the life God might have expected from you.'

'It's a bit late now,' said Julie.

'Oh no it isn't,' Christopher said, anxious to bring something like good news to the newly dead and comatose people around him.

'Quite,' said Clemitius, who was enjoying himself. 'If you do well, work through your problems and come out on the other side, you may get a second chance. Ours is a merciful Lord, and if he thinks you can learn from what has gone before and, more importantly, what goes on here, you may be allowed to go back to your life.'

'You are not serious?' said Julie who, even as she said it, thought, None of this can be serious!

'Is this one of those weird psychology experiments?' asked Yvonne.

'How do I get out of here?' said Gabriel.

'Well it's not like a hoop you have to jump through. It's about confronting yourselves in this group, but I warn you it's rare for people to go back. Mostly they pass through this therapeutic group into the kingdom of Heaven. Or Hell. Now I think maybe we need a few introductions. Gabriel, would you like to start?'

'Fuck off.'

'Gabriel, please,' said Christopher.

'No, hang on,' said Yvonne. 'I have a question.' She sat back in her chair and crossed her legs, looking directly at Christopher.

'Of course,' he said.

'That man over there murdered me. He is a murderer. That is a sin, it is the biggest sin. It makes him a bad person. Why isn't he in hell?'

'Fair question,' Christopher answered, but before he could say anything else, not that he was sure what he was going to say, Clemitius inhaled deeply and loudly, raised himself up in his armless, wine-coloured chair and took over.

'Indeed. The thing is, whilst the old sins are still important, they are not what we would call the whole story.'

'Not the whole story?' whispered Yvonne.

'Think of it like this. A modern God, a God in touch with the nuances and struggles of modern life, would know that the things people do are not necessarily indicative of who they are. That sometimes, quite often in fact, we need to look beyond the actions of a person and see inside them to truly understand what motivates them and who, in fact, they are. Moreover, a

43

modern God would recognise that it is by addressing the inner turmoil that can haunt you all, that one might truly address sin.'

Everyone stared at Clemitius. Gabriel shook his head and muttered something under his breath. Kevin nodded vigorously.

Finally Yvonne spoke. 'Oh my,' she said softly. 'Someone has killed God and replaced him with a social worker.'

'What exactly do you expect from us?' asked Julie.

'We expect you to work,' Clemitius said.

'What does that mean?' she snapped at him.

'You'll come here twice a day and we'll talk. We'll share and hopefully support each other in that sharing. Together we will try to understand why you lived as you did. Why you missed the opportunities to be ... what you could have been.'

'Do you do this for everyone who dies?' Julie asked.

'You're not dead yet,' Christopher told her. 'You and Gabriel are still alive. Do well here, and maybe you can go back.'

'No,' Clemitius said as if Christopher had not spoken. 'We don't do this for everyone who dies. This is a pilot project. We hope it takes off in a big way, but that partly depends on people like you. You should be proud. There is a lot riding on you.'

'Are we the first?' asked Kevin.

'Oh no,' Clemitius said. 'You're not that special.'

'Is this Hell?' Gabriel had stopped staring out of the window and was instead staring at Clemitius. 'Because it feels a lot like I would imagine hell to feel. Not that I believed in hell up to today, you understand.'

And Clemitius looked back at him almost pityingly. He licked his dry lips and said slowly, 'Oh no, this isn't Hell. Hell is far, far worse than this. Let's see if we can help make sure you don't ever find that out, shall we?'

5

After the first group session Christopher took each of them back to their rooms. The same quiet walk down the white corridor. Julie could see another group of miserable dead people through the windows at the corridor's other end. She thought they looked broken and realized that she probably looked the same.

None of them spoke much. Kevin was happy; Yvonne was angry; Julie, bemused and in shock. Gabriel was the nearest to despair. In his room he was restless: he lay on the bed, stood up and paced around, lay down again, turned on the TV, flicked through the channels, and turned it off again.

Finally he just sat on the bed, brought his hands to his eyes and his knees to his chest, and was still. He wanted to scream but hadn't the breath in his body. He rocked to and fro, whispering to himself, 'This can't be real, dear god this can't be real.' And then, even quieter: 'Ellie.' The whispering turned into gasping as he cried.

Ellie and Gabriel met more than seven years ago at her best friend's birthday party. Izzy was turning thirty and decided to hire a bar in Soho and invite loads of people. Unfortunately, however, she didn't actually know loads of people, so she made her boyfriend Sam invite people he knew. This made Izzy appear more popular than she actually was and also meant there would be some unknown men at a party full of women—always a plus for both sides after a few drinks.

Ellie had known Izzy for years; they had trained together as psychiatric nurses. During that time they had shared a flat, some clothes, a couple of men and five holidays. Inevitably, they had also shared approximately 668 bottles of wine, a small amount of cocaine, and 345 conversations about what simple beasts men are.

'Men want oral sex and the football results,' Ellie would say drunkenly.

'But not at the same time,' Izzy giggled. 'That really pisses them off.'

Tall and slim, Ellie had gone for the stunningly-sexy-best-friend-of-the-host approach to Izzy's party. She wore black trousers with a sleeveless long white top that covered her bum. Not that she needed to. She had shoulder-length black hair and a slightly turned-up nose. As faces go it was probably average, but she had this teasing smile that seemed to say to women, 'I am genuinely interested in what you have to say and am completely satisfied with your company, for we are sisters,' and to men, ' I am so good at sex, it's scary.'

Ellie's casual elegance inevitably annoyed Izzy a little. Not that she was going to show it, at least not until she had drunk half a bottle of tequila and been sick on Sam's new Paul Smith shirt. Izzy had gone for a floral print smock over black jeans. It might have worked if the pink carnations had been smaller, or if her hips were a little narrower, but as it was she felt from the moment she arrived that she had chosen the wrong combination and thus felt out of place for the whole evening.

Izzy had managed to hold on to the complexion of a sixteen-year-old and no amount of Clearasil was changing that. Spots, for people who are spotty, are like that; when you really need them to keep a low profile, they decide to throb and show off a little, pretending to be garden peas sellotaped to a face. Despite this, or perhaps because of it, Izzy was slipping between people, kissing them theatrically on the cheek and asking them, in a voice only half a cocktail away from sobbing, 'Are you having a good time? It's so lovely to see you. You look great, where did you get that top/lipstick/boobtube/cravat/poncho? It's so pretty/vibrant/ironic/retro/aromatic.' Given the right amount of tequila and enough nervous energy to power a light aircraft,

Izzy always knew the right thing to say. Except about ponchos, obviously.

All women are genetically programmed to know what to do at their best friend's thirtieth birthday party. They know it is their job to be there until the end, to bestow the right amount of hugging, reassuring and agreeing, and to spend some time late in the evening needlessly reminiscing about great times, which weren't terribly great but are worthy of mention merely because they happened. It often takes a drunken thirty-year-old woman with garden vegetables stuck to her face to realise with absolute clarity that all times are precious.

Gabriel was there as a near-friend of Sam's. They worked in the same building: Sam worked for an advertising company that occupied most of it, while the website for which Gabriel wrote about sports was based in the basement. They met following an e-mail that went round the building asking if anyone fancied starting a football team. The team never materialised, but over the summer a bunch of men from around the building had got together for a kick-about in the park, some coughing and a couple of beers.

Sam and Gabe went along, and still turned out every Tuesday. They didn't know each other well but that didn't really matter; they had drunk together and laughed at a bloke called Barry who played football in a Phil Collins on Tour t-shirt. More importantly, both supported Chelsea, which meant they could talk uninterrupted for four or five hours at a time without becoming bored.

Parties in bars are like parties anywhere: everyone circles each other for the first hour or so, moistening themselves with vodka and bottled beer, talking to the people they know the best about nothing. It's a bit like the first five laps of a 10,000-metre race—a little light jostling for position, establishing a rhythm, then settling in for the duration before the inescapable late sprint for the finishing line.

Inevitably there is someone who goes off too fast. In this case it was Izzy's little sister, Moira, who set off at a blistering pace. The more experienced chasing pack let her go and ran their own race. Consequently, Moira stepped off the track on lap 12 or, more precisely, was sick on the pavement and her Nicole Farhi velvet smock and was put into a taxi by her big sister at 10:15 p.m.

Gabriel was a tall man with thick lips and dark hair. Seven years ago he had a bit of a quiff thing going on; even then you could tell his hair was only reluctantly stuck to his head, and some of it was beginning to leave. On the whole though, he was a good-looking man who took a suntan well and knew how to carry his I-go-to-the-gym-just-for-evenings-like-this body. In his early twenties, he had decided to base his walk on that of James Coburn in *The Magnificent Seven* and spent some time cultivating it. Gabriel believed every man should choose how to walk, as opposed to just ambling about; it is our capacity to determine the way we carry ourselves, he thought, that separates us from the apes—that and trousers anyway. He was, or at least was back then, the kind of man who thought of lines like that in bed at night and saved them up for parties like Izzy's, secure in the knowledge that he would never, ever use them.

Ellie and Gabriel spoke for the first time about 10 p.m. They were drawn to the increasingly watchable Moira, whose tousled brown hair had begun to unfurl into a jug of piña colada. She had already been sick and was caught between the two irresistible desires that can overcome someone in that position: to sleep or to sing 'Dancing Queen'. Poor adorable Moira lay her head on a small round metal table, closed her eyes, and heard a voice that existed only in her head say, 'Tonight Matthew, I am going to be Agnetha.' She burst into a high-pitched, disco-diva mumble, disguising bravely the fact that she didn't know any of the words other than 'queen' and 'dancing.'

Ellie and Izzy floated over to Moira, being sweet, caring, and a tiny bit patronising and Sam, who was talking to Gabriel about Ruud Guillit, glanced over and said, 'Oh Moira.' He walked the short distance to the table and Gabriel, having long ago noticed Ellie and seen she was involved with the drunk kid with a bit of pineapple on her head, inevitably followed.

He could have said 'Do you need a hand?' in that fake, helpful way that always comes out as condescending. He could have said 'What's the matter?' and thus given the impression that he was not only a moron but had also never been to a pub before. However, after watching with his hands in his pockets, as Sam joined Izzy and Ellie, who were talking to Moira as though she were deaf rather than drunk, Gabe chose to start singing along.

This immediately got Moira's attention. She started banging her hand on the table, bellowed 'Dancing queen!' and fell backwards off her chair. Mind you, credit where it's due, even while sprawling on the floor with her frock round her hips, Moira managed to let out another 'Dancing Queen!' before she smiled at Gabriel and threw up.

As Izzy and Sam went to help her, Ellie said to him, 'Nice touch.'

'It's the effect I have on women. If that had been a date I would have considered it a raging success.'

'Even the throwing up?' asked Ellie

'Oh yes,' smiled Gabriel. 'At least we hadn't just kissed.'

Izzy and Sam were busily arranging a taxi and an escort for Moira.

'Do you want a drink?' Gabe asked.

Ellie looked at Gabe and quite liked what she saw. 'Flushed with success, the man who sings at drunk girls moves on to his next conquest,' she answered, and did her smile.

They were sitting together and drinking pink cocktails by the time Izzy and Sam came back into the bar. For Izzy, the possibility of her best friend getting off with a mate of Sam's should perhaps have constituted a wonderful girlfriend moment. Especially since it was a mate about whom she had heard no unsavoury 'he split up with his girlfriend when she found him in bed with her dad' stories. However, Izzy's heart sank, and it stayed that way for seven years and counting.

Sam, meanwhile, glanced at the potential couple and—summing up beautifully that moment when new love may just burst into the world—patted Izzy's bum, nodded in their direction, and said, 'Aye aye.'

Ellie and Gabriel exchanged numbers, but Ellie decided that it would not be appropriate to go home with a bloke she had just met at her best friend's birthday party, it being traditionally a ridiculously emotional time. Izzy certainly appeared to be giving her that message anyway. Ellie got in just after 2 a.m., tired but not ready to sleep, drunk but perfectly able to put the kettle on. The phone rang at 2:11.

'Hello,' said Gabriel.

'Hello.'

'Did you get home OK?'

'Apparently.'

'Good.'

There was a long pause before Gabriel said: 'Well, I'm pleased you gave me your real number. The last time a beautiful woman gave me her phone number it turned out to be Pizza-a-Go-Go.'

'That's a line.'

'Sorry.'

'Come over.'

'OK.'

He was there inside 24 minutes and stayed the weekend. On Sunday morning they walked around Regents Park exchanging bits of life story. On Sunday afternoon they watched a black-and-white British film, eating Kettle Chips and doing impressions of Margaret Lockwood and James Mason.

By Sunday evening they had pretty much sailed through all the requisite tests that qualify the contestants to move on to part two of the preliminary rounds of the relationship game. These tests included the giggling-while-having-sex test, and the falling-asleep-together-unexpectedly during 'Antiques Roadshow.'

Izzy had phoned Ellie the morning after the party but Ellie had ignored the phone. She called her back soon after Gabriel had left. Izzy's discomfort was demonstrated by the first words she said on finding out that Gabriel had been at Ellie's since the party: 'Well, I hope you had safe sex.' Dead giveaway that—any excited friend would want to know what happened or what was going to happen, or at least do some mandatory squealing. They would not pretend to be a health-promotion leaflet.

Ellie knew this and, with the sole purpose of irritating Izzy the spoilsport, said: 'I'm not stupid, Izzy, when we ran out of condoms I took it up the arse to be on the safe side.'

Within three months of meeting, Gabriel and Ellie took their first foreign holiday together. Within two days of being abroad they had their first argument. It was about putting away underwear. Ellie felt that putting away pants once you had finished with them was a simple and reasonable act. Gabriel felt that putting away pants was not something one should prioritise when on holiday. As all good first arguments should, the Great Pants Debate of 2003 became something of a motif. They would trot it out at dinner parties or when teasing each other in front of family or friends. In fact, the Great Pants Debate was to Gabriel and Ellie what 'Yesterday' was to the Beatles—not their greatest or most relevant work, but certainly something familiar and easy to remember them by.

By year two, Izzy had reluctantly decided that Ellie and Gabriel were not just a passing fad. They had, after all, moved in together after first spending three months travelling round India. They had even had tattoos done at the same time: not matching tattoos, obviously—that would be ridiculous—but something indelible nonetheless. Consequently, Izzy, Sam, Gabriel, and Ellie occasionally socialised together. One New Year for example, they hired a cottage together in Wales and spent a long weekend drinking pretty cocktails, walking on windswept beaches, and playing Trivial Pursuit and charades. Izzy's discomfort with the Gabriel-Ellie axis receded over the years, and became a bit like an unsightly mole: most of the time she forgot she had it, in fact she had to look for it just to make sure it hadn't completely disappeared, but when she found it she resented it; somehow it made her feel imperfect.

At least for the first couple of years, Gabriel and Ellie could easily have passed for the kind of couple who appeared in bottled-beer adverts with other nice-looking, linen-wearing, laid-back people. However, as they edged into their mid-thirties and beyond, they wore less linen, Gabriel found himself with less hair, and Ellie's bum was ... less 'gathered' is perhaps the best way of putting it. After vaguely trying to get pregnant for a year, and then really trying to get pregnant for another year and a half – temperatures, legs-in-the-air, vitamin-supplements, come-home-at-lunchtime-and-have-really-mechanical-sex trying – they appeared less laid-back. Izzy felt they had been reminded of the struggle, the struggle that less-blissful people have with life most of the time. This feeling really kicked in when Izzy and Sam managed to get pregnant before, as Izzy said, 'I even got my pants off.'

Gabriel was a man of few sperm. As he had recently said to surprised guests who had come round for dinner to celebrate Ellie's 37th birthday, 'I have so few sperm I could name them after the Waltons and still have a couple of names, maybe a Jim Bob and a Mary Ellen left over.' They had, after four years of hopeful distracted sex, turned to Dr Science and his modern bag of tricks. Dr Science, being a busy old sod, had taken his time to get back to them.

They spent a good six months attending an NHS clinic that, after a lot of hanging about and a few tests, had proved to be about as useful as a piano in a canoe. After a handful of appointments, a stale-smelling old Russian woman who said she was a doctor told them: 'It's a shame, but you two cannot have children. We recommend donor sperm. We can get you donor sperm.' She sounded like she was selling watches in Stalingrad.

'But what about ICSI?' Ellie mumbled. People this infertile always do their homework, and both Ellie and Gabe had worked out for themselves that the technique whereby one of Gabriel's limited but able sperm was injected directly into Ellie's willing and ready eggs was the only chance they had.

The Russian shrugged. 'We don't do ICSI, why you worry about this ICSI?' She looked around the room with disdain; to Ellie she looked as if she were trying to find her spittoon.

'Can you recommend anywhere that does?' Gabriel asked.

'So you don't want donor sperm?' she said. 'It really is very good quality.'

Gabriel and Ellie left before the woman offered to show them samples and decided, in anger as much as anything else, to go private.

So for the past few weeks they had been attending St Catherine's College Hospital in the middle of London. The new place seemed much better; it had a waiting room for one thing, and furniture. As Gabriel said when they first came in, 'I like a place with carpets.'

Their first visit had gone well. The most noticeable thing about St. Catherine's was that when you saw a member of staff, they smiled at you, and when you spoke to the woman on the front desk, she knew your name.

'Hello, Ellie,' the young, smiling receptionist said. 'Would you and—'

'Gabe. Gabriel. Gabriel,' Gabriel said.

'Would you and Gabriel like to come through? Dr Samani will see you now.'

Dr Samani was a tall, middle-aged Middle Eastern man with thin black hair that had a distinctly orange tint, who was wearing an expensive suit. He sat behind an oak desk with his fingers to his lips. When Gabriel and Ellie entered, he got up, shook both their hands, and offered them a seat. If he knew how nervous they were, he pretended not to, speaking in a matter-of-fact way.

'I understand you have had some difficulty at a previous hospital.'

'We were told that there was nothing that could be done,' said Gabriel.

'Who told you that? The cleaner?' laughed Dr Samani.

'She was a doctor.'

'She was an idiot, an idiot in doctor's clothing. There are lots of things that can be done, but I think given the semen report your GP so kindly sent us, Mr Bell, ICSI is the best course of action. Might I suggest you go and provide another sample?'

He waved Gabriel out of the room. Outside, a waiting nurse escorted him to a small, wood-panelled room with a plastic seat, a small specimen container, and some old porn magazines. To the nurse's eternal credit, she didn't look him in the eye.

Gabriel started flicking through the magazines. Far from being arousing, they were vaguely amusing—a woman who may have once been in Bucks Fizz was playing with herself. Try as he might, Gabriel couldn't get 'Making Your Mind Up' out of his head. Over the page, a man with a curly perm and handlebar moustache was thrusting himself unconvincingly at a blonde girl with a centre parting, flicks, and blue eye shadow. Gabriel imagined a queue of embarrassed men beginning to form outside the door, and the nurse whose job it was to police the masturbation room waiting impatiently to go for lunch, where she might meet her boyfriend, who would ask her how her morning went, only to be told, 'Well there was this one weird guy who stayed in the wank room for half a day; not that it was worth the wait, according to the lab.'

Gabriel put down the magazine, closed his eyes and thought of Ellie. Did it every time.

Meanwhile, Dr Samani was running through the proposed procedure with Ellie. 'If we go with ICSI, we need to test you thoroughly first: two scans and some simple tests. If all is clear, you could start on the drugs after your next period. It will take four weeks to develop the eggs for collection; two days later we should have some embryos ready to implant.'

'That quickly?'

'Why wait? Surely you have waited long enough?' He smiled with a mix of reassurance and pride in his work. 'First we need to take control of your ovaries, stimulate them, and encourage them to produce more than just the one egg. Then we harvest the eggs, add one of your husband's sperm directly into the egg, and wait 24 hours to see how many embryos we have. ICSI is good for creating embryos—something like an over 90% success rate—then we implant two and hope.'

'What are the chances?' asked Ellie nervously.

'About one in three, but it all depends. Statistics don't mean much once you have started—you just aim to get from one part of the process to the next, and we see if we can help you have your baby. OK?'

Ellie was crying when Gabriel returned, having deposited his jar with the nurse and, to his credit, not looked her in the eye, either. But he knew it wasn't an unhappy kind of crying.

Dr Samani went through the explanation again gently, before saying 'I suggest you wait in the waiting room. He shook their hands.

Within twenty minutes he called them into the reception area. 'Yes, ICSI. You have few sperm but enough, don't worry,' he said to Gabriel. 'Ellie, we have booked you an appointment for a scan next week and a hysterosalpingogram one week after, as you have to have that just before a period. If all that is clear, you begin the drugs after that, but you will come back and we will teach you. Goodbye.'

And with that, he was off. The man with the slightly orange hair had given them more information, more help, and more hope in thirty minutes than they had found anywhere else over the past two years.

That night, they went to their favourite restaurant and laughed together for the first time in months. They got drunk on two and a half bottles of wine and had careless sex in the kitchen when they got home. But carelessness never lasts.

Gabriel didn't list the emotions he experienced in the face of infertility and all that it entailed. If someone has lots of emotions they rarely waste time naming them, instead they waste time trying to cope with them, or to hide them, or to live in spite of them or to gather them together into little emotion bags to be buried at the bottom of the garden. Mainly Gabriel became quieter, more bitter. He thought about sperm sometimes, but mostly he thought about Ellie; he found that when he struggled with life, life seemed to move faster; time changed gear and put its foot down, and the quicker it went, the fewer options there were.

Ellie, on the other hand, simply became more serious. It wasn't that she felt she carried the weight of the world on her shoulders, it was more that she had come to believe that she should behave as if she did, as if austerity and a straight face were some kind of penance. Feeling bad was her communion with God. A God, incidentally, she had no belief in whatsoever. Perhaps she imagined she was being watched by the heavens, to see if she was worthy. So she became more ascetic. She lived as though she was on her way to an interview, and that is no way to live.

6

Ellie had been lying in bed half asleep for a couple of hours before giving up. She always struggled to doze off when Gabe wasn't there, and the drugs from the IVF were making her feel a little nauseated anyway. So she had got up and gone to the fridge, got some chocolate ice cream and sat in front of the television, flicking between 'America's Next Top Model' and 'Wife Swap' and enjoying neither.

She heard the doorbell before the police rang it. Maybe she'd heard the footsteps, perhaps the police radio squeaking out its annoying white noise. For whatever reason, she was up from the sofa and heading for the door when the bell rang.

Opening the door, she saw a short blonde policewoman with strikingly red cheeks and thin pink lips, looking grave and sympathetic. A young policeman, tall and thin-faced, stood just behind her looking embarrassed. Ellie felt an electric cold.

'Where is he?' she managed to say.

'Ellie Field?' asked the policewoman.

'Where is he, what's happened?'

'I'm afraid there's been an accident. Can we come in, please?'

Before she could open the door and stand aside to let them in, Ellie was sick on the hall carpet.

No matter how hard you try, how much you concentrate, when a stranger is telling you that someone you love is on life support, you don't hear full sentences. Ellie sat hunched on the sofa, trying not to be sick again, trying to breathe the way she had told a thousand patients to breathe when they were close to panic. She heard a few key words: 'Hit by a car,' 'Shoreditch,' 'head-injuries,' 'internal bleeding' and—from the embarrassed young policeman who was probably trying to join in but not actually helping—'bagels.'

She threw on some clothes and kept asking questions that made no sense but reinforced the words she was taking in: 'What car?' *'Shoreditch?'* 'Head injuries?'

'We don't have any more details, Ms Field,' the woman said.

Ellie had never been in the back of a police car before. The policeman asked if she still felt sick, She shook her head, not really understanding the question. He didn't look convinced. As they drove to the hospital, Ellie stared out of the window at the lights. Cars, shop windows, street lamps—she didn't really go out at night much these days. She didn't recognise the lives after dark that were going on around her nightmare. They stayed in a lot, arguing. Waiting. Hiding. They: her and Gabe.

'Shoreditch,' she said out loud. 'What was he doing in Shoreditch?'

The A and E department was bright and ugly. They are always grubbier and more desperate than the ones they show on TV. Ellie noticed a couple of anxious-looking parents gathering around a pale child, and a couple of drunks in the corner shouting at nobody in particular. She could have been dreaming ... except she was so cold and she had a policewoman guiding her toward the receptionist.

To whom, with a lucidity she hadn't expected, she said, 'My partner, Gabriel Bell, was admitted earlier,' then spoiled the momentary picture of calm with 'Is he dead?'

The receptionist looked at the policewoman and then to her computer.

'He went straight into surgery,' she said. 'Third floor.' She began talking to a man with a very bloody head who had appeared beside Ellie and had asked how long he would have to wait, and could he borrow a cloth.

'Surgery,' murmured Ellie. 'That's probably good.'

58

The policewoman smiled. 'Is there anyone you want to call?' she asked.

'No, thank you. Not just yet. I'll just go up.'

'I'll come too.'

'There's no need,' lied Ellie.

'I think there is.'

They walked away from the lights and the shouting, down the main corridor to the lifts. Opposite the lifts was the hospital shop run by the League of Friends. Closed. Ellie stared through the window and saw a jar of fudge. She used to eat the same fudge with her granddad when she was a child. Who on earth would have thought you could still get fudge in a jar? She was staring at the shop, wanting her granddad to pick her up and take her home, when the policewoman said quietly, 'Ellie, the lift.'

7

Kevin had decided to embrace the therapy with a vigour he had not shown since the time he garrotted a stoned drug dealer for £1,500.

'It was when I turned forty-two that I realised forty-two felt very symbolic to me,' he said, pausing briefly for dramatic effect. He wasn't someone used to having people listening to him, and he wanted to make the most of it. Gabriel stared out of the window at the still, grey lake. Julie shuffled in her chair. And Yvonne glared at Kevin, who found himself feeling quite exhilarated.

'Elvis,' said Kevin.

'What?' said Julie. 'What about Elvis?'

'Elvis was forty-two when he died,' said Kevin. 'Tragically young.'

'And remarkably big,' said Gabriel, distractedly.

'Yes, he had a weight problem,' acknowledged Kevin, 'but let's not forget the impact that man had on the world, an impact that lingers even now. How does it go ... 'If all the world was a stage ... The King ... "Are You Lonesome Tonight?"''

'Shakespeare actually,' said Yvonne.

Kevin ignored her. 'He may have died young, but he had lived a life that was full.'

'He'd travelled each and every highway,' smiled Yvonne.

'Yeah, looking for biscuits,' said Gabriel. And they both— much to their own surprise—started laughing.

'He's being sarcastic,' complained Kevin.

Clemitius looked at Kevin solemnly. 'I don't think they are laughing at what you have said or what you have experienced, Kevin. I think they are laughing because they don't know what else to do with the things they are feeling. In my experience, people find coming into a group like this both profound and threatening.' Clemitius paused for a moment, looked intently around him, and tapped himself on the chin. 'It is a great testament to your courage that you are able to speak about your experiences so soon. If I may say so, my sense is that everyone moves at their own pace, and Yvonne and Gabriel are struggling to come to terms with this experience. Please try to be tolerant if you can.'

'Yes,' said Yvonne. 'Don't kill us! Oh, too bloody late.'

Kevin, who was still riding the crest of the wave that was finding he hadn't gone straight to hell for the twenty-one lives he had taken for money, closed his eyes and remembered what it had felt like to hit Yvonne with that ashtray. It helped somehow; it even made him smile. He had come across people like Gabriel and Yvonne many times in his life. Sometimes he had envied them their comfort with themselves; other times he had murdered them. Once or twice he had pitied them their detachment from the rawness he felt; he knew himself to be in touch with the realities of life in a way people like them never could be. They thought they were sophisticated, they thought they were clever, but they weren't. Rather, they were muffled: wrapped up in something insulating and protecting. They could not feel life the way he could.

Mostly because they had never killed anyone. Kevin believed courage and understanding came from being able to sustain yourself alone. Separate from the world. Without anything like love or even company. Gabriel, Yvonne, and probably Julie were not the types to have spent long periods of their lives alone; they were too pretty—and too needy. This Clemitius, he seemed understanding, and of course quite possibly the person in the room most likely to help him. Kevin glanced over at Clemitius and decided to press ahead.

'Anyway,' he continued. 'Elvis had lived a full life despite dying by the age of forty-two, and I hadn't done a damn thing;

well, nothing of note. I'd been in the army and done what I was told. I'd worked, eaten, and slept. That was pretty much it.'

'Tell us more,' said a very earnest Clemitius.

'Well, I travelled a bit, I marched in and out of countries, blew some of them up, did the things soldiers do, but I never really visited anywhere. I never really did anything and I never really felt happy, or comfortable. It may seem strange to you,' he said loudly and self-consciously, 'but I was never very happy around other people.'

'So you decided to kill them?' asked Julie.

'Not straight away, I didn't. I was working as a security guard at the time—easy work, crap money. I knew I had to do something different. I kind of thought: What kind of life is it that feels unlived, you know?' he said, looking at Julie.

'I don't know,' said Julie, genuinely confused.

'Exactly,' said Kevin. 'So I knew I had to do something, something that made me feel my life stood out, something that made me feel in control, if you like.'

'How do you do it?' said Yvonne.

Kevin paused for a moment, staring at the floor, seemingly deep in thought. Finally, he looked at Yvonne shrugged and said, 'S'easy.'

'How can killing someone be easy?' said Julie.

Kevin's face loosened somehow, his jaw slackened and his eyes slipped further back into his skull as he stared at her and then at Clemitius. He shrugged again, and everyone was silent.

Until finally, Gabriel said: 'What the fuck did I do to end up anywhere with you?'

8

The only time Ellie left Gabriel's bedside was to go home to wash and to give herself hormone injections. Shock and grief numbed her. She had forgotten how to think. She just was. She hadn't so much as wondered what use the treatment was without Gabe, and none of her friends had found a way of asking her. She clung to what felt like the important things: the artificial hormones—the life bringers—and going to see Gabe—the reality bringer. Beyond that she was not eating, not sleeping, not thinking, and not conscious of talking to anyone. She was simply taking medication designed to make her super-ovulate and waiting for Gabriel to wake up.

On the third day the doctors came and told her that they didn't think he was going to. The operation had lasted nearly seven hours. His skull was fractured and his brain was swollen. Worse, it was likely to swell more post-operatively, and the surgeon felt sure there would be a bleed. The optic nerve in his left eye was severed and his left cheekbone was shattered, as was his eye socket. His pelvis was in five pieces, his hip in two, his liver had been pierced by a shattered piece of bone and was bleeding. There was more, but it made Ellie dizzy to hear it.

He was still breathing, albeit through a ventilator, and his heart was still beating. And so she waited. She waited until she could decide what to do. She waited for something about which she might have a decision to make. She nodded as the doctors spoke and seemed to understand the words she heard, but made no sign to suggest she understood what they combined to mean. The doctors were not unfamiliar with this kind of response from grieving relatives; they knew she would come to understand. They had seen dozens of people struggle to accept terrible truths, sometimes after those truths had made themselves more than apparent.

However, there was something different about this case. As the consultant and his registrar got to the door, Ellie said: 'I need his sperm.'

'I'm sorry?'

'I need you to give me his sperm.'

The consultant, a thin-faced man with the most pointed chin Ellie had ever seen, and the registrar—Indian, much younger, chubby-faced and seemingly more anxious—looked at each other. At least one of them was slightly irritated about still being in the room.

'What do you mean?' asked the older man.

'We are in the middle of IVF treatment.'

'I'm sorry to hear that,' the consultant said. 'But you must understand, this young man is in no state to continue with that process.'

'I've been jabbing myself in the bottom with a needle every day for a fortnight and sniffing drugs for four weeks,' said Ellie. 'I am having my eggs harvested in two days—the same day I need his sperm to make us a baby. I need you to give me his sperm.' She wondered if what she imagined he saw, an empty grey-skinned woman on the verge of collapse, illustrated her point well enough to make him change his mind.

The consultant sat down beside Ellie. 'We can't do that.'

'Yes you can.'

'No, we can't. We don't have his permission.'

'Yes, you do.' Her voice began to shake. 'He is undergoing IVF treatment; he has signed the forms. What clearer permission can a man give?'

'He would need to give permission for us to invade his body and take the sperm, and he hasn't done that.' The consultant spoke softly, aware of the fact that the tired woman in front of him, full of borrowed hormones and crashing grief, was just barely holding herself together.

'Hell, he's got tubes in every orifice! What is that if it isn't invading his body?'

'Those tubes are there to keep him alive.'

'This is a man who has already signed up to a course of treatment that involves his sperm being added to my eggs in a lab.' She could feel reason leaking out of her. 'He has said it's OK!'

'Yes, but not to us taking the sperm without his consent.'

'Well sir, it wouldn't actually be without his consent, would it?' said the registrar. The consultant ignored the registrar—who probably realised he had just made the rest of his time working with the eminent and deeply traditional doctor hell—and said, 'I think you need to talk to a solicitor if you insist on continuing with this. I certainly know I cannot extract sperm from this man without legal clarification.'

Ellie could feel her breath quickening. 'I don't have the time. You just said he might not wake up, and I am having my eggs taken the day after tomorrow. They'll be wasted unless you give me his sperm.'

The consultant looked away. 'I'm sorry,' he said. 'There is nothing I can do. I can talk with the medical director for clarification, but I am sure he will agree with me.'

'Well, do it anyway,' said Ellie. 'And I'll do the same.' She knew she wouldn't do anything of the sort. She didn't have the time. She would have to find another way.

'I'm sorry,' he said. And both the consultant and the embarrassed-looking registrar left the room.

And for the first time since she had arrived at the hospital, for the first time since the police had called round to her house to tell her what had happened, and for the first time since she had seen her lover being kept alive by a machine, she cried. From the bottom of her belly to the top of the sky she wailed, and Gabriel didn't even hear her.

9

Izzy's sister Moira, five years younger and with none of the complexion problems, had always stood out from the crowd. Mainly because she dressed each morning as if Stevie Wonder were picking her clothes. For Moira, colour coordination was for interior decorators; she believed that one dressed most comfortably if one chose each item of clothing in perfect isolation from each other. She looked a bit like a cross between one of those people who had had their colours done ('no, really, purple *is* you—in another life you may have been a plum') and an art student who had run out of grant. In fact, she worked for the Citizens' Advice Bureau as a debt adviser, which came as a surprise to just about everyone who came through the door.

Look a little closer or, indeed, ask her why she has such beautifully clear skin, and she will tell you that everything good about her, from her generous spirit to her spotless bottom, is down to complementary therapies. Moira is as close to being an expert on Reiki, crystal healing, reflexology, aromatherapy, Bach flower remedies and homeopathy as one can get outside of a yurt. Her fascination with all things alternative began when she managed to rid herself of a wart on her thumb at the age of fourteen with a dab of ylang-ylang and a crushed dandelion. Quickly converted, she steadfastly refused to go to hospital with severe stomach pains at the age of seventeen, instead insisting her close friend Patricia come round with some crystals and her healing books. When she woke pain-free the following morning, she quite understandably felt redeemed and not a little proud of herself. Izzy maintained that wind passes regardless of whether you place a rock under your pillow or not, but that was the kind of cynicism that Moira knew she would have to get used to.

'It wasn't wind, it was peritonitis.'

'Oh right, a burst appendix was miraculously reformed by your friend Patricia and some glass stones on your bed,' mocked Izzy.

'It must be horrible being so cynical all the time, Isabel. You know, I think that's why you keep getting those big spots. It's all that bile you carry about all the time trying to get out.'

Moira had grown into a woman of many interests and few ambitions. She had formerly been a sub-editor on a series of business magazines ranging from *Cement Monthly* to *The World of Wound Care,* but while the social life that existed in magazine companies probably suited her best, she couldn't help but find herself frustrated by the absolute pointlessness of what she was doing with her time. Particularly when she was working for *Cement Monthly,* which had an editor who behaved as though he were putting out *The Washington Post* each month, only focusing pretty much on the cement-centred stories.

To train up to work at the Citizens' Advice Bureau, she had to do three different courses and take an £11,000 pay cut. Everyone she worked with considered her ridiculous for the first three days of her tenure. After one month they considered her indispensable, albeit badly dressed. After three months she was simply Moira.

Her relationship history was as chaotic as her clothes. She had lived near and had a lot of hurried, largely unsatisfying and guilt-laden sex with a married father of three who was twelve years her senior—a man she continued to sleep with long after any inkling of attraction had passed, partly because, as she told Ellie and Izzy: 'I feel a bit sorry for his wife, the only time she gets to herself is when he comes round to shag me.'

She fell hopelessly in love with a part-time croupier, part-time drug dealer who could only write his name in capitals and who used to rifle her purse when she was in the bathroom. She stuck by him for nearly three years, half of which he spent in prison.

She also had a couple of half-hearted affairs with friends of Sam's, explaining later that she didn't like to let Sam down by telling him that she thought his friends were dull and, most lately, she had agreed to marry a Croatian asylum-seeker who she said 'looks a bit like George Clooney but with just the one eye.' A marriage of convenience that couldn't take place because one-eyed George, who it turned out was actually from Limerick, was already married to three other women.

As if all that weren't enough, Moira differed even further from her older sister in that she adored Gabriel. It was never a 'wish he were mine' kind of thing: she simply didn't think about the world in that way; although she kind of assumed that she would have shagged him under other circumstances. But she really, really liked him. They made each other laugh and while they never, ever arranged to go out together, just the two of them—somehow that would have been odd—but whenever circumstance, or Sam and Izzy, brought them together, they behaved like long-lost best friends and immediately slipped into what seemed to Izzy, at least, some kind of private comedy language. All of which probably made Izzy dislike Gabriel all the more.

However, caricature Moira as the fly-by-night, dizzy little sister if you like (it's OK, everyone does), as soon as she heard Gabriel had been hurt, she became the most focused, ordered, and generous friend anyone could have wished for. She went straight to the hospital and sat with Ellie. She came back the next day and the next. She brought tuna sandwiches and spare knickers and a constant flow of coffee and bottled water. She didn't cry once, at least not in anyone else's company. She spoke charmingly with nurses and, on the one occasion that Ellie slept for an hour, Moira sat beside Gabriel and spoke to him about work, football, and the Croatian George Clooney bloke, whom Gabriel had met and been very nice to even though he thought he was 'a one-eyed mad bastard.'

When Ellie woke, Moira quietly slipped away for more coffee or more pants or whatever. It's often—Ellie might have reflected if she had been capable of cogency—the quiet ones you don't expect to have to rely on who are the only people there when you need them.

10

A few days before the accident, Julie had, ironically under the circumstances, decided to change her life. In a cottage in the Norfolk countryside, James Buchan, the man she was living with, had just got off of the telephone, the words of his accountant ringing in his ears.

'My advice,' the accountant had said, 'would be to make some money, proper money, fucking quick.'

Julie was sitting on the sofa leafing through the Norfolk Herald and not really helping. 'Get a job,' she said.

'I'm not qualified for anything. What do you want me to do, apply to be a bus conductor? A milkman? A hospital bloody porter?'

'What's wrong with that?'

'Oh don't be so fucking stupid, how's that going to look? James Buchan, one-time pop star, now reduced to being a bloody bus conductor. If the papers get hold of that, I'll be a laughing stock.'

James was an overweight man with thinning, just too long, black wavy hair. His fat had gone to his face first, forcing his already slightly withdrawn chin into what looked like full-blooded retreat. When he sweated he went red, and when he went red, the bald spot on the crown of his head looked like a strawberry gateau. When Julie looked at him, she wondered why she had ever spoken to him, let alone slept with him or moved into his silly bloody house.

She breathed deeply and decided not to call him a deluded twat. 'You were never that famous. And anyway, my father was a bus conductor,' lied Julie, whose father had been a maths teacher.

70

'You told me your father was a maths teacher.'

'Not all the time,' she said and returned to her magazine. Julie knew a job was out of the question. James was forty-five and had no useful skills. All the jobs that didn't require skills were either taken or about to be taken by twenty-three-year-old geography graduates. She knew he was unemployable but sometimes, just for fun, she left job adverts around the house. Most recently, ones for a trainee estate agent and a bus conductor. He hadn't pursued either opportunity.

The phone started ringing. Julie looked at James. He made no move to answer it, secure in the knowledge that it was either his bank phoning to remind him that he was £8,876 overdrawn, which he had promised to rectify two weeks ago. Or it was the building society phoning to tell him he was now three months behind on his mortgage payments,* and while it really didn't want to repossess, it would. Or it was his accountant phoning back to remind him about the £500 he had been stupid enough to lend James to tide him over the previous month.

The ringing stopped, and for a moment James imagined all of his creditors had, as one, decided to let him off. Either that or the phone had been disconnected.

He could always sell the cottage. That would clear his debts, get the building society off his back, and perhaps leave enough for a small deposit on a two-bedroom flat in King's Lynn. But the cottage was all he had and besides, if he sold that, he also sold his livelihood, pathetic as that was. Without it this time next year he would be in the same position, except worse: he'd be in King's Lynn. Fuck, he was annoyed. This shouldn't be happening to him, it never happened to Sting for chrissakes, or any of Adam's Ants. Why should it happen to him?

Nearly twenty years ago, James had been the voice of post-post-punk pop outfit Dog in a Tuba. The high point of his and their career had come with the single 'Red,' which reached No. 3 in the charts and was No. 1 in Japan for four weeks. As a result of that single, the ridiculously titled album 'The Animals are

Coming' (yes, it had a big picture of lots of animals, including a pink rhino and a giraffe with a really big scarf on running after Dog in a Tuba on the front cover) sold quite well and spawned two other, less-successful singles 'Insect Control' and 'Partytime' (16 and 28, respectively). The low point of his career came when that whole Manchester baggy-jeans thing took off. Overnight Dog in a Tuba went the way of Gerry and his sodding Pacemakers.

Since then, he had eked out a living renting out a small recording studio and rehearsal space to wannabe bands who didn't mind paying that little bit extra for being in the presence (or at least the converted barn) of a man who had not only been on Top of the Pops, but had also shared lipstick with The Cure's Robert Smith and, allegedly, urinated into Dave Lee Travis's thermos flask at a Radio One road show in Great Yarmouth. Rock 'n roll.

However, in the past few years, recording studios in converted barns had become rather old hat. While he still played host to the occasional metalheads, most people recorded at home these days, on computers. Converted barns were for games rooms, holiday lets, or housing tractors. Countryside recording studios were to music what the Spinning Jenny was to the manufacturing industry. And anyway, it would be fair to say his studio was not exactly state of the art.

Last night, as he lay on the floor upstairs in his quiet room—the place he went to think, to smoke grass and, more recently, to sleep—he played Dog in a Tuba's last (second) album. It had sold about 700 copies. More, James liked to point out at the time, than Mick Jagger's solo work. The sleeve lay on the floor beside him; pinned to the inside of the cover was a faded review ripped from the pages of the *NME*. It said: 'Truly awful. If you have ever wanted to make someone an interesting ashtray out of a crap record, this is your chance, because you are sure as hell not going to play it more than once.'

72

And a possible desperate solution had, through the mists of cheap grass, suddenly come to him. Only 720 people had heard that record, most of them must have forgotten it; hell some of them might be dead. If Dog in a Tuba were remembered, it was as the band that recorded 'Red'. The band that had once been described as Norwich's answer to the Psychedelic Furs, albeit by James himself.

'Hell,' he had said aloud to the empty room, 'if Go fucking West can do it, so can I.'

Meanwhile, Julie had sat on the bed in the room next door and contemplated her escape. She knew that she could not muster the energy for any heartfelt goodbyes; ideally she would leave when he was out, but he didn't go out very much. She gave no thought to leaving James, beyond the practicalities of where to go, but she did think about herself, the habitual leaver. She glanced in the mirror, but quickly turned away. She was 35. She knew that if you look too often or too long at yourself at that age, then you are looking for decay. Julie had naturally pale skin, stroked by delicate, near-invisible freckles. She was tall, thin, athletic; she could have been a contender except that her eyes were not fashionable eyes: they weren't big and moist and always close to surprise. They were bluey-green, but they didn't shine; even when she smiled they didn't shine, and that detracted slightly from what would otherwise be considered a conventional English beauty. Her eyes were thin and half-alive; if an interesting man shot Julie an admiring glance, invariably she responded with a wince, whether or not she meant to.

'There's only one thing to do. I'm phoning Bernie,' James announced.

'Is that a good idea?' asked Julie sarcastically; she had absolutely no idea who Bernie was.

'Only one way to find out,' said James.

The former manager of Dog in a Tuba, Bernie Skyte was a recovering alcoholic and one-time club owner whom James had last spoken to in 1991, when the words 'fuck', 'off', and 'die' might have been uttered. James phoned what had, ten years earlier, been The Bernie Skyte Management Agency. It was now a kebab shop.

So James called The Roadie. Despite the fact James had not spoken to him for at least five years, The Roadie seemed unsurprised to hear his voice. Nothing surprises a roadie, thought James. 'Hello Jimmy, how's it hanging?'

'By a thread. I need Bernie's number.'

'What for?'

'I just need to talk to him.' James remembered why roadies always irritated him. It was because they were irritating.

'You thinking of getting the band back together?'

'No, well maybe, I don't know. Where's Bernie?'

'Margate.'

'Margate?' repeated James.

'He's got a bungalow, runs a little antique shop,' said The Roadie.

'Margate?'

'Last I heard.'

As this conversation droned on Julie ignored him. She was reading an article about a woman who had had fifteen sessions of plastic surgery. Face lifted, eyes Botoxed, legs and stomach drained of unsightly fat. She'd had her breasts enlarged, the skin around her neck tightened, and something done to make her bottom look more tapered. The photographs looked as though she were walking into a strong wind. And her teeth went straight past white on their way to transparent. She looked awful. Julie touched her neck, looked up at James to see he wasn't looking, and felt her breasts. She couldn't remember how they felt fifteen years ago so how did she know how they'd changed? She still worked out, although not as often. They felt OK she thought.

'What are you doing?' asked James.

'Nothing' she said pulling her shirt down tightly to her waist.

James paused, shook his head, dialled a number, and said to Julie—as if she cared—that he was calling 'his' old guitarist.

'Gary Guitar! Hey Gary. James here. James Buchan. Jimmy B. Gary... Gaz ...'

James dialled again, and at least this time Gary Guitar spoke, albeit to say: 'Fuck off, tosser.'

After he had hung up, James poured himself and Julie a drink and tried to think what to say to Bernie. James was perspiring. It would be a lie to say that Julie, who watched impassively from behind the magazine, pitied James. That would imply more feeling than she could muster for the bloke.

James and Julie had lived together for nearly a year. They had met at a yoga class. James was sleeping with the teacher, Julie didn't like the teacher, James was having one of his good patches, Julie looked good in a leotard; it was bound to happen. But that was ages ago. If Julie had been the type of woman who reflected earnestly on her past decisions, then she might have considered James to be one of those transitory relationships that had lasted longer than it should and had been ascribed more significance than it deserved simply because she had needed a place to live and he had needed rent.

But she wasn't much given to reflection, not about relationships anyway. Julie believed that one's capacity to form and maintain relationships existed beyond reason, it just happened, and it was best to let that part of you take care of itself. Julie trusted her instincts: wherever she was, whenever it was, if her instinct told her to go, then she left. She didn't always have a plan as to where she was going, but she believed that that didn't matter. She reasoned that if whatever filled her present wasn't pleasing her, then it was not worth building a future on. Julie had done a lot of leaving.

'I know!' shouted James, clearly chastened by Gary Guitar's reluctance to engage. Julie jumped a little, spilling gin on the tight-faced freak in the local paper. 'I'll visit Bernie, see him face to face. You can't hang up on someone who's standing in your shop.'

'No, but you can throw things at them.'

'Nah,' said James. 'Bernie's not the throwing type. He's too short.' As James picked up the phone again to get an address for Bernie, Julie made her way upstairs to her bedroom.

That evening, Julie's last in the cottage, they had guests over. Guests being Michael—Julie's favourite person in the whole of Norwich—and whoever happened to be with him. James did the cooking while Julie stayed in her room—packing, hiding, wondering what she would be doing next week.

Julie came downstairs about five minutes after hearing Michael and his date arrive. She usually made an effort to avoid the introductions, as they always brought the worst out of James and that made her irritable for the rest of the evening. James was always a little competitive around Michael, and when he brought a woman round James would often greet her with things like: 'Good lord, you're beautiful. Why are you with him?' Or on one occasion: 'Christ, you look just like Kim Wilde, and believe me I should know.'

So she waited for the embarrassing air-kissing to stop, and by the time she came down, James, Michael and a dark-haired woman with bright red lipstick and, Julie thought, a slightly-larger-than-necessary arse, were standing staring at James's latest acquisition—an elaborately framed poster that he had bought at a car boot sale, of a Rothko painting called "Blue and Green." It was about the size of Belgium, and James had bought it shortly after seeing the original on the wall in the background of a TV interview with Sting. Consequently, Julie referred to it as his 'lucky Sting poster.'

Nobody noticed as Julie came into the room. She was heading for the gin when she heard James say, 'I don't know what it is about it, but sometimes I feel I could just jump right into the middle of it.

76

Julie said, 'You don't want to do that, Jim, you'll bang your head and fall in the fire. Think what the papers will say, "Former pop singer killed in surprise collision with crap poster."'

Michael smiled and gave her a hug, being careful not to hold on for too long, then introduced her to Lipstick Girl while James wandered off to the kitchen, which was probably the room in which he was happiest. They drank gin and tonics, and James worked hard at making everyone feel good about being there. As Lipstick Girl was the outsider, she was the target for most of his charm. James was a good host: what might have first looked like showboating for the attractive stranger increasingly came over as a genuine attempt to make Lipstick Girl comfortable. He asked all the right questions: 'What do you do?'

'I teach media studies.'

'Where did you meet Michael?'

'At a book launch.'

'Can I get you another gin?'

'Yes.'

Julie listened politely but thought that anyone who said the words "media studies" without spitting afterwards should be taken to the kitchen and put in the oven. And she didn't like Lipstick Girl's dress, which she thought looked like the one the girls wear in WH Smith.

By the time dinner was ready, Lipstick Girl seemed quite relaxed in a 'This is my fourth gin' kind of way. James, pleased with his hosting skills, was in such a good mood he let Julie pick the CD. She opted for something by 'My Morning Jacket', which was clearly perceived as taking advantage, because after three songs James replaced it with the Police's greatest hits.

'I met him recently,' said Michael.

'Who?' asked James.

'Sting.'

'Really?' said James, quite impressed. 'Did he know who you were?'

'He said he recognised me.'

'Really!' even more impressed. 'You see the band is still kind of out there floating around in the ether, we are still lodged in the consciousness of people of a certain age.'

'What band?'

'Our band.'

'He recognised me from "The Late Show," not Dog in a fucking Tuba.' Michael inadvertently screwed up his nose when he said the word Tuba. James looked embarrassed. Michael quickly added: 'Christ, Jim, I was just the bloody bass player, maybe he'd have recognised you.'

There was a silence, which Lipstick Girl filled by asking loudly, 'Were you two in a band together?'

Michael had had no clue what he was going to do when he stopped being in Dog in a Tuba, but he knew that he would rather not work for a living, and to get away with that, you had to plan ahead and be lucky. A friend of his persuaded him to write something and put him in touch with a features editor at *The Guardian*. They asked him to write a piece for the Saturday review about what it was like to be in a band when it finishes. They probably expected some maudlin liturgy of recrimination, name-calling, and sulking. What they got was quite a funny, lively piece about how surprised he was when flares became fashionable again and how ridiculous it feels to be playing to 2,000 Japanese teenagers on your thirty-second birthday.

Other work followed, and he became quite popular, even appearing on 'The Late Show' a few times talking about Spanish film, some crap exhibition of Brit Art—his key line being 'someone pins their trousers to the wall and calls it 'Legless' and that's art?'—and the new series of 'Holby City.' He never claimed to be a proper journalist, but he took time to learn to write, reading the people who obviously did it well and figuring out what made them good. He never lied about anything, never pretended that the things he talked about were important, and always delivered what he was asked for.

However, having made it into his forties with most of his hair, a few decent suits and two homes—a flat in central London and a cottage in Norfolk—it had finally occurred to him that he might want something a little more substantial in his life; something like a family or a cause or at least a nudging, self-defining belief system. He had begun to sleep badly; he had grown—reluctantly—a gnawing ball of self-doubt. He had tried to ignore it. He had filled the night-time hours with as much sex as he could find without feeling too sordid or seeming too desperate. He had slept with an awful lot of women. Quite recently he had slept in the same week with two women who he considered plain and more worryingly, quite dull. He didn't know why. The second he imagined was to eliminate the thought of the first. He found himself touching her flesh softly not through tenderness, but through curiosity. Almost asking himself, what am I doing here? Consequently, he did things he perhaps shouldn't have done. Thrown himself into the fleshy project with a fervour that might later require a restraining order from the shaken and stirred woman.

Lipstick Girl was cute. It worried him a little that that didn't matter to him as much as it should.

Michael had decided he needed to spend more time out of London. It was partly to avoid the easygoing, going-nowhere circle of hack acquaintances that he enjoyed hanging out and talking rubbish with, and partly because he had decided there was no point in having a cottage in Norfolk if you never went to it. He figured if he wanted to change his life, the first thing he should do was to spend part of it in a different place.

One of the consequences of spending time in Norfolk was seeing more of James, although that wasn't difficult as he hadn't seen him at all between 1989 and 1995. They met again by accident in a record shop on Oxford Street, swapped numbers, and had seen each other once every six months or so until Michael had bought the cottage. Now they saw each other every six weeks or so, usually at James's for dinner and only, from Michael's point of view, so he could hang out with Julie.

Later, just after the lemon cheesecake, Julie turned to Michael and said quietly: 'She has lovely hair.'

'Who does?'

'Whatsername.'

'You don't like her, then?'

'She seems perfectly nice.'

'That's a no.' Michael always liked this bit of the evening best.

'I prefer her to that American you brought last time.'

'I thought you got on all right with her.'

'Of course I got on with her, that's just good manners.' Julie said in mock wide-eyed surprise.

'Or being two-faced.'

'Or that. But *like* her? *Pur-leeze!* She had a bloody eating disorder, made Ally McBeal look like Bette Midler. She kept picking at her food, hardly ate a thing, and only drank white-wine spritzers. I wanted to force feed her a chunky Kit Kat.'

Michael laughed. 'I'd have paid to watch that.'

James and Lipstick Girl, on the other hand, were talking cake. She loved his cheesecake, which James was milking for all it was worth. 'I'm probably happiest in the kitchen, wouldn't you say pet? Julie! Julie! I was just saying how I'm happiest in the kitchen.'

'Yes,' said Julie. 'Jim does like to bake.'

'Either the kitchen or the recording studio,' lied James, who hadn't been in his own recording studio for weeks and certainly hadn't done any recording.

'You have a recording studio?' asked Lipstick Girl. Julie rolled her eyes.

'Oh yes, would you like to see it? Mike, Mikey, I'm just going to show your lady friend the studio. If we're not back in ten minutes, let yourself out, ha ha.' And James and Lipstick Girl wandered off toward the barn.

And it was a barn: dark and cold, with straw on the floor even though the place hadn't had an animal in it for years. Lipstick Girl shivered as she walked into the middle of the room and looked around. There was a hole in the roof, big enough to see a couple of stars through, and a puddle on the floor to prove the hole worked even if the rest of the place didn't. In the middle of the barn was a semi-circle of guitar amps. There were three amps, one of which was covered in cigarette burns, and all of them were dusty and old. At the far end was the blacked-out console room. 'Doesn't look like what I imagined a recording studio would look like,' said Lipstick Girl, who was wishing she had brought a coat.

'Yeah, a lot of people expect something shiny with machines everywhere. But a studio is a place of work. Come on, I'll show you the nerve centre.'

James marched off toward the end of the barn, bumping into what appeared to be an oil drum. 'Fuck.'

'What is that?'

'Bloke up the road asked me to store some stuff for him when he was having his place inspected. He was paying, and I thought they might make an interesting noise if you banged them. That's the thing about music, you're always looking for a sound.' And when he said it, he actually believed it. 'So you and Michael, you serious?'

'Oh I don't know,' she laughed. 'What's serious?'

Which was far too hard a question for James. 'Here, sit here. You look cold ... Here.' He took off his cardigan. It smelt of cannabis and sweat, but it was thick, and Lipstick Girl was cold. She sat down in a dusty imitation leather chair in front of the console and James stood behind her. She could feel him leaning on the chair, forcing it to rock gently backwards and forwards, and she could see his breath in the cold, which meant he was closer than he needed to be. She looked around: to her left was a drum kit, to her right an old upright piano. Almost exactly between them were three microphone stands standing in a puddle. She looked up and saw another hole. As she did so she felt James's warm breath on her exposed neck. She got up quickly.

'You've got another hole up there.' She didn't turn round. If she had, she would have seen James half-falling over into the chair as it tipped back. Recovering quickly, he glanced up. It was another hole, right above where the singer would stand.

'Oh fuck,' he mumbled. 'Let's go back, shall we? Don't want the others to worry.' Which was music to her ears. Or at least the nearest thing to music anyone was likely to hear in that place.

Back in the house Julie and Michael were still half whispering. It was a hard habit to break. 'He's putting on a bit of a show, isn't he?' said Michael.

'Yeah, he's got this idea into his head about getting your old band back together.'

'You're joking.'

'No, he's been phoning around, he's going to see someone called Bernie.'

'Bernie? Bernie hates James, James videoed himself and Bernie's young and stoned god-daughter fucking … . Sorry.'

'Oh Christ, Michael, I don't mind. James and I haven't been near each other in months. I see myself as a lodger, not sure what he sees me as. Actually, I was going to ask, you doing anything tomorrow lunchtime?'

'You asking me for a date?' joked Michael.

'One step at a time,' smiled Julie. 'I'm moving to Norwich tomorrow and, no, James doesn't know yet. I'm going to stay with one of my students.'

'Is that allowed?'

'I'm a part-time adult art teacher and she is a seventy-five-year-old woman. Believe me, I've encountered worse cases of teacher-student abuse. I wondered if you fancied meeting for coffee?'

'Sure. Twelve-thirty by the clock tower?'

'Fine,' said Julie, who looked up and nodded toward James and Lipstick Girl as they returned.

'Hey Mikey, your lovely friend wants to hear what we sounded like. I can't believe you haven't played her any of our stuff.'

'I haven't got any.'

'What do you mean, you haven't got any?'

'I mean I haven't bloody got any.'

'Well how about a little show? I'll get you a guitar.'

'And I'll get my coat,' said Michael.

'Oh well,' said James, remembering that he hadn't sung outside of the shower for a decade, 'It'll have to be a record, I'm afraid.'

'Oh Christ,' murmured Michael.

'I'll get you a drink,' said Julie, trying not to laugh and failing. 'And then you can tell us all which bits are you. Hey, I've got an idea, I could go and get a tennis racket and you could act it out for us.'

11

The next morning James had woken with a rare enthusiasm for life and Margate. He was a bit nervous about getting down there and seeing Bernie, but if his brief flirtation with Zen had taught him anything, it was to try to live in the moment. The moment he should be in by now was on the B1108 four miles from the A11. Unfortunately, he was still stuck in an altogether unexpected moment where Julie was telling him that she was moving out and that there was a cheque for a month's rent in the kitchen.

'I don't want your money,' lied James, reading the cheque. 'Anyway, you paid a month's deposit; I suppose you'll want that back.'

'You can send it to me.' Julie knew that if you wanted a quick getaway sometimes you had to pay for it.

'Where will you be?' asked James in a whiney voice.

'In town for a while, staying with a friend.'

'What friend? Not Michael!' Which surprised them both. Being left was one thing—actually it was a big thing. Pop stars, James felt, sang about being left; they weren't actually left. Well, except Bryan Ferry, and he could get away with it. But being left for your bass player?

'No, of course not,' said Julie, but she felt herself blush slightly and wondered momentarily if James did actually notice things going on around him after all, before rejecting the idea as absurd.

'Is it another man?' he asked.

'No, her name is Brenda,' sighed Julie. She was getting bored. She looked at her watch, then out the window. 'Let's not make a fuss, eh? We both know this has gone on longer than it should have.'

'But …' said James.

'But what, James? You love me and you want us to be together for always?'

'No, but …' He was fingering a buttonhole on his cardigan and wincing. He looked as though he wanted to go to the toilet.

'Because at no point has there been any love between us. Some sex yes, but that wasn't anything to write home about was it?'

'No, but …'

'Oh for goodness' sake, you hardly know I'm here, and now you've got this band thing to be getting on with, and I wish you well with that, I really do. It's nice that you have something to be concentrating on, but it's time for me to be moving on.' And she looked at his redder-than-it-should-be skin and the slope between his bottom lip and his throat, the space where other people have chins, and thought, He is the least attractive man I have ever slept with. Which made her feel sad.

'Well, you don't need to move out, Jules. I mean, we've been living more like friends than anything else, and we don't really bother each other.' James let go of his cardigan and looked at her evenly. And Julie looked as though she might cry, but she knew that was not because of James.

'I know, James, and that's sweet of you, but I think it's best.'

A car pulled up outside. 'Look that's my cab, I'll give you a call sometime, when I'm settled in,' she lied, slinging her bag over her shoulder and dropping her house keys on the kitchen table. 'I'm going down to London tomorrow, visiting a friend for a few days, but I'll be back for the start of term. Take it easy, let me know how the reunion goes.' And before James could say anything else, such as to clarify how long she was prepared to wait for her deposit, she was gone.

James wandered from room to room trying to remember the good times. By the time he got to Julie's bedroom, he'd realised that he couldn't actually remember any, so he had a quick wank and decided to advertise the room when he got back, resolving first to see if Michael had any friends—Lipstick Girl for example—looking for somewhere to live. Within forty-five minutes of Julie leaving the house, James was in his car and heading for the A11. There'll be other women, he thought, especially if Dog in a Tuba get to tour the Far East.

About an hour later, a happier Julie arrived at Brenda's house to a warm and comfortingly matter-of-fact welcome. Brenda was lovely, she didn't make any kind of fuss, simply showed Julie to her room, told her to make herself at home and to come down if and when she wanted a cup of tea.

The room was exactly what one would expect of a spare room in a nice house in the middle of Norwich. It smelled of potpourri and the wallpaper was embossed—lilac and cream carnations on a white background. She rubbed her hands across it: it felt like the walls she had had at home as a child. She remembered drawing round the flowers with a pen, and her mother being furious with her.

Julie put her bags on the floor, sat on the bed and phoned Lynne, her oldest friend. They didn't speak regularly, but whenever anything happened in their lives they were used to telling each other first.

'Hello, we still OK for tomorrow?'

'Yeah, I've got wine, and I've moved again.'

'Why? Man trouble?'

'Not an important man.'

'They never are. Why you staying up there at all?'

'I like the work, got some friends.'

'Name four.'

'Can't, just got two.'

'Names?'

'Michael.'

'Friend friend or friend?'

'Friend ... at the moment ... and Brenda. Look, I'll tell you about it when I see you. How's work?'

'I love it, I really do.' Lynne was a training to be a nurse. She'd been a nun, an exotic dancer, and a traveller. What else was she going to try, she'd said to Julie—telesales?

'Is around 10 p.m. too late?'

'Perfect. If you get lost, call me from Brick Lane and I'll guide you in. Oh, by the way, what happened to that singer bloke?'

'Coming to a bingo hall near you soon.'

'Eh?'

'Nothing, see you tomorrow night.'

The next day Julie was early, it was a habit of hers, but Michael was earlier. He was sitting on a bench under the clock tower, trying not to watch a couple of drunks on the other side of the cobbled road, knocking back sherry and working themselves up into a lather about who had the funniest shoes or something. Michael was wearing a slightly absurd black Hawaiian print shirt with yellow and orange dahlias on it. Julie approved. She sat next to him, stared at the cool blue sky, and said, 'What a beautiful day.'

'Hello, how you doin'?'

'I'm well, how about you?'

'Good, thanks, but then I haven't just split up from my live-in lover.' Michael hadn't planned to bring that up quite so soon, but he did think he ought to find out what kind of mood he should be in with her. Sad, comforting, reassuring her that she would not end up living with lots of cats in a bedsit in Cromer? Or pretty much the same as usual? All the signs were that usual was the order of the day.

'Oh, did I tell you I was doing that? I forgot. Anyway stop it. Do you want to get coffee or do you want to sit here and admire the wildlife?'

'Coffee. I know just the place.'

He led her through the market square and down behind the high street to a small, secluded square with an art shop, a shop selling stamps, and what appeared to be a very exclusive retail outlet specialising in gloves. There was also a nice, quiet coffee shop with imitation leather seats and homemade cake. Once they were sitting down with their skinny lattes and shortbread biscuits, Michael asked how the 'leaving' had been.

'It was fine. James is worried about money and preoccupied with this band thing. He was more worried about the rent than he was about me.'

'Oh, I'm sure that isn't true,' said Michael without thinking.

'It's all right, Michael, this was no big romance; it was mostly about convenience—a lot of relationships are. I would have thought you knew that.'

Michael laughed. 'Well I don't tend to have relationships. Dates sometimes, phone calls occasionally, a browse through the personal ads. But relationships?'

'Now what is that supposed to make me think, I wonder? That you are the archetypal commitmentphobe? "Wherever you lay your hat that's your head" kind of man? Or that you are the slightly vulnerable, sensitive type on the lookout for love but tragically destined instead to sleep with lots of attractive young woman who are never quite... enough?' Julie was smiling, and managing to eat shortbread without getting crumbs stuck to her lips at the same time. That didn't mean it didn't sound a little cruel though.

'I've been married, you know,' said Michael, slightly more defensively than he meant to.

'So have I,' said Julie. 'A long time ago.' And as she said it she closed her eyes for a moment so as not to let the memory in. They drank coffee, quietly, comfortably. Michael glanced out of the window as his drunks marched by, walking with a pace and determination reserved only for an adequately resourced trip to the off licence.

'How old are you?' asked Julie.

'Forty-three.'

'Christ,' she hissed.

'Quite.'

'Do you feel forty-three?'

'Dunno. I don't feel I have the life a forty-three-year-old should have.'

'What life is that?'

'Wife, couple of kids, a hobby. I'm not sure.'

'Do you actually want any of those things?'

'Not sure.'

'Yes you are.'

'No, I'm not really. I mean I think I'd like those things; well, maybe not a hobby. I can't quite see myself in a garden shed carving mermaids out of driftwood. But if I wanted it bad enough, I suppose I'd have made it happen. Anyhow, I may be quite set in my ways.'

'Oh that's bollocks, Michael. People can do what they want, change if they want, live differently if they want. You just like getting laid a lot. No harm in that.' As she spoke she looked away from him, dismissive but not cold.

Michael felt momentarily embarrassed. He wasn't used to anyone providing a commentary on his lifestyle. He didn't know if he should be offended or touched that she was paying attention. 'Well it keeps me off the streets. Sort of,' he shrugged. 'So what do you want? Where do you go from here?'

'Two different questions, I think. From here I go home, throw some stuff in a bag, go and pick up my hire car and head south. I'm going to visit a friend in London: I'll stay down there over the weekend and be back for work on Tuesday. As for what I want? Something different to what I've had before, I suppose.'

'What have you had before?'

'Freedom, or what you call freedom when you are young. I don't know, I've never been very good at plans.'

'So how do you know you won't get to London and decide to stay down there?'

'I don't like London.'

They paused again, this time less comfortably, both aware they were not speaking and both frustrated by the complete lack of drunks to pretend to look at.

'I think we need more coffee,' said Michael, hoping that Julie would not say she had to go and unpack.

'OK, my turn.' Julie wondered if maybe Michael simply didn't fancy her. She found herself wondering about Lipstick Girl and for the first time wondered what she must have thought of Julie. Living in the cottage. With James.

Michael watched her as she walked to the counter. He watched as she chatted with the girl making the coffee and as she laughed naturally at a joke about Danish pastries. And he looked at the shape of her arse and the long black skirt that clung to it and the slightly faded, golden skin of her arms and smiled to himself as he wondered what he was doing looking at her arse—which felt, frankly, a bit tacky, and acknowledged the fact that he was quite interested in the colour and texture of her skin and that he did—no big surprise, so why does he feel a bit surprised—fancy her quite a bit. Bugger.

'So how's Lipstick Girl?' Julie asked, sitting down and handing him a blueberry muffin.

'We're not seeing each other or anything ...'

'Just sleeping together?'

'No. Well yes, but no. I mean ...'

'Oh come on, Michael,' Julie was looking him in the eye. 'If it's a delicate subject, we can talk about the weather or something ...'

'No, it's not. We have, but we're not. Really. I don't imagine we'll see each other again.'

'Sorry, it's not really any of my business.'

'No, but I think I wish it was,' which was not the sort of thing Michael had remembered saying for a very long time. It occurred to him that the whole black-skirted arse thing may have gone to his head—or the other bit of him that did the thinking where women were concerned—but then he thought, oh what the hell.

Julie smiled and thought to herself, I knew that. I've known that for ages, and said: 'You think you wish it was.' Teasing, feeling as if she were ten years younger.

Michael grinned. 'Yes, I think I do ... if that's not too much trouble ... thank you.'

'Yeah,' she said. 'That's OK.'

'I mean the James thing ...'

'Oh shut up and eat your muffin.'

Michael bit into the top of his cake, chewed quickly and said, 'Fancy a drink then, when you get back?'

'Yeah, course. I'll be bloody thirsty by then.'

'Ha ha. When suits you?'

'I don't believe I have too much planned socially for the next six years or so, and I imagine you have a slightly busier diary, so you tell me.'

'When you planning to get back?'

'Monday evening or Tuesday morning.'

'Tuesday evening OK?'

'Yeah, where?'

'Clock tower. Eight p.m.?'

'Fine. Do you know anywhere else in the city by the way?'

'Don't knock it, I'm coming to think of it as my lucky clock tower.'

12

The group began with silence. Christopher didn't like silence, and so had an announcement ready should it go on for too long. As it was, to his surprise, Clemitius beat him to it.

'We, and by we, I mean the therapists, have what you might call a supervisor here. His name is Peter. When I say supervisor, I don't mean in the clinical sense.' He paused and looked around, perhaps realising that nobody in the room had the faintest idea what he meant. 'Anyway, Peter wants us all, clients and therapists, to meet outside in the compound at 5 p.m. I'm sure Christopher will come and get you all, won't you, Christopher?'

'Of course,' said Christopher, who was hearing about this gathering for the first time, although he tried not to show it.

'What are we meeting for?' asked Kevin.

'It would be hard and probably pointless to try and explain,' Clemitius answered. 'Needless to say, everything will become clear. Now I suggest we press ahead ... unless there is anything else?'

'Well yes, actually, there is,' Christopher said. 'I wanted to invite you all to dinner this evening. I, I mean we, realise it is a very difficult transition. I thought a relaxing informal dinner, maybe a little wine ...'

'Wine, you say?' Yvonne said.

'Yes, and a little conversation.'

There was silence. Gabriel stared out of the window, Julie played with the hem of her blouse. 'Or no conversation, just some decent food and the aforementioned wine? It's that or reruns of "Last of the Summer Wine" again.' Christopher knew that both Julie and Gabriel had half-heartedly watched TV the night before. He looked at Julie, who looked straight back and tried to smile.

'OK,' she said. 'Anything is better than "UK Gold." '

'I look forward to a nice glass of Rioja,' said Yvonne.

'I'd be delighted,' added Kevin in what was presumably his telephone voice.

They all looked at Gabriel. 'I'm a vegetarian,' he said.

'I think we can cater for that,' Christopher answered, smiling.

He shrugged, which was as close to a yes as Christopher was going to get.

'Will you be joining us?' Kevin asked Clemitius.

'No,' said Clemitius. 'I don't think it would be appropriate. There are therapeutic boundaries to consider.'

'What about *his* therapeutic boundaries?' Julie pointed at Christopher, who tried to concentrate on not blushing.

Clemitius smirked. 'Christopher has a vital role in this group, at least equal to mine but slightly different. Christopher has, I would suggest, designed for himself a role as part facilitator, part befriender. He attends to needs, he helps you settle. In choosing that role he helps design my own role. I cannot be a friend *and* a therapist. It simply doesn't work like that. I'm sorry.'

'It's OK,' said Gabriel 'I think we can cope without you.' And he turned to Christopher. 'Actually I am a bit surprised, I thought people who shared therapy groups weren't supposed to socialise together?'

'I didn't know you had had therapy before, Gabriel,' said Clemitius.

'I haven't,' Gabriel said. 'But my girlfriend, Ellie, she used to run groups and I remember her telling me once about some problems because two people started sleeping together and it made things a bit difficult or something.'

'Not much chance of that happening here,' said Kevin.

'You must miss Ellie very much,' said Clemitius.

Gabriel stared at him. Clemitius took that as a cue to continue. 'You've mentioned her before, and you clearly love her very much. In fact, it almost feels to me as if she were in the room.'

Kevin looked around him.

'I don't mean literally,' Clemitius said.

'No, of course not,' said Kevin. 'It's just that ... well, I imagine you could do stuff like that if you wanted.'

And Christopher watched and thought, Clemitius is right, I do create a different role for myself, I am more befriender, facilitator: I try to soften the blows, which he thinks is pointless and cowardly. But I can't help myself.

Now, looking at Gabriel, Christopher wondered if he was right. Being here felt almost cruel, watching that confused silent scream. He felt uncomfortable. He thought Gabriel might cry, and he had a sense that the others were uncomfortable, too. 'This is what these groups are for,' he told himself, although deep down he wasn't certain. But Gabriel didn't cry: instead he looked around, shrugged, and said, 'It wouldn't be much of a love if I wished her here would it?'

Nobody said anything else. There wasn't, Christopher thought, anything else to say.

13

After the group had finished, Christopher led them all quietly outside. The light was somehow bracing and the air fresh; Gabriel thought it smelt of lilac and cut mint. As they stepped from the dark, the sun welcomed them in what was essentially a misleading way. It looked like a beautiful summer's day, with all the promise such a day brings. But it wasn't.

They were not the last to arrive. Dozens of other equally surprised-looking people were emerging from the semicircle of two-storey, whitewashed buildings onto the pale yellow stone path. And there they all stood, facing across a round patch of grass a little larger than half a football pitch, about eighty near-dead people and twenty angels.

'Please stand still and be quiet,' Christopher said nervously.

'Quite a crowd,' said Gabriel. 'Are we going to do the hokey cokey?'

'Ahhh of course, Gabriel, you use humour—of sorts—to cope with anxiety-provoking situations. I do wonder how helpful that really is.' Clemitius had arrived behind them, his arms folded, his hands resting inside the wide cuffs of his robe. He nodded at everyone and stood beside Christopher.

'Do you know who it is?' he asked him.

'No,' Christopher whispered. 'Do you?'

'Oh yes.' Clemitius smiled smugly, adding, 'Don't worry, it isn't you.'

'I didn't think for one moment ...' spluttered Christopher.

Then Peter appeared, emerging from the end door of the building on the far side of the grass. He was a tall, thin, black man who walked with a measured elegance that somehow made him look sad. As he did so, everybody stopped whispering amongst themselves. Peter had presence. His height helped, but it was his physical grace that spoke to you first. Christopher always thought he looked as if he had been a dancer and, while he probably hadn't danced for a millennium, his walk said that he could if he chose to. His brown, slightly hooded eyes glistened with thousands of years of seeing. Peter never rushed anywhere. When he got to the centre of the clearing, he paused for a moment, looked up, and said,

'Welcome. I should start by telling you that what you are about to witness is—I am pleased to say—not common. Indeed, as new residents, there is a strong case suggesting that you do not need to see it at all. This really has nothing to do with you.'

He paused. Christopher watched anxiously. He liked to think of Peter as a force for good. This elegant old black-skinned angel embodied the calm certainty that was godliness. He spoke with the words of God. Words the angels already knew but expected to hear now and again anyway. Everyone looked up to Peter.

'However, this is a place of openness. And as some of our more senior therapists pointed out, how can we tell you that in being here you are engaged in a transparent process of healing and sharing only to hide from you the indiscretions of one of us?'

He paused again. He seemed to be wondering if he had said enough. He apparently decided he hadn't. 'Others said that this could create the wrong impression for you and hinder your understanding of what this place is about. It is a place of hope, of clarity and self-improvement. And I sympathise with that view, but if seeing this means it will take longer for you to feel safe here ... which it needn't, but it might ... well then, we will take more time with you.'

Peter looked around, knowing that anyone present who wasn't an angel couldn't possibly understand what he was talking about. He smiled. Julie noticed he had yellowing teeth. 'I'm sorry,' he said, 'I'm talking too much. You are here to witness a banishment.'

Christopher felt sick. He didn't fear for himself, although he did feel a floating uncertainty about himself and the rules of therapy. But banishment didn't come on the back of some wrong words or an uncertainty. Someone had broken the rules. The light clouded over a little and Peter looked across the grass to a breaking angel and nodded. He said, 'I think you know who you are.'

She was a short, handsome woman, a brunette with long separate curls running past her shoulders and large eyes that glistened in the sunlight. She had been a watcher of people, like Christopher. She looked down at the ground for a moment then, raising her eyes to meet Peter's, she strode purposefully toward him. There was a quiet murmuring. Christopher glanced at Clemitius. He was licking his fat lips.

The broken angel stood beside Peter and stared at him: defiant, afraid, and powerless, as if she had already stopped being an angel. Peter placed his hand on her shoulder and looked at her for a moment, before turning away to address the crowd.

'Estelle. You have been a watcher for more than ten thousand years. You have been a friend to many and a saviour to more.'

Christopher thought that what should have followed was some warm applause, some kind of Angel of the Millennium award and an embarrassed speech, but instead there would be only ritual humiliation and exile.

Peter looked into Estelle's eyes. 'All the things you have done, all the service you have offered and the devotion you have shown amount to nothing now ...'

'What did she do?' whispered Julie.

'Sshhh,' chided Clemitius, before asking in a whisper, 'Do you think Peter is good at this?'

'At what? What is happening?' asked Gabriel.

'She is being banished. She broke the rules.' Clemitius was staring at Peter. He began bobbing up and down very slightly on his toes.

'Do you have anything to say?' Peter asked her.

Estelle shook her head quickly. She was still staring into Peter's eyes. Holding on to herself, just. Then she seemed to change her mind. 'Yes,' she said quietly. Peter gently put his hands on her shoulders and waited.

'What I did,' she said hesitantly, 'I did for love.'

Clemitius grunted with contempt; a few other angels murmured. Peter just gazed into her eyes and said quietly, 'But not love of God.'

Estelle seemed to wilt, buckle, but Peter held her steady for a moment, before nodding and releasing her. As he let go, she seemed to pale. Any colour, whether hers or lent to her by the light of eternal September, simply left her. Slowly she turned away from Peter and faced the still, dark lake that rested at the foot of the compound and walked toward it. Everyone stared.

'Is she going to be cleansed?' guessed Julie.

'Oh no, she's way past that,' said Clemitius

'What's in the lake?' asked Gabriel.

'I bet its crocodiles,' said Kevin. The group all looked at him. He shrugged. 'Well, if it was my lake, it would be crocodiles.'

'It's not crocodiles,' said Clemitius irritably.

The broken angel reached the lake and half turned, raising her hand as if to wave, then changed her mind and let it drop back to her side. She paused for a moment and then stepped into the black water. She didn't stop again; she waded out as the clouds grew darker and a slight wind picked up and made the water ripple slightly. She was quickly up to her shoulders. Again she turned. Her face was pale.

Christopher moved his arm as if to wave but didn't quite, returning it to his side and watching her carefully, looking for some peace in her expression, thinking he could see it. A few more steps and she was under the water. The wind stopped, the clouds faded, and the lake was still again.

The compound was silent. Peter stood still in the centre, his shoulders slightly hunched. He might have sighed. Then he turned and walked slowly back the way he had come, back inside and out of view. After a moment the angels began to lead their groups away as well. Julie turned to Christopher.

'What did she do?'

'I don't know,' said Christopher.

'You must.'

'She sent an email,' said Clemitius without looking at anyone.

'What?'

'She was a watcher, like Christopher here, and she became a little too involved with her clients. Very poor.'

'Who did she send an email to?'

'The daughter of a member of her group. The girl was distraught at the loss of her mother. Estelle felt she was at risk of taking her own life. She was spending more energy watching the child ...'

'Child?' said Yvonne.

'Yes she was about fourteen, I think, very close to her mother, but she would have been OK. I mean, if we can't show a little faith who can, eh?' He smiled at his little joke.

'What did the email say?'

'It said, "hush Deedee, know I love you, make me proud." Her mother was the only person who called the girl Deedee. Dreadfully irresponsible.'

'How do you know all this?' Christopher asked.

Clemitius smiled. 'Peter sought my counsel.'

'And she was banished for that?'

'Oh yes, it's not our job to interfere or comfort, it's not for us to get involved. Anyway'—his tone changed from judgmental to contemptuous—'she showed no regret. She had to go.'

With that he turned away. 'Enjoy your dinner, see you tomorrow. We have work to do.' And he went inside.

14

Izzy was trying to persuade an exhausted Ellie to leave Gabriel's bedside and go home with her to get some rest. 'If he wakes up they will phone,' she had said about a hundred times, before trying a wide range of strategies geared to moving Ellie out of the oppressive room with wires and machines and into something like the real world. Her tactics had ranged from 'You have to get some rest or you will make yourself ill' to 'Do you want him to see you like this when he wakes up' and then, 'Ellie, you can't stay here forever.' Finally, she looked at her friend and said quietly, 'If you are going to give yourself any chance of getting pregnant, you have to get rest. You have to stay healthy.'

Ellie stared at her, at first just trying to understand the words. Izzy had said so many things but Ellie hadn't heard one of them until the word 'pregnant' passed her lips. Then, as she saw Izzy for maybe the first time since the accident, a plan began to emerge, a plan to take back some small control of a life that had been wrested from her when she wasn't even looking. It was a daring plan that required delicate timing, good planning, a fast car—and a sterilized specimen pot.

'I need your help, Izzy.'

'Of course sweetie, anything.'

'I need you to help me get Gabriel's sperm.'

'Of course you do, darling ... What? What do you mean, exactly?'

'Look, the doctors won't help me: they say they can't invade Gabriel's body to get his sperm. I need it; I need it the same day I have my eggs taken out, but I can't be in two places at once. So I need you to take Gabriel's sperm, put it in a jar, and bring it to the clinic.'

'Darling, that's ... insane,' said Izzy, touching her friend's arm.

Ellie pushed her hand away and stared at her.

'How ... how do I get Gabriel's sperm, sweetie?' asked Izzy, already frightened that she knew the answer.

'You take it,' said Ellie, 'the usual way!'

'Well excuse me, but giving your best friend's boyfriend a hand job while he's in a coma isn't actually the usual way!'

'Oh come on, Izzy, you're a *nurse*.'

'Not that kind of nurse, I'm a psychiatric nurse, not a willy nurse! And in my professional opinion this is madness.'

'Izzy, please, I'm begging you.' Ellie began to cry. 'Please help me.'

Izzy sat down beside her friend and held her as she sobbed. She tried to imagine helping, but she couldn't. Yet neither could she imagine being able to say no. Finally, Izzy said quietly: 'Ellie, sweetheart, even if I agreed, how do you know his bits work? What makes you think anything will happen?'

'Because I have been here when they've washed him and after they left, I touched him ... I thought, you know a bit of stimulus might help wake him. I didn't, you know, fiddle about or anything—but there was definitely a response.'

'Well, maybe on some level he recognised you. He won't recognise me, will he?'

'He's in a coma. His life systems are functioning, but he isn't.'

'It feels weird.'

'Izzy, this is a matter of life and death. Weird doesn't come into it. I have lost everything, everything—this is all I have, a slim chance it may be, but it's all I have.' Ellie's eyes were red-rimmed and staring. A few moments ago she hadn't thought of this; now it felt like the very idea was keeping her alive.

Izzy stared at her friend and looked at Gabriel's body.

'When?' she asked.

'The day after tomorrow.'

'What do I do with it once I've got it?'

'You bring it to the clinic. They "wash" it, find the healthy ones, and add them to my eggs. Then we wait. You have to get them to the clinic inside twenty minutes and you have to keep them warm. Hold the pot under your arm.'

'Ellie!'

'What?'

'How do I get them to the clinic in twenty minutes?'

'You'll need a fast driver. Sam.'

'Sam! Sam? What am I going to tell Sam?' Izzy cried. '"Listen darling, wait here, keep the engine running—I've got to run upstairs, give our comatose friend a wank while the doctors aren't looking, and then you have to drive us with his seed to Ellie"?'

'Well why not?' said Sam, who had arrived a few moments earlier and had stood quietly at the door, holding a bag full of fruit and water. 'How about for now though, we get Ellie home? You need some rest and some proper food if you're going to try to grow a baby.'

15

The dining room was three-fifths IKEA restaurant and two-fifths college refectory, with wooden floors polished in red and metal-legged tables for six lining the sides. Only one table was occupied when Christopher brought the group in. In the far corner, five miserable-looking non-angels were eating pasta and listening to their angel, clearly the old and nervous-looking one in the long white smock. Only two of them looked up when Christopher and the others entered, and they didn't look for long. Christopher knew that this was Estelle's group. It occurred to him that if he were banished today, nobody would look that sad about it. He wondered what that said about Estelle. And about himself. He ushered his people to a table beside the window.

The table was laid, with silver cutlery on a crisp, thick white tablecloth. There were two bottles of wine, one red and one white, and a large jug of water along with a basket of rolls and a bowl of olives.

'What do you think of our restaurant?' Christopher asked, adding before anyone could answer, 'Wine?'

'Oh about bloody time,' said Yvonne, pouring herself a large glass of white.

'You're not trying to get us drunk, are you?' said Kevin.

'Red, please,' said Gabriel.

'Yes, red,' seconded Julie. 'So is this still therapy?'

'No, no. This is dinner,' Christopher said feebly. 'It's a chance to relax a little. We do realise what a shock this is, and we would like to make you feel as comfortable as possible. And give you a chance to get to know each other outside of the group.'

'You were saying earlier that you thought this was unusual?' Yvonne said to Gabriel.

'Yes, sorry about that, I thought it was … just thinking out loud. My girlfriend is a psychiatric nurse. She used to talk about work, not so much lately, but I remember her telling me that in the more serious groups, the ones she described as "full of rich well people in need of some attention", they have a rule that members shouldn't mix together outside of group.'

'Well, you are right—' Christopher began.

'What's her name?' interrupted Yvonne.

'Ellie.'

There was silence for a moment, before Gabriel asked: 'How about you? Do you have anyone?'

'A son, Anthony—he is twenty-one, studying in Spain. Well he was a few days ago, presumably someone would have called him.' Yvonne stared into her now-close-to-empty glass. 'He won't know what to do; he is a young twenty-one going on seventeen. I may have been a fussy mum. Going to Spain was an enormous adventure for him, studying Spanish and European literature. He's too young to be arranging funerals.' She drank, and poured herself another. Turning to Julie she said: ' Do you want some of this, love?'

Julie took the bottle of red. Gabriel said to her, quite softly given that she had run him over, 'How about you?'

'Not really. I was...' She trailed off and shrugged. She found herself thinking about Michael and wondering what the answer to that question would have been if the accident had happened a month, a week later.

'Me neither,' said Kevin, ignoring the fact that nobody had asked him. 'An ex-wife and two kids who I don't really have much to do with. Well I send gifts, you know, and write, but we're not close.'

'How old are they?' asked Gabriel.

'Oh Christ, the boy must be twenty-three, no twenty-four, and the girl twenty, just about to turn twenty-one.'

'Do you see them?'

'Yeah, once or twice a year, we go out for something to eat. The girl writes me emails. That's nice. It's the only reason I have a computer. It's her birthday coming up.'

The starter, mushroom soup, arrived. Yvonne ignored hers, pouring her fourth large glass of wine instead. The others ate, commenting on how good it tasted. Julie wondered out loud how they could taste anything when in truth they are not physically there.

'Well it's something we gave a lot of thought to and I won't bore you with all of the reasoning,' said Christopher. 'Suffice to say we need to bring as much of whatever constitutes "you" here as we can, and that includes your tastes and your responses to them. For example, if you drink … a lot … you will get just a teensy bit drunk.' He looked at Yvonne. She ignored him.

'But our bodies are still on earth?' asked Julie.

'Yes, but you are here.'

'Can we feel anything here that happens to us there?' she followed.

Gabriel jumped in. 'Can we see ourselves? Can we see our … can I see Ellie?'

'Well, actually you can. Eventually. If we think it would be helpful to the therapeutic process,' Christopher said. 'There is a viewing room that enables you to look at where you are, if you know what I mean. However, we have to be sure that the act is in the best interests of the work you are here to do.'

Gabriel, who had been hunched and distracted since he arrived, finally came to life. He started drumming his hands on the table and said loudly, 'When can I see her?'

'Not yet, I'm afraid. You need to do some work first, and maybe not even then if we don't think will be helpful.' Christopher felt embarrassed. He didn't bring them here to make them even more unhappy, and particularly not before the main course.

Gabriel was staring at the floor, Julie was staring at him. Christopher looked out of the window. When he saw the trees beside the lake, he always imagined he could smell them. Wet bark and orange blossom. 'I'm sorry. I know this is hard, but please be patient.'

Gabriel said nothing. Everyone except Gabriel finished their soup in silence. He poured himself another glass of wine. Finally, Yvonne spoke, a little louder than normal: 'As this isn't actually really my body, can I ask, do you have any cigarettes?'

The main course was a walnut-and-squash bake for Gabriel and Julie, and grilled king salmon for Yvonne and Kevin. The accompanying vegetables were steamed and dressed with a little butter. It smelt delicious and was prepared perfectly, yet it was wasted. The quiet introspective misery from the table in the far corner seemed to have infected Christopher's group. Yvonne was chatty, talking about Spain and her son, but then she was drunk. Kevin was trying to please by nodding and handing out bits of bread roll, but Julie was continuing to be reserved and Gabriel was completely silent.

'So, what do you two do for a living?' Kevin asked Gabriel and Julie.

'I teach art,' she answered.

'Oh, in school?'

'No, in a day centre. I used to teach in a prison and I do some evening classes. It's not exactly a career, I just found myself doing it. I like the people,' she said dreamily. She was thinking about the old people in her art group, how genuinely sad they would be about her accident. And Brenda. Would someone think to call Brenda?

'What about you?' Kevin said, looking at Gabriel.

'Actually, I'd just lost my job. All in all it wasn't a very good day.'

'Oh, sorry to hear that,' said Kevin.

'Doesn't much matter now, does it?' and Gabriel smiled for the first time since he'd all but died.

'I used to lay people off,' volunteered Yvonne. 'Horrible business, hated it.' She was slurring. 'I'd do it to their faces, but every time I did it I felt worse than the last time. Strange, you'd expect it to get easier; people I worked with said it did, but not for me. I think because every time I had to lay someone off it felt like I had failed in the business and it was more my fault than before. After all, I was experienced, I should see the odd recession coming, know what I mean?'

Nobody did, but they weren't going to say.

'I was just a sportswriter on a website,' shrugged Gabriel.

'Oh well, you know, the dot-com industry, a disaster waiting to happen,' said Yvonne dismissively.

'Yeah, except it was on pretty solid ground we thought, good advertising revenue, part of a big company committed to developing properties on the Web. Still, it's all bollocks isn't it really? I mean I loved writing about football and cricket for a living, but it wasn't exactly a job for a grownup.'

'Well, what is?' said Yvonne.

'Ellie and I were in the middle of IVF, I hadn't even told her I'd lost my job; I didn't want to worry her.' His voice grew quieter. His eyes were reddening.

'You'll find something,' said Yvonne. Everyone stared at her. 'I mean you would have found something, you know … oh fuck it, what do I know, I'm just a fucking drunk. I'm sorry.'

'It's OK,' said Gabriel quickly. 'You haven't said anything wrong.'

Julie looked as though she were going to cry. 'I'm so sorry. I'm so, so sorry for running you over. I'm so very sorry.'

'It wasn't your fault, Julie,' Christopher said.

'Nothing is ever anyone's fault,' said Julie. 'I fucking hate that.'

'Well,' said Yvonne. 'Anyone else fancy a cigarette?'

'She won't give up, you know,' Christopher said without thinking. As soon as he said it, he realised he shouldn't have. Yet he felt no regret.

'Who?' asked Yvonne, lighting up and tossing the pack of cigarettes along the table toward Julie and Gabriel.

'Ellie,' Christopher said, looking directly at Gabriel. 'Ellie won't give up on you that easily.'

'What do you mean?' Gabriel sat up straighter 'What can she do about it?'

'She is going ahead with the IVF.'

'How? Who with? For fuck's sake ...'

'With you Gabriel, she plans to finish the treatment with you. This I know. It's my job to know. She is planning to steal your sperm ...'

'What do you mean, "steal" it?'

'The doctors looking after you won't let her have it without going to court, something to do with informed consent, so she has hatched a plan with her friend Izzy.'

'Izzy won't help.'

'She says she will.'

'She won't; she hates me.'

'What do you mean, she hates you?' asked Julie.

'Well she doesn't like me; she won't help.'

'Well Moira's around, maybe she will. And Sam's definitely involved.'

'What kind of plan?'

Christopher breathed in and looked at the trees outside again. He thought of Estelle. He missed her already. He said 'I don't think it's appropriate to go into details right now, especially as the crème brûlée is just coming, but suffice to say she hasn't given up on you.'

'Quite a woman,' said Julie, picking up the cigarettes and taking one before offering them to Gabriel, who started to pluck one out then stopped.

'No, it's OK, thanks. They're bad for your health.'

16

The next morning everyone was on time, and nobody was hung over. The silence at the beginning of the group was short. Yvonne looked around, raised her eyebrows, shrugged, and said, 'If it is talking we are here for, then I can talk—if nobody else has anything they want to say?'

Everyone shook their heads. Yvonne began, 'Between 1983 and 1988 I probably made over four million pounds from property deals and I lost most of it in two months in 1989. Of course I wasn't the only one, and to be honest I don't think it hit me as hard as it hit others; I mean, it didn't ever cross my mind to shoot myself or anything. It never really felt like my money, not deep down, which is perhaps the feeling that guided my later actions.'

'I heard you had your hand in the till,' said Kevin.

'Yes well, if that made your job easier I imagine you relished that kind of information. It wasn't true of course.' She paused before adding, almost gleefully, 'Although from their point of view I can see that it was.'

'It wasn't supposed to help me kill you,' Kevin explained. 'It was just something someone said.'

'Whatever.' Yvonne thought of, and treated, Kevin as if he were something sticky on her shoe. 'Anyway I started again. During the '90s I—quite cleverly, I thought later—ignored the dot-com revolution. If I couldn't clearly see the revenue stream I didn't want to hear about it. Instead I went into business publishing and it was, if I say so myself, a very good decision, financially at least.'

'And what happened?' asked Clemitius, who was relishing some proper talking going on at last.

'I set up business magazines that serviced the public sector. I started with a teaching magazine, then a nursing magazine, then another nursing magazine for nurses who thought they were too clever to read the first one, then a social work magazine and so on. At my peak I owned 11 magazines. You probably wouldn't have heard of any of them. Not all big sellers, but all profit makers.'

'What's so clever about that?' asked Julie.

'Recruitment advertising,' said Yvonne. 'I mean, none of the public sector groups are exactly A-list consumers for the mainstream advertisers, but all of them are massive recruitment areas. And ultimately the recruitment drive was a publicly funded, unlimited resource—particularly through the 90's when all those public-sector professions had staff shortages. I made more money in 1996 for example then I had in the whole of the 1980s.'

'You must have been very happy,' said Julie uncertainly. She had never really thought about money very much. Nor why people built their lives around it.

'You'd think, wouldn't you?' sighed Yvonne.

'Did I tell you my girlfriend's a nurse?' said Gabriel, for no reason other than that he was thinking about Ellie, as he had been since he got there.

'Maybe she read my magazines,' said Yvonne.

'Maybe.' Gabriel sounded unconvinced.

Yvonne waited to see if Gabriel would elaborate. He didn't. 'What is interesting to me is that nobody ever, not once, asked if we were doing anything morally questionable.'

'What do you mean?' Clemitius asked.

'We were stripping millions from public services.'

'You were selling a service,' said Kevin. 'Nobody made them pay you.'

'Yes well, you would say that, wouldn't you. Of course we were selling a service that had to be provided, but the money we brought in was taxpayers' money, it existed to provide people with social workers or teachers and yet was being filtered off to me, my partners, and ultimately—when we went public—to our shareholders. Our share price was bolstered by taxpayers' money, which made it a pretty good share to have, so it became more and more popular and, as a consequence, shareholders got greedy and put more pressure on us to provide more profit, providing the bare minimum in terms of content, reducing staffing, selling even more ads. Nobody ever asked if what we were doing was morally wrong.'

'What did you do when you started to wonder?' asked Clemitius.

'I started drinking too much for one thing,' said Yvonne. 'That was a mistake, because apart from the fact it made for some pretty undignified moments in my life, it also made it easy for my company to get rid of me. I got kicked upstairs, became an executive director, which is business-speak for pointless suit. They should have had the guts to fire me but didn't. I decided to set myself up as a project director. At first I tried, quite legitimately, to persuade the company to fund educational projects, awards, career development funds, stuff like that. Things that would pump just a little money back into public services and also give us a more positive profile, but the idiots couldn't see the point, or the profits, and refused me.

'So I went into competition with my own company, I essentially went into business with the government to set up a series of free websites and newsletters for recruitment advertising. I had every contact I needed in the business, all the people had long resented paying money to the likes of us just to staff the public services. I undercut my own company by 45%, I negotiated agreements with all of the appropriate unions, and I didn't say a word to anyone. It took me seven months of bloody hard work and nobody once asked me what I was doing. I wasn't answerable to anyone.

'Somehow they got wind of it, about three weeks before the network was due to launch. I knew they would, of course. The head of marketing escorted me from the building. I'd hired the chinless prat. They got even dirtier than I anticipated in employing you, Kevin. It's a shame, I would have loved to have been there for the first six weeks of the sites and the papers. But unfortunately I missed out on that.'

'So,' said Clemitius, trying to be charming. 'You are something of a Robin Hood figure, stealing from the rich and giving back to the poor?'

'No,' said Yvonne. 'I just got tired of freeloading off of the state and getting praised for doing it. Christ, if I'd been a single mum living on benefits, I'd have been considered the lowest of the low, but as it was I was a candidate for Businesswoman of the Year simply for taking millions from the government to advertise jobs.'

'I have a question,' said Gabriel.

Yvonne looked at him and pursed her lips.

'Why are you here? It sounds to me as though you were pretty much in control of your life, and you tried to do the right thing, something I don't remember doing lately, not that I am any kind of right-thing role model here, but ... well I just don't get it?'

'Yes, why do you think you are here?' Clemitius asked Yvonne. 'Think about yourself, try to take an overview of your life and the things about you that have perhaps stopped you from fulfilling your human potential.'

Christopher shuffled in his seat a little, he felt a mild anxiety, as though he should be saying something, but he couldn't think of anything. He had rather enjoyed Yvonne's story. He found himself liking her.

'I'm a drunk?' suggested Yvonne dispassionately.

'Yes,' said Clemitius, 'but that in itself isn't what has prevented your personal fulfilment. Everyone looked confused. 'Why do you think you drink?' he went on, helpfully.

'I get thirsty?'

'I'm thinking beyond that.'

'I like the feeling it gives me.'

'I'm sure there is more to it than that. What feeling? More confidence perhaps?'

Christopher wanted to say something, anything. He shuffled in his seat again and even opened his mouth but nothing came out. He realised he was uncomfortable. Not for himself, but for Yvonne. Because when Clemitius spoke it felt to Christopher as though he were assaulting someone.

'No, I'm pretty confident most of the time,' said Yvonne. She felt no anxiety at the questions, no embarrassment at the answers. 'If anything, I like the fact that when I'm a little drunk I may be a little more vulnerable, you know, to the unknown. Maybe I'm a bit of a control freak.'

Everyone sat in silence.

'Is that it?' said Yvonne. 'I'm a bit of control freak?'

Clemitius nodded sagely, a man who had today at least done his job.

'So,' said Yvonne. 'You're suggesting that my tendency toward wanting to retain a certain control in most circumstances has in effect prevented me from living a more fulfilling life?'

'No,' said Clemitius, a little smugly. 'You are saying that.'

Julie screwed up her eyes. Is that it? Self-knowledge as delivered by angels? Because it felt to her just a little like a daytime television show.

'Well maybe,' said Yvonne. 'Or alternatively, it's given me the drive, confidence and ability to move beyond the career in telesales I had at twenty-three, to break into business?'

'But you'll never know what might have been.'

'What do you mean?'

'I mean that if you had found it within yourself to challenge yourself in a different way, perhaps you might have found a path to a greater personal fulfilment?'

'How do you know that?'

'I don't, but ...'

'You don't.'

'Seems to me that you're guessing,' interjected Gabriel. 'She's done all right, she is who she is, she hasn't done any harm to anyone ...'

'Harming others is a slightly outdated way of measuring good,' said Clemitius.

'Oh, sorry for being old-fashioned,' said Gabriel.

'Is it?' Julie asked.

They looked at Yvonne, who was shaking her head.

'No,' she said. 'No sorry, you're wrong. I know I have a drink problem, I will buy that I am a control freak, hell if you like I'll even get into the fact that I cannot sustain a decent relationship— although as I sustained one long enough to give me my son, on reflection I'd say I did OK there. On the whole I don't have any big regrets. I can even cope with being dead, because I feel as though I have lived. Being killed by that insidious little creep annoys me, but dead is dead. Beyond that? It was a pretty good life I think. Sorry, does that mean I've failed?'

'You can't really fail in therapy,' Clemitius said with a shrug. 'It is for you to do what you want to do with whatever emerges from the process.'

Yvonne was quiet and so was everyone else. It may have been a thoughtful silence, it may have been a comfortable silence, but Julie looked at her as she stared at the floor in front of her and if she had to guess, she would have guessed it was a confused silence. She had felt like she was stoned ever since she got here, but now she was waking slightly. And as she looked around the group she found herself thinking two things: firstly that Clemitius was, well, a bit of a prat. Secondly, she found herself wondering about Michael and it made her ache, really ache, and those two things combined to make her feel as though she were going to be sick.

17

James Buchan's meeting with Bernie, his former manager and currently an antiques dealer, hadn't gone as badly as it might have, but neither had it gone as well as he might have hoped. Mind you, James had hoped for quite a lot. As he had driven to Margate, his dream scenario involved Bernie sobbing at the sight of James, whom he had always thought of as the son he had never had. Furthermore, and this bit came to James when he got to the Medway towns, Bernie had by coincidence received one or two calls lately from journalists anxious to know what had happened to the 'years ahead of their time' Dog in a Tuba, and in particular to their 'enigmatic, distinctive, some would say misunderstood genius' front-man James Buchan. What's more, Bernie would reveal that Dog in a Tuba had been invited on the '80s Revisited tour with Adam Ant, Paul Young, and Go West. And Sting himself had called to see if Bernie knew where James was, in the hope that he would co-write some of the songs for his forthcoming album.

Consequently, it wasn't going to take much for James to be disappointed.

Bernie, meanwhile, had always anticipated punching James if he ever saw him again. James being the man who, in Bernie's head at least, had not only driven him to drink, but had also driven his innocent young god-daughter Alice to drugs and then, even worse, into a modelling career. However, the years had mellowed him, and it is quite possible that sitting in the pub with James had made him forget the bad times and remember— if not the good times they shared, because frankly there weren't any—the fact that when they were all together, they were young and thin.

'Have you spoken to any of the others about this reunion idea?' They were huddled round a small table in the corner of the near-empty pub. An old man in a cap was playing a fruit machine; three others were listening to a horse race on the radio. In the pub it was the 1970s. James felt quite at home.

'No, not really. Gary Guitar hung up on me.'

'Well Gary Guitar hates you.'

'Yeah, yeah, he does,' said James, genuinely bemused.

'You pissed a lot of people off, James. You were playing the rock star.'

'Well of course I was, Bernie, that was my job, wasn't it?'

'You took it a bit too far.'

And James thought, 'Did I?' He remembered drinking and smoking a lot. He remembered staying up late and having bad sex with plump girls whose names he didn't ask. He remembered a messy thing with Alice, who was about sixteen and came on to him like a tank with lips. Maybe he should have resisted, and the three-in-a-bed-video with Alice and her friend ... Brigitte? Brenda? Brian? And given his time again, he wouldn't have slipped the video on instead of 'Life on Earth' on the tour bus, but by that time Alice was coked up to the eyeballs from about 10 a.m. onward and needed help, which she wouldn't have got if Bernie hadn't seen her burning her candles at both ends, so to speak, in glorious Technicolor.

Bernie was, thankfully, thinking of something else. 'We knew we were in trouble when you tried to rename the band James Buchan and Dog in a Tuba.'

'Well, other bands were doing it.'

'Who?'

James's mind went blank. 'Herman's Hermits?' He smiled.

Bernie stared at him in disbelief and then burst out laughing.

'You silly sod, Jimmy. Why don't you forget the band thing, mate, and get yourself a job?'

'I would Bern, I really would, but the band was all I was ever any good at.'

'Yeah, well football was all that George Best was any good at, but he had to stop playing, didn't he?'

'Well yes he did, but you can't play football when you're pissed, whereas you can sing. Look around you Bern; they're all getting back together—Blancmange, Dollar, Heaven 17, and the Psychedelic Furs ...'

'They're not, are they?'

'I think they might be. I saw a poster.'

'Thought they'd stayed in the U.S.'

'Even Tears for Fears are talking again.'

'Really? I thought those boys hated each other.'

'They probably did, but you know, the band is bigger than the sum of its parts, isn't that what you used to say? ABC, Culture Club, Bananarama — they're playing big places, Bern, that's got to be good money. Just think about it, that's all I'm asking.'

'Did I ever tell you about me and the Banana girls, James?'

'Yes mate, yes you did. But if you want to buy me another drink you can tell me again.'

Consequently, driving back from Bernie's, James felt something close to excited. Bernie wasn't exactly on board. But he wasn't so far off as to require a yacht and a strong wind to reach. Of course James knew persuading the others would be difficult. They hated him, especially Gary Guitar. But that kind of inter-band animosity had kept some of the greatest musical combos in pop history at the cutting edge. Anyway, he was pretty sure he'd be able to talk them round. He always had in the past. All except Michael, anyway.

But the further north he drove the, more miserable he became. It wasn't simply the thought of moving further away from what was most interesting him at the moment, getting the band together, it was also the realisation that he was going home to an empty house. That and the possibility that debt collectors might be hiding behind the hedge. By the time the M11 turned into the A11 he was almost depressed, and by the time he stopped outside his house, the only thing stopping him from turning round and heading south again was the fact he was really hungry. And that he didn't have anywhere to go in the south.

The first thing he did when he got into the cottage was to turn all the lights on. He hated the place dark and, as he hated the place quiet too, he put a Police CD on. The answer machine was flashing but, given the number of people he owed money to, it always was. In fact he had got to the stage where he was almost reassured by the flashing, demonstrating as it did that the phone hadn't been cut off. He ignored it and headed for the kitchen. The fridge was virtually empty, just some tomato puree, mustard, and half a pint of stale milk. He checked the cupboards: a tin of lentils bought by Julie for a curry she never made and a packet of custard that had been there since before he moved in. He put his hand in his pocket: £1.32. No takeaway then. They certainly wouldn't take a cheque again.

He wanted to phone Julie. Mostly to see if she'd lend him some money. She might, if she felt a bit guilty about leaving him. But she hadn't left her number. He could call Michael, but he didn't really want to yet, not just to borrow money anyway. Of course if Michael had phoned him while he was away, then returning his call would be OK. But Michael never called. James hadn't noticed that until now.

He sighed. He decided he'd check the answer machine, just in case. He pressed the button and walked back toward the kitchen, secure in the knowledge that it wouldn't be Camelot telling him he had won the lottery. The first message was from his accountant, who appeared to be dropping the thin veneer of professionalism and was being rude now. The next caller rang off without leaving a message and the third had nothing to do with money.

'Mr Buchan, this is Police Sergeant Doyle. I'm afraid there has been an accident involving a friend of yours, Ms Julie Eden. We are having trouble locating any family, and according to our records her last known address is with you. Local officers have been round but you may be away. When you get this message, please phone us on the following number ... .'

James froze for a moment. What kind of accident? How serious? He should phone, and he would. But he didn't, not straight away. He paced up and down in front of his lucky poster, thinking. Why were they phoning him? Did Julie ask them to? He couldn't see it. He felt confused, surprised, but—and this didn't occur to him immediately—not much else. He picked up the phone. He paused. And then he phoned Michael.

When Michael answered, James waited, he wasn't exactly sure what to say. In the background he could hear music; he couldn't place it. 'What's that you're listening to, Mikey?'

'Er, Magic Numbers.'

'Is it new?'

'Not that new. Good though.'

'Oh. I'm, er, listening to the Police.'

'Righto. Thanks for letting me know.'

'Yeah sorry, Mikey, I'm in a state of shock, Julie's had an accident. I just got back from visiting Bernie—he says hi—and there's a message saying Julie has been hurt ...'

Silence.

'Mikey ... Mikey?'

'How hurt?' Michael had forgotten how to breathe.

'I don't know, there's a number I need to call, but I called you first. I thought you might want to come over.'

'Right, but she was going to London.'

'I know,' said James.

'I'll be right over. You call and get details and we'll go down.'

'Down where?'

'To London.'

'Right. Well I've only just got back ...'

'Are you going to call?' snapped Michael.

'Of course I am, she was my girlfriend, wasn't she? But we have split up, you know that, don't you?'

'Yeah, I heard. Look Jim, do you want me to call the bloody number?'

'No no, I'll do it, you come over and we'll take it from there. OK?'

'OK.' And Michael hung up. He felt cold, his hands especially. He sat down, putting his hands under his legs and for a moment felt like a schoolboy waiting to see the headmaster—not that he had any real sense of himself—then he stood straight up again. He had, while he waited for Julie to come back, begun to get a sense of her as 'significant.' He had wondered about her in a way he hadn't wondered about anyone in a while and he had even caught himself feeling embarrassed by the fact that he was so excited.

And now he couldn't remember what her mouth looked like, her lips, or the noise she made when she laughed. He could remember the shape of her in that skirt and he could remember how he felt at the coffee shop; enthralled, young, uncertain. This wasn't fair, it hadn't even started yet.

He grabbed his jacket and drove over to James's cottage. He didn't have much petrol but decided not to stop yet. He needed information first; he needed to know how bad it was even though deep down he felt he already knew. James was waiting at the door when Michael knocked.

'Not good, Mikey, apparently she was in a car accident in the East End. She's in a coma, has been for two days.'

'Where?'

'St. Francis, in London.'

'OK, I'm going down there.'

'Me too,' said James without thinking.

The two men looked at each other. Michael considered speaking; he thought about saying something, anything, about how he felt about Julie but he didn't have the energy. James spoke instead.

'Well, just because we aren't together, it doesn't mean I don't care. I mean you care, don't you, and you're not together or anything ... are you?'

Michael looked at James. He was trying to see the place where James kept his concern for others. It wasn't something he had ever come across before, nor was it a place he believed in now.

'No,' he paused. There was no time for this. 'I'll need to get petrol.'

'It's OK, we can take my car,' said James, and he went inside to grab his coat. He turned off the Police and the lights, and felt a massive sense of relief when he closed the door and headed back outside.

They began the drive in silence, Michael biting his lip and staring out of the window; James wondering what it was he was supposed to be feeling. Increasingly uncomfortable with the silence, he finally broke and said, 'Do you mind putting some music on? Helps me drive.'

Michael pressed the play button on the car tape and 'Don't You Want Me Baby' beeped out. It made Michael jump a little. 'Quite popular again I understand,' ventured James.

Michael was looking at the endless black row of trees that lined the A11, wondering how much variation existed in the word 'coma': could there be some comas that were less bad than other comas? He'd heard stories of people staying in comas for years and then emerging unscathed.

'Mikey? Mikey?'

'Hmm, sorry ...'

'What sort of music do you listen to these days?'

'Er ... I don't know Jim, whatever's on I suppose. It doesn't mean much to me anymore.'

'Really? You used to know all the new bands before they'd even formed, mate. What happened?'

'I grew up, or at least out of it.' He paused. 'Did they say anything else?'

'Who?'

'The hospital. When you called.'

'No, just that she was in a coma and had had an accident and that the next forty-eight hours were very important.'

'You didn't tell me that before—why are they important? Do they think she may come round? Is there a better chance of her being OK if she gets through the next forty-eight hours? What?'

'I don't know, Mike. You know what hospitals are like; they are always vague. I think it's in case you sue them if they say something that doesn't happen.'

'I don't know anything about hospitals,' said Michael quietly. And he went back to staring out of the window. The trees were gone and now there were just empty grey fields for as far as he could see. The empty space surprised him.

James, meanwhile, was trying to decide what to feel. He knew he should feel something, more important he knew he should be showing Michael that he felt something, but he wasn't sure what it was. So instead he said: 'A lot of the bands from the 80s are touring again, you know.'

'Hmm.'

'Human League, ABC, Culture Club.'

'Yeah?'

'Pulling in the crowds too, apparently.'

'Well I suppose lots of people like to revisit their youth,' said Michael without thinking.

'But not you, eh?'

Silence. They came to a well-lit road and the empty space began to fill again. Michael could see the fields dip into the distance, and then more trees, this time not in lines but rather a forest of thin saplings. He wondered what it would be like to be in there, lost and cold and frightened. Better than being here now.

'Mikey?'

'Yes? Er, sorry no, not me.'

'You never miss the good old days?'

He didn't. In truth he couldn't really remember them. He felt he should, as everyone should, but he couldn't. Not the real things, not the way he felt or the things he believed or what distinguished one day from another. He remembered events— getting laid, cutting their first single—but not the life. Maybe that was his problem, he was never really that much in touch with things. Too many books, too many records, too much talk about nothing. 'No Jim, I don't. They weren't all that good, I guess. Or at least, I was always hoping for something more. Doesn't everyone?'

And they drove on in silence, listening—or not—to hits from the 80s. The road broadened past Cambridge, it seemed to turn orange, and James drove faster. Michael assumed it was to get there quicker.

Finally, James said, 'Mikey, about you and Julie.'

Michael sighed.

'It's all right, I'm not hassling,' said James. 'It's just I was wondering, how long has it been ...?'

'It hasn't,' said Michael. 'There is nothing going on, not really. But I wish ... I really like her, Jim.'

'Yeah, well so do I,' said James defensively.

'No Jim,' said Michael, turning to face him for the first time since Norwich. 'I really like her.'

18

James and Michael arrived at the hospital just before six. James's immediate concern was finding money for the pay and display; he mumbled something about not having change, so Michael went to the machine and sorted it out. He handed James the ticket. Up to eight hours! That's not a hospital visit, thought James, that's a short holiday.

Michael set off for the main entrance to the hospital, James struggling to keep up.

The hospital felt strangely like a shopping centre. There were a couple of shops, one of which appeared to be selling clothes. Who comes to hospital for new trousers? There was a choice of cafés, a sweet shop, a magazine stand. Michael half expected a cheese counter. Julie was in Intensive Care, which was near Nightingale ward on the second floor and, according to the security man at the front desk, could be found by following a blue line along the corridor floor. Michael hurried on.

Further inside, down the main corridor toward the lift, the building stopped pretending to be anything other than a hospital. It was the smell at first: a mix of urine and cheap disinfectant. After that it was the staff, everyone was wearing a uniform. And finally it was the austerity. The corridor was sparse, the lift functional, and the blue line that they had to follow was fading and chipped. The further he went, the faster he moved.

When they got to the ward James stood back so that Michael could ask the nurse at the desk where Julie was. This was partly because James wasn't comfortable among sick people, he always worried that he might say or do something inappropriate like accidentally pull out an important tube or sit on a dialysis machine and break it. But it was also partly because James didn't want to give anyone the idea that he was still involved with Julie. He wasn't. She had left and that was fine. If she needed a kidney or somewhere to live with wheelchair access, then that was not really his problem any more.

He needn't have worried; Michael apparently wanted to be involved. James couldn't hear exactly what he and the nurse were saying, but he caught the words 'coma,' 'forty-eight hours,' 'friend,' and 'over there.' James followed Michael's gaze to a bed in the corner of a bay of four, a bed surrounded by bits of equipment and tubes. James immediately imagined himself becoming entangled in the tubes and stepped backward. Michael, however, took a deep breath and walked with the nurse to the bedside. After a moment James followed.

Julie was white and lifeless-looking with green rings round her eyes and a tube coming out of her mouth. Beside her sat a shaven-headed woman who glanced up at Michael as he stared at Julie.

'Are you the singer?' asked the bald girl.

Michael shook his head. 'I'm a friend,' he whispered.

'I'm the singer,' said James. The woman turned round, looked him up and down, turned away and sneered. 'Of course you are.'

Michael must have stood at the side of the bed staring at the bloodless, sallow Julie for nearly five minutes; he didn't move. Finally the woman sitting beside Julie looked up at him and saw that he was crying. 'I'm Lynne,' she said.

'Was it you she was coming to visit?' sniffed Michael.

'Yes. Was it you she was going back for?'

Michael couldn't even nod properly.

'I'll get some coffee,' she said. Her face softened as she added, 'You keep guard.'

She ignored James completely, which might have offended him if he had been planning to stay, but he wasn't. Being here didn't feel right and he had found that time seemed to stand still in hospitals: he'd only been here for five minutes but it felt like days. The question was, should he say anything or just slip out? He decided he'd have to say something, if only because he needed directions to Gary's house. And with the 'friend' out of the way this seemed the moment.

'Mikey … Mikey … I'm sorry mate, I don't think I can handle this, seeing her like this, I didn't realise it would be so … so … hard.'

Silence.

'I think maybe I'll just go out for a while, OK?'

Michael nodded.

'Actually, come to think of it maybe I'll go see Gary Guitar … You wouldn't know how I'd get there, would you?'

19

Less than sixty feet from Julie, Ellie sat holding Gabriel's hand, while Moira sat on a chair in the corner as she had done all afternoon.

'Do you know,' said Ellie quietly, 'he's been a right pain to live with for the last six months or so, maybe more: irritable, sarcastic, positively misanthropic. The only time I even saw a glimpse of the bloke I moved in with was when we would go out at the weekend for a drive to the coast, or a wander round the park or something, and after a few crap attempts to have a conversation about anything we would settle on wondering what it would be like to be parents. You know, where do you stand on boys' names today? If we had a child would we stay in London? Could you imagine teaching him or her to swim or read or play football or whatever? He was fine then, Mr Bloody Chatty. The rest of the time … I didn't know how we were staying together.'

'So why were you?'

Ellie didn't say anything. She'd thought about leaving, she'd thought about how it would feel to leave a man with no sperm and potentially go off and get pregnant by some other bloke, and she thought about whether or not it was that that kept her with Gabriel. But she had never thought about being a mother in isolation from Gabriel. Somehow it wasn't the same project, it didn't feel as right. And anyway she did still love him. That may have annoyed her these days, but it remained a glowing unalterable fact. 'Dunno, why do you think?'

'To annoy Izzy.'

Ellie nodded. 'She never really took to him, did she?'

Moira ignored the past tense. 'No.'

'Why do you think that is? And don't say she fancied him.'

'She probably did, but I don't think it was that. Christ, I fancied him, when I first met him ... '.

'When you first met him, you were so pissed you'd have fancied Andrew Lloyd Webber!'

'Bloody wouldn't 'ave. Anyway I meant after that, but the point is, I liked you two together more than I liked the idea of being with him myself.'

'Really?'

'Yeah.'

'Christ, I don't think I could ever feel like that for anyone. I'm too selfish,' said Ellie.

'It's not about selfish, it's about how you see the world. I think of all things as being in pursuit of harmony, of some kind of precise balance, if you like. You and Gabriel look like harmony.'

'So why does Izzy dislike him so?'

'Because where I see harmony, she sees a couple of good-looking people laughing a lot. If you are unhappy or insecure or generally tense the way my sister is, there is nothing quite so annoying as seeing people laughing all the time.'

'We did used to laugh a lot, didn't we?' But as she said it she couldn't remember what laughing felt like.

'Yeah you did.'

They fell silent. After a minute or so Moira said 'Do you want a coffee?'

Ellie tried to smile and said, 'What do you think of my fiendishly desperate plan to get Izzy to steal his sperm while I lay in a hospital bed having my eggs removed?'

'I think it's a great idea,' Moira said softly.

Ellie glanced across the room at Gabriel and said quietly, 'So do I,' then asked, 'Do you think Izzy will do it?'

'I think so,' said Moira, not entirely convincingly. Ellie was quiet again.

'Of course,' said Moira. 'I could always kind of help, if you want?'

Ellie started to cry softly. Moira came over and put her arms around her, feeling her sob into her chest. Ellie pulled her head back long enough to nod almost violently through the tears. Moira stroked her hair, looked at Gabriel, and whispered, 'It's what friends are for.'

20

'I don't *feel* dead.' Gabriel was looking around him as he spoke. It was hard to tell if his heart was actually in what he was saying, but his position was that this constituted an effort.

'Well, of course not,' said Kevin. 'And you don't look it. I've seen enough dead bodies to know what dead looks like, and it doesn't talk. Smells after a while though.' He smiled at his little joke.

Gabriel ignored him. 'I mean I felt ... like I was in the middle of something ... in the middle of lots of things ... not at the end.'

'I know what you mean,' said Julie.

'We were in the middle of IVF for one thing, and it feels like, well ... you didn't let me finish anything.'

'Well, who gets to finish everything?' said Clemitius. 'The nature of life is that you are always in the middle of something when it ends.'

'Yeah I get it,' said Gabriel irritably, 'but I'm talking about how that makes me feel, which was I thought the fucking point of the group.'

Clemitius held his expression and shuffled his feet uncomfortably under his robe. 'Of course,' he said, forcing a smile.

'In fact, I don't think there was a day in my life when I could possibly have felt more in the middle of my life than I did the day I died. Is that the lesson I'm supposed to learn? I shouldn't have started anything for fear of getting run over? "Don't take life for granted?" Because I'm infertile, mate, and that teaches you pretty bloody quickly not to take anything for granted.'

'It's not our job to teach you any lessons.'

'No of course not, that would be a bit too Old Testament, right?'

Everyone was silent. Christopher found himself struggling not to speak and he thought about why. He felt embarrassed. Embarrassed to be listening to things he could have seen just by looking. Gabriel was staring at his feet; Julie looked at him, perhaps still struggling with the fact that she'd run him over. Kevin seemed as though he was going to burst unless someone said something.

'Funny, I felt like I was maybe at the start of something,' said Julie. 'That's probably easier in some ways but ...'

A sticky silence descended, cloying and awkward. Julie thought it was like being in a lift going a long, long way up, except in therapy you can't all stare at the door hoping nobody speaks. You face each other, aware that the doors won't open and nobody is going to get out, not for a while yet anyway.

'Well if there's one thing my job has taught me, it's that nobody gets to choose when they go,' said Kevin, looking at Clemitius for approval.

'Hmm, I wonder if you had to become a murderer to learn that?' said Yvonne, curling her mouth to add extra venom.

'Tell me more about feeling unfinished,' said Clemitius.

'You see,' said Gabriel, 'that's what annoys me. It's so false, that kind of question, it makes my teeth itch, and I can just feel myself getting irritated. "Tell me more about feeling unfinished"—for fuck's sake!'

Christopher listened but didn't move. If he had, he would have found himself nodding and so he stayed perfectly still.

'That sounds like a defence mechanism to me,' said Clemitius, a bit defensively. 'A way of acting that prevents you, or excuses you, from saying or thinking about things that are too hard.'

'Or maybe the problem is the words simply sound like a lie dressed as a question?' Gabriel looked up at the smooth white ceiling, then at Clemitius.

'How can a question be a lie?' said Clemitius.

'If the person asking it does so believing they already know the answer?'

Another silence. Kevin struggled the most when nobody was speaking, he almost changed colour, from his usual pinky grey to a bright puce.

Finally Gabriel said, 'So you're saying I'm in some kind of denial.'

'I didn't use those words.'

'But that's what you mean.'

'I just mean that you say you haven't been happy, and when someone asks you anything about yourself you get cross, which serves to prevent you thinking about why you were unhappy.' Now Clemitius was in his element.

'I'm not unhappy, I wasn't unhappy, I was ... frustrated, irritable maybe, not in control of my life. I wanted to be a dad, I wanted to be the father of Ellie's child, and I couldn't.' He paused, thinking hard. 'I couldn't figure out what to do about that. But I wasn't unhappy.'

'So you got cross and stayed that way for about a year and a half?' Christopher asked.

'I don't know. There's more to it than that.'

'Which is why you're here,' said Clemitius.

'I don't think I could have handled it, mate, firing blanks, too embarrassing,' Kevin said. 'I admire you for even admitting it. I mean, I was all right in that department; my first wife said I got her pregnant by looking at her from across the room.' He laughed.

'Yeah, I hear that kind of thing a lot,' said Gabriel, unmoved.

'I can't imagine any woman wanting you to get any closer,' shuddered Yvonne. 'Did it never occur to you that maybe that was her way of telling you that it was someone else's child?'

Gabriel continued, 'I did think about things, not just the fertility stuff but why I was, well, moody ...'

'And what did you think?' asked Clemitius.

'I thought of a hundred reasons why I was behaving the way I was, but knowing them doesn't change anything, knowing them just gives you something to talk about while you are behaving that way.'

'What do you mean?' said Kevin to Yvonne.

Gabriel ignored them. 'Worrying about getting older, and more unsure about things, less in control of my life. I mean my hair started to fall out, I know it's not important in the scheme of things, other people are losing kidneys and loved ones, what's a bit of baldness? But it was *my* baldness, and I got to thinking: Well, it's the first thing that has happened to my body that I didn't choose, and it felt like a sign of things to come, you know? Dodgy knees, arthritis, getting fat, a fucking lack of sperm ...'

'What do you mean someone else's child? She didn't, she wouldn't have dared,' said Kevin.

'Because you'd have killed her?'

'Yes, actually.'

'All the more reason not to tell you.' Yvonne smiled.

'There seem to be two conversations going on at the same time,' said Clemitius.

'You see it's always the bloke's fault isn't it' said Kevin. 'We can't do right for doing wrong.'

'Oh yes, you poor little contract killer you,' sneered Yvonne.

'If I'd met you before I'd been paid to kill you, I'd have done it for nothing,' spat Kevin.

'Yes I'm sure you would, you have the demeanour of an amateur,' she said.

Kevin clenched his fists and looked at Clemitius, who said, and he had probably been practising this for a long time: 'I sense some hostility in the group.'

21

Gary Guitar was—as Eighties pop refugees go—quite a success. And a lot of it was down to a reliance on cough medicine.

In the last throes of Dog in a Tuba, Gary was rarely seen without a bottle of cough medicine in his hand. He could get through seven bottles a day when things were at their worst. That constituted a £70 a week habit. After Dog in a Tuba split up, he found his way into drug rehab. He loved it. Not only did he manage to kick the linctus but his cough cleared up, too. And if that weren't enough, he met Brett BigHair, lead singer with American AOR 'legends' Karma. Brett was doing battle with the evil twin axes of cocaine and sex addiction. He was also quite pissed off by the defection of Karma guitarist Stevie 'Strings' Logan to a bunch of Seventh Day Adventists who liked Stevie's cash but not the devil's music he played to earn it. Brett needed a guitarist; Gary Guitar had a guitar. A union made in rehab that earned Gary more than $5 million over the next seven years.

He needed Dog in a Tuba about as much as a polar bear needed an anorak. Nothing would get him on stage with James Buchan again. He had better things to do. He wasn't exactly sure what they were at the moment, which is why he found himself watching 'U.K. Style Horizon' more than he might have anticipated and, as a result of 'Watercolour Challenge,' trying to teach himself to paint.

Gary Guitar had returned from the U.S. after a messy divorce expecting to lose himself in meaningless sex, song writing and some music production. Only the song writing had materialised. As a result he had 24 new songs, mostly about his ex-wife and estranged daughter, although one or two touched on the sensitive subject of addiction (example: 'My Coughing Soul').

He had imagined that a few young women might want to sleep with him. However, he didn't get out all that much and, when he did, it appeared that the local females saw not a rock star but a forty-five-year-old fat bloke with a mullet wearing pressed denim and some cowboy boots. It hadn't been much better in the States either. Brett had banned girls from the backstage area as part of his recovery. Gary Guitar had considered this unfair, as he wouldn't dream of demanding the other band members renounce cough medicine if they needed it. But it felt unsympathetic to say anything.

So anyway, Gary Guitar did what he did and waited. At first he had been waiting for someone to call about producing a new band who had always admired him, or wondering if he had any plans for some solo work, but as the days turned into weeks, and the endless re-runs of 'Last of the Summer Wine' turned into endless re-runs of 'Dad's bloody Army,' he realised he was waiting for just about anything. And then, after the phone call, Gary Guitar realised that perhaps he had been waiting for James.

James left the hospital with a mix of relief and excited nervous energy normally the preserve of new fathers. Of course he was worried about the possibility of getting punched by Gary Guitar. And he was even more worried about Gary not even answering the door. But he was also looking forward to seeing the silly sod. The prospect of seeing the man he had once thought about calling Lennon to his McCartney, but hadn't because he didn't want to give Gary delusions of equality, warmed him.

By the time he had got out of the West End and up past Hampstead Heath, Julie and her coma couldn't have been further from his mind. As he drew nearer to the address Michael had distractedly given him, all other thoughts and feelings had drained away, being replaced by an overwhelming 'creosote-my-bollocks-and-call-me-a-coconut-because-that's-how-much-this-hurts' jealousy. The houses weren't just houses, they were small mansions, estates even, and in London, which made them worth about as much as Luxembourg. This was the stuff of 'Through the Keyhole', the stuff that James believed was meant for him.

Most of these places had security systems. Many had closed gates; some had yellow signs threatening trespassers with large dogs. Gary's house, he was relieved to discover, had none of that stuff. Bloody big, though. In order to get from Gary's gate to his front door, James was better off staying in the car. He had to drive up his guitarist's front path, that was obscene, and all the way he was driving he was surrounded by a garden, more a field really, with a couple of trees. The drive was lined with large ornamental urns, each about the size of James's bath, and they were all full of flowers. James decided he would piss in one of the bloody things if Gary wasn't in.

The grass was freshly cut, which James thought probably meant a gardener, and the drive had gravel. James wasn't certain why this above everything else annoyed him the most, but it really did; as he cruised up the driveway the sound of his guitarist's gravel under the wheels almost made him throw up. Still, this was no time for bitterness or retribution: all that could come later, along with some carefully placed Benylin in Gary's hotel room. Jammy bastard. First things first, thought James, let's get Dog in a Tuba back together again.

The doorbell chimed 'Eye of the Tiger.' It wasn't being ironic. James waited. He thought of ringing again, but who wants to hear that repeated? And anyway, it was a big house; Gary Guitar might have been down in the cellar, or in the fucking sauna.

When Gary finally answered they just stared at each other. They had met nearly twenty years earlier, written bad songs together, shared poverty, pot noodles and instant mashed potato, and whilst they had also grown to hate each other, there are moments when you forget the loathing and remember the mashed potato. Moments when you romanticise your past or, as James would say, 'go a bit soft in the head.'

It may be that Gary was having one of those moments, because he neither slammed the door shut nor hit James. He did say, 'Whatever you're selling I ain't buying,' with a slightly mid-Atlantic twang to his voice that made James want to tell him he sounded like Sheena Easton.

'Nice house Gary; is it yours?'

'No, I'm squatting. What do you want?'

'To talk.'

'What about?'

'Any chance of coming in? Or you worried I'll see you don't have any furniture?'

'Oh, I've got furniture, I just don't want you sitting on it.' But as he said it Gary Guitar turned away from the door and walked through a large hallway into the living room. As he hadn't closed the door or set any killer dogs on him yet, James took that as the nearest thing he was going to get to an invitation to come in.

In the living room Gary was already lounging on a long, cream-coloured leather sofa. Behind him were enormous French doors leading on to the garden. It was a lovely room being slightly strangled by crap, thoughtless furniture. A series of three large rugs—one burgundy, in the middle of the room, one off-white, and one multi-coloured African style affair over by the French doors—gave the impression that Gary had decided to spend what he saved on interior designers down at the 'Lucky Dip Carpet and Rug Emporium'. On the wall, above an original and quite stunning fireplace, was the same picture James had back in the cottage, the Rothko poster.

'Hey' exclaimed James 'I've got that at home too!'

'I doubt it,' said Gary. 'He only did it the once.'

'Yeah well, I mean I've got a copy.'

Gary enjoyed the following silence, and couldn't resist smiling and saying in a stage whisper: 'That's the original. I bought it off Sting.'

James coughed, then realised that perhaps coughing was insensitive. So he coughed again. 'Nice house Gaz, bit different to Dalston Road, eh?'

'Long time ago. What do you want?'

James had the spiel ready. How Dog in a Tuba had been, even if Gary didn't realise it, a seminal part of all of their lives, and how the advantage of a reunion is that people only remember the good things the band did, they don't remember the crap, and even if they do remember the crap they don't remember it as crap because they remember how happy or hopeful or thin they were when they were listening to it.

'Christ, I've even heard "Prince Charming" referred to as a classic and people were throwing up in the streets when that came out.'

Gary didn't look at James while he spoke, which made him feel a bit like a vacuum-cleaner salesman, but he did pour a couple of glasses of scotch, almost distractedly, and James took that as a sign to carry on with even more enthusiasm. He talked about maybe writing some new songs together, about seeing and being with the others, about playing with old friends like Blancmange and those fellas out of Spandau.

'We never met them, did we?' said Gary.

'No I don't think so, but we probably will this time—all in the same boat and all that,' said James.

'But you're missing one vital thing,' said Gary, handing James a glass. 'Why bother? I mean what would be the point, it sounds like some kind of hell to me. Singing songs I can't remember to an audience of tired, bald, fat people who won't be asking for an encore because they have to get home to the babysitter by eleven. I mean why? What would be the point?'

'Fun.'

'You call that fun?'

'The musical challenge?'

'Pur-leeze.'

'Money.'

'Ah, money. Now we are getting to the point. James, you haven't changed: still full of bullshit and still crap with money. Well sorry man, but I don't need the money.'

'Everyone needs money, Gary, even rich people. Let's face it, it won't do your profile any harm to be seen in your old band again.'

Gary Guitar laughed. 'Well, it depends what you mean by profile, James. A load of overweight has-beens doing Eighties cabaret? I think if you want a profile that says "loser," that's a pretty good way to go about getting it.'

'Oh don't be such a snob. OK, it's not ideal, but you are not going to tell me that the manufactured crap around at the moment is better pop music.'

'I am not interested in pop music James, pop music is for the young, it's for the impatient for chrissakes; that's why it's always just three minutes long.'

'Well, the audience won't be young, they'll be adult. We don't just have to play the old stuff, do we?'

'What? New songs?' For the first time Gary had stopped sneering.

'Yeah new songs, new audience; I haven't actually written much yet but ...'

'No, but I have.'

James's blood froze. People didn't buy Rolling Stones records to hear Bill Wyman songs. They didn't go to see The Police to see what Andy Summers was writing about, and they weren't going to welcome Dog In a Tuba back into their lives if they had to listen to the interminable mid-Atlantic drivel that Gary Guitar would almost definitely inflict upon them.

'Nah, hang on mate, I'm the songwriter. You're the musical craftsman. It's what made us such a good band, we knew our roles.'

'We didn't know jack shit, James, we were kids. Well I've been playing pretty much non-stop since then; have you? If I'm going to do this, and I'm not saying I am, I'm doing my own songs.'

James nodded. Like fuck you are, he thought, but this wasn't the time. That will come later, with the cough medicine. 'Be great to get together again after all these years. We'll be better this time round, I know it.'

22

After the group, Gabriel wandered outdoors and down toward the lake. From the semi-circular building it was about 150 metres to the pale uncut grass. The ground sloped a little as he drew nearer to the water, and the smell of honeysuckle and lavender faded, but the beginnings of a path, made by the near-dead who had gone before him, was clearly forming. Gabriel followed it and quite naturally turned to the left toward what city dwellers might call a wood, but Gabriel knew was simply a few trees and some bushes. He had begun to develop a habit of heading for the side of the water and coming to rest among the trees; he liked the illusion of being out of sight, as if anyone can be out of sight so close to heaven. When he thought he was out of view, he sat down on the grass and threw bits of fallen bark into the water.

Julie tended to go back to her room after a group but sometimes, like today, she would wander out, too. Unlike Gabriel she didn't have a fixed routine, she would just stroll around and would often stand for quite a while staring at something. Looking at the light on the trees and the shadows on the water, she wondered what it would be like to paint there. In fact she wondered sometimes if she was actually in a painting, able to move freely around as long as nobody was looking, trapped and still if someone stopped to stare. It made as much sense as God had before she had found herself surrounded by angels. After gazing into space she moved on and walked away down toward where the dry bush was at its most dense, near where Gabriel sat, lobbing wood at water.

When she saw him she paused. She hadn't spoken to anyone alone since the accident and, given the circumstances, talking to

Gabriel seemed the hardest place to start. But she had always gravitated toward the more difficult choices and anyway, he seemed a decent bloke. She moved closer and said, 'What is it with men and water?'

'Pardon?'

'If you put a man in front of water for long enough he will eventually start throwing things into it. Why is that?'

Gabriel thought for a moment. 'It's genetic,' he said. 'We throw stuff; women need to pee. It's just one of those gender-difference things.'

'Excuse me?'

'Women: show them an expanse of water and within five minutes they need to go for a pee.'

'That's rubbish.'

'Is it?'

'Yes.'

'Fair enough.' Gabriel carried on throwing bits of bark and Julie turned to go.

'See,' said Gabriel.

'What?'

'You're off for a pee, aren't you?'

'No I'm not, I was looking for something to throw,' said Julie.

Gabriel smiled. 'So, what do you make of all this?

Julie didn't answer.

'I've been wondering if I'm mad,' said Gabriel. 'Ellie is a mental health nurse; she says that a lot of madness revolves around religion. Being God or Jesus is a very popular delusion. I've wondered if maybe I am in some kind of delusional state.'

'And what about the rest of us?'

'I don't know, you either don't exist or you are just people who I imagine to be other dead people in a therapy group with me.'

'Does madness work like that?'

'I don't know, I've never been mad, unless of course I am mad now.'

'I'm not convinced.'

'Got any better ideas?'

'No. I wondered about it being a dream, it even crossed my mind that I was part of some sicko experiment, you know, been kidnapped ... or something ...'

'What, we are here being forced into therapy by some rogue group of psychology students?' smiled Gabriel.

'Something like that. But the longer I am here, the more I wake up in the room, and the more I have to sit in a circle with you and the others the more it occurs to me that this is what Pinky and Perky say it is. The tragedy is, I don't feel the things I know I should feel.'

'Like what?'

'I don't feel grief. I just feel numb.'

'I feel sick; I feel as though I am going to explode, and just start screaming.'

'But that would make sense, why don't you do that? It would make sense to go crazy.'

'I don't know ... something stops me. Every night I go back to my room, I try to cry, but I just stare at the ceiling until I sleep and then like a moron I show up for toast and therapy in the morning.'

'Well we have to go to the group,' said Julie.

'Why?'

'Because it is the only way out of here and it feels like an unbreakable law.'

'But what if it isn't a way back? What if Pinky and Perky, as you so rightly call them, just want to run a fucking therapy group for eternity? Christ, what if this is hell? It does feel a bit like hell listening to Kevin talk about killing people, and having to look at Clemitius nodding his fat head like a pig watching a bungee jump. And what if there is something else I could be doing to get back to Ellie?'

143

'Maybe that's why I don't feel the way I think I should feel, and maybe that's why I don't quite believe this is happening.'

'Sorry,' said Gabriel. 'I don't quite follow you.'

'Well, you have Ellie. You obviously love her very much, and from what Christopher said the other night at dinner she must love you, too.'

'Christ knows why ...'

'Whatever, but she does, and I don't have anyone like that. Nothing anchored me to life, or no one ... and maybe I was just realising that ... I had wondered if someone I had met might become ... you know ... hell, I can't even think about that. When I hit you I was on my way to stay with a friend I hadn't seen for ages. She was a constant, but apart from her I think I had realised I felt quite lonely. I didn't want to be that way, I was going to do something about it, I think, but I didn't. I was just living in Norwich waiting for my life. Maybe I deserved this.'

'Norwich, you were living in Norwich? Talk about out of the frying pan.'

'Have you ever been to Norwich?'

'No, sorry, it's kind of a habit, saying stuff like that.'

Julie smiled. 'Take it to the group.'

She sat down beside him and started making a small pile of twigs. The water was flat apart from the ripples growing around Gabriel's tiny missiles, and the lake seemed to go on for miles. She wondered what would happen if someone walked into the water and started to swim. Not stopping, not looking back, just kept on going until you couldn't go any more, the way that angel had. You can't die twice. Maybe you'd just wake up in your bed like nothing had happened, or maybe you wouldn't wake up at all, having passed on your last chance. Or perhaps it took you somewhere else? It wouldn't make sense to have a trap door from heaven, nor would it make sense for there to be choices for any of them that were not already explicit. But you can't change the beliefs of a lifetime, and Julie believed that there were always choices; you just had to be brave enough or desperate enough to make them.

'I want to see this viewing room,' said Gabriel.

'Me too.'

'Then I might start believing ... or I might not, but that is what we should be saying.'

'What, to Pinky and Perky?'

'Yes, that it's hard to take all of this in and to work on our issues and concentrate and all of that. That what we need is some kind of proof or—'

'—perspective,' offered Julie. 'We could say we need a little perspective to come to terms with our changes in circumstances.'

'Yeah and then, well ... then we'd know.'

'Let's do it,' said Julie turning to go.

'No not now, we should do it in the group.'

'Yes, you're probably right, but what about the others, should we talk to them?'

'I don't know. Yvonne, maybe, but Kevin? I don't think that would be a good idea, I think the bloke is pretty eager to please and this might seem too much like a plan.'

Julie stared some more at the water and thought *There is always a choice.* And said, 'I don't trust people who kill other people anyway. Let's do whatever we need to do to see what's left of our lives, eh?'

Although at the back of her mind she wondered, 'Can any conversation here be secret?'

23

James and Gary were on their fourth whisky, and while James felt the nice warm glow that came from not having been thrown out yet, he was pretty uncomfortable with the idea of Gary providing songs for the comeback.

'So what do the others say?'

'Haven't asked anyone yet; I thought I should come to you first. After all, you were the guitarist.'

'And you did shag my girlfriend.'

'Oh for fuck's sake Gary, I didn't mean to ...'

'Oh it was an accident was it—your dick accidentally slipped?'

'No I mean ... Christ, you know what it was like.'

'I know what you were like.' They sat in silence. James wanted to say more, explain away his mistake, but the truth was he couldn't really remember it very well. He knew that Gary was kind of seeing Alice, but everyone was kind of seeing everyone in those days. It was quite a small bus, and it wasn't like Gary and Alice could hide away together, or did they? He couldn't remember.

He was pretty sure it was Alice who made the first move, or they were drunk or something, one evening when the others had gone up to the hall for a sound check. Leicester? Coventry? Fuck knows, somewhere in the middle of the country. And he remembered that she had a long skirt on and took her knickers off remarkably early in the proceedings, like before they'd even kissed, and he certainly remembered Gary and Bernie coming back because they'd forgotten strings or more likely, Gary's spare cough linctus. There must have been one hell of a row but he couldn't remember it, so he said the only thing he could think of under the circumstances: 'Shit happens.'

'She's with Matthew now, you know.'

'Yeah I heard—hard to imagine.'

'Yeah, 'til you see them together, then it makes some kind of sense.'

'What, you see them?'

'Oh yeah, they were up for the weekend earlier this month. Did you hear about their lottery win? Really pleased for them. They're quite religious, you know?'

'Blimey. So anyway'—James didn't really take in information about other people's lives— 'all I'm asking is that you'll think about it.'

'Well there's a lot to think about, James, and I have other responsibilities.'

'Like what?'

'Well for one thing I am contracted to tour with Karma for the first four months of next year, and we are recording from October through to February of the following year, so I have to build any other projects round that.'

'Yeah right, of course,' said James.

'Mind you, it might be worth thinking about.'

'Yeah that's right, just think about it, Gary, that's all I'm asking.'

'I mean it could be a way of showcasing some of my new stuff.'

'No, hang on Gary. I mean, each band on these reunion tours ... they are only getting like four or five-song sets.'

'Well we only had one hit.'

'Two.'

'One.'

'"Partytime" made Number Three in Germany.' James was staring at the rug, wondering if it was real animal. Everything in this house was expensive: tasteless, but expensive. It was probably a big sheep, he thought. Not a baby polar bear.

'Yeah but Germany ... And either way that leaves two or three songs.'

'Yeah, but they would be my songs, Gary.'

'No James, they would be mine.'

'Sorry, I can't allow it! I mean, I'm the bloody songwriter; Christ you don't go to a Rolling Stones gig in the hope that Bill Wyman is going to step forward and do "Je Suis un Rock Star," do you?'

'No you go to hear Keith Richards, and anyway Wyman left the Stones.'

'I know, but the point's the same.'

'No it isn't. For all you know, he left because Mick wouldn't sing his songs.'

'He left because he was about seventy-eight.'

'I want to do my songs, James. That is the only circumstance under which I would consider it. Think about it.'

James looked at Gary and whilst a big, big part of him wanted to punch the linctus freak in the mouth and remind him that he was just a fucking guitarist, he knew that you only did that kind of thing when you were actually in a band, not simply talking about being in one again. Anyway, Gary was thinking about it. As things stood, this constituted a result.

There would be plenty of time for fighting later. Dog in a Tuba would just be a stepping-stone anyway. When James went solo, Gary could do his songs as much as he liked. 'All right Gary,' he said. 'Can I ask a question?'

'Yep.'

'Did that rug used to be a polar bear?'

24

Ellie was, in the words of her consultant Dr Samani, 'ready to pop', which meant that her eggs were ready to be harvested and she would need to come into hospital the day after tomorrow to have them removed. Dr Samani had asked where Gabriel was; he had, after all, been with her every time she visited the unit up until these last two visits, and although Ellie had decided that she was going to lie if and when this came up—and she was sure when they started looking around for the right semen, it would most definitely have to be mentioned—she had not actually thought up the exact lie she was going to tell. She had thought of taking Sam along and saying she had changed men, and she had thought about saying that Gabriel had broken a leg and wouldn't be able to attend, but would most definitely be sending sperm on a motorbike when the big moment arrived.

However she was so tired, so full of fear and loneliness and stuffed to the gills with artificial hormones and grief, that when Dr Samani finally asked directly about Gabriel, no doubt expecting something like 'Oh he's at work', instead he got 'He's in a coma' and the whole story poured out.

She tried not to mention the doctors who said they would not supply the sperm. She tried to talk round that bit but Dr Samani said, in that irritatingly direct way that doctors have, 'I assume his doctors know that you are in an IVF cycle?'

'Yes.'

'And are they being helpful?'

'Not really. They say that Gabriel has not given consent for his sperm to be taken and therefore they can't do anything, and so I am going to ... to be supplying the sperm myself.' She was clinging to a chair in his office, holding the seat hard because hearing her own words actually leaving her mouth was making her dizzy, and she realised that it could all end here. She might think she could trick the doctors looking after Gabe, she might think that she could smuggle some sperm from his sleeping testes whilst they were looking the other way, and get someone to drive it across town while her eggs waited impatiently in a dish, checking their hair and putting on some lippy. But without this man's say-so, without him willing to put the assorted gametes together and then putting the cells they make back into her, she was lost.

'Really?' It was the first time she had seen him surprised. 'How are you going to do that, grow testicles? Only joking. What do you mean, they say he has not given consent? What do they think this is, some kind of silly farce? What is the consultant's name? I will talk to him.'

'No really, please, I have tried.'

'Yes, but I will succeed. We will get your husband's sperm, not just anyone's sperm.'

'I wasn't going to get just anyone's sperm for chrissakes,' shouted Ellie.

Dr Samani stopped and looked at her. He was not used to being shouted at, but he seemed startled rather than angry. His brown eyes softened. Ellie began to cry.

'I'm sorry, of course not. I will talk to this doctor of your husband's.'

'He won't do anything without it going to court, he said so, and by then Gabe could be dead and I ... I ... please don't call him. Please.'

'I do not have time for people like these, we make babies for good people, they think what they do is better than that? Nothing is better than that. Court case ... pah!'

'Please listen,' said Ellie, composing herself. 'If you phone him and he agrees, great, but I don't think he will. He will argue and report what is going on to his superiors, he's the type, believe me; he may well keep even more of an eye on Gabe, and maybe even stop me from being with him, and I need to be with him and so do my friends.'

'Of course you do ...'

'No, not just because we need to sit with him. We need to be with him because we need to take his sperm and bring it here, so you can put it with my eggs.'

'How are you going to take his sperm?'

'The same way he would; my friend will do it and her husband will drive here with the sperm. He has been practising, he can do it in eighteen minutes.'

'Eighteen minutes is OK, ten would be better. Can you not find a motorbike?'

'I don't think so.'

'Well, I think *I* can.'

'But ... if you help, won't you get into trouble?'

'Don't you worry about that. When the time comes we will be ready. These people try to make difficult science impossible, they try to stop dreams from coming true. Don't worry Ellie, we will get the sperm here and we will make the embryos. Then we pray.'

'I pray a lot these days,' said Ellie. 'No idea who to.'

25

'The point of therapy,' said Julie as soon as everyone had sat down. 'It's about revelation really, isn't it? About strangers telling other strangers about things or events or feelings that they wouldn't otherwise talk about. Isn't it?' She looked at Christopher as she spoke, rolling her finger and thumb together on both hands.

'Well,' said Christopher. 'It can be about that, or at least include that, but it isn't only about that.'

Julie shook her head, seemingly ignoring the answer. 'You see, I'm confused. If there is a God, can I assume he is an all-knowing God?' She paused. Nobody spoke. She raised her hands to exaggerate her question. 'Anyone?'

Clemitius and Christopher stayed silent. 'OK, I will assume he is, or she is, all-knowing; we can but hope, right?' She glanced at Yvonne, who nodded supportively. 'Because if he is all-knowing, what is the point of disclosure? I mean if we bring something to the group that has haunted us, surely you two men of god will already know about it?'

'No,' said Christopher. 'We don't know everything that ever happened to you, that wouldn't be possible, it wouldn't work.' He looked as though he wanted to carry on, but Julie interrupted him.

'Right,' she said. 'What happens to dead babies?'

'Pardon?' said Clemitius.

'I think you heard me.' Everyone looked at her; she looked at Clemitius, who inhaled deeply, sat up slightly in his chair, and looked back at her calmly.

Julie had decided it was her turn to say something; she had decided this the previous night, as she lay in her bed curled up in a ball the way she used to when she was young. But she didn't know what to say. She wasn't used to talking about herself; in fact she wasn't used to thinking about herself, at least not in the way therapy or modern life seemed to demand. She didn't turn her life into a series of short fables and she couldn't imagine how all the things she had found herself doing combined to form a whole that made sense to anyone, least of all herself. She just did what she did because it seemed the right thing at the time. She was comfortable with that.

But that was no use to her here. And so she had wondered through the previous night what could she 'bring to the group' or more accurately, to Clemitius. Uncertainty? The quiet purr of disappointment? A list of past lovers and cities long since faded? Or do you ask about your baby, who would, incidentally, have been eighteen this year.

'Yes Julie I heard you, I was just taken aback by the question.'

'Well now that your surprise has passed, maybe you could tell me what happens, or more specifically what happened to my dead baby. I'd really like to know.'

Yvonne lifted a hand to her mouth; Julie stared at Clemitius.

'Could you explain to the group what you are talking about?' Clemitius said gently.

She held his gaze and spoke coolly. 'When I was seventeen, I had a baby in difficult circumstances, a little boy who was stillborn. I had married my English teacher who was nineteen years older than me. When I went into labour he was at the home of a fifteen-year-old student of his, helping with her homework. Or at least, that is what he told the judge when her parents pressed charges. Anyway, I was thinking last night that if there is a heaven, and you say there is, what kind of heaven … '. She stopped; composed herself. ' I was thinking about what might happen to dead babies, babies who have not had the chance to do good or bad or to fuck up or whatever it is we've done. I was wondering ... why?'

Christopher looked at Clemitius and found himself feeling sorry for him. Clemitius didn't know what to say: he might think he did, he might try a few words from his psychotherapy manual, but nobody, man nor angel, knew what to say to that.

'I'm so sorry,' Christopher said softly.

'Can I ask,' said Gabriel, who seemed engaged with the group for the first time, 'do you have any other children?'

'No,' said Julie quietly. 'Didn't want children, or didn't find myself in a position of thinking wanting them would be OK. Does that make sense?'

Gabriel nodded. 'Yes, perfect sense.'

Julie's eyes were shining. Yvonne said, 'So what happens?'

Silence.

Kevin burst, the way a big boil bursts, 'I imagine it's the same as with babies who are aborted or something, isn't that right?'

'Shut up, moron,' hissed Yvonne. 'Jesus, what kind of ...'

'What happens, please?' said Julie, defiant, contained.

'They ... he ... to be honest, Julie,' said Clemitius. 'I think there are other things happening here, not least you wanting to revisit what happened to you. And what effect did that event have on your life for example?'

'Really? You see I don't think those things matter at all. I think I am sitting here staring at God, or at least as close as I'm likely to get, and I just think a good question is, what happened to the baby I nearly had when I was a kid? The dead one.'

'Julie.' Christopher said.

'What?' Julie turned to him, and he stared into her eyes.

'They become the light. So you can see.'

He spoke softly. He didn't know if she believed him. He didn't even know if she heard him.

Clemitius looked at Christopher. Christopher could feel his eyes burning into him but he carried on looking at Julie. He knew the rules. Rule No. 1: Never lie. Rule No. 2: Be careful

154

how you care. Rule No. 3: Do not bring feelings to the group; it is not here for you. Rule No. 4: Don't bloody lie!

Christopher half expected Clemitius to call him a liar. To say in that sanctimonious way he had, 'Well that isn't actually true is it? I wonder what made you say that?' Except Christopher knew that he wasn't a patient, and you're not really allowed to confront your co-therapist; it's not done.

Instead Clemitius said, 'How have you lived with that, Julie? With the loss. How has it moulded you, would you say?'

Julie's face hardened. 'You don't live with it; you live in spite of it.'

'I don't know what that means. And I'm not sure you do either.'

This was a different silence, not uncomfortable in the way they usually were. This was more purposeful. It felt like a gathering of energy. Christopher expected Julie to leave or shout. She did neither; she just looked at Clemitius coldly.

It was Yvonne who spoke, and she did so quietly. 'I think the most generous thing I can say about that is that it is unkind, maybe cruel. However, I don't feel you deserve that much generosity. I think you are an unthinking, unknowing, bumbling shithead. If you are an angel, then God is a fool.'

'Why … my baby … why does that happen?' whispered Julie, looking at Christopher.

He shrugged, 'There is no reason.'

And she knew that, she had always known that. It was bad luck; she was too young, and she was alone. But knowing it, living with it for most of her life, didn't actually make much difference. She had grown used to the hole it had left in her, the way you become used to a limp after a while. You change with the life that happens to you, and sometimes you see it happening and maybe even understand it, and sometimes you don't, because you are simply too busy trying to breathe. And she knew that somewhere, a long time ago, she had decided to just carry on doing that and now, this, was simply too late.

26

Moira, Izzy, and Ellie were sitting in Gabriel's room, staring out of the window across the dusty landscape of London, watching the sun go down.

Ellie was tired. She knew that this part of her grieving was coming to an end soon. When the eggs and the sperm were added together she would sleep, and wait, and see if there was any kind of God anywhere. See if the exchange that she and Gabriel were being offered stacked up or not. A life for a life? Gabriel's burnt-out, cynical screaming life for a new one. Was it sick to think of it like that? Perhaps, but it was the nearest thing to sense Ellie could muster, that somewhere something good might happen, and somehow that would make sense of all the bad.

'So is there anything I should know?' asked Izzy.

'What do you mean?'

'About Gabriel's penis, is there anything I should know?'

'Yeah, it makes a kind of whistling noise when he comes.'

'What!' said Izzy.

'Well for God's sake, what kind of question is that?'

'Well I don't know what I might be letting myself in for—is it big, little, misshapen?'

'Izzy!' said Moira. 'For fuck's sake just rub it and catch what comes out.'

'Oh, listen to my darling little sister.'

'It's only weird if you let it be weird.'

'No I'm sorry, I beg to differ: it's just weird!'

'Izzy, you can't let me down, you know,' said Ellie. And she got up and left the room to go the toilet.

Izzy carried on staring out of the window. If anyone had ever asked Izzy and Moira if they were close, they would both have said no and gone into a routine about how 'different' the other was. How unfocused, dippy, impractical, and hopeless Moira was; how uptight, unsympathetic, tethered, and neurotic Izzy was. The truth was they needed each other to be what they were. It helped them define themselves and take satisfaction in what they had become. If they weren't related, they probably wouldn't be friends, but they wouldn't feel complete without each other.

'Do you want me to do it, Iz?'

'No, it's my job.'

Moira laughed. 'Christ, you used to do that when we were small! Mum would give us jobs to do around the house, and you'd moan about having to hoover, so I'd say, "I'll do it," and you'd go "No, it's my job," like I was stealing your favourite toy.'

'Well this is a bit different, I'm the best friend; if anyone is going to wank her boyfriend off, it's going to be me. Anyway you've always fancied him and that would make it a bit sordid.'

'Yeah well, what about you?'

'What about me?'

'I fancied him, no big deal, no harm done. You, you bloody hate him!'

'Don't be stupid.'

'You did. You were always rude, unfriendly, and unsupportive of them when they found out they couldn't have kids. You've never liked him.'

'Of course I didn't hate him—he isn't who I would have picked for Ellie, and he could be an arrogant sod sometimes, but I didn't hate him. That's a terrible thing to say about a man in a coma.'

'Well, you looked like you felt a lot of stuff about him. Maybe it wasn't hate, eh?' Moira teased. 'It's a thin line, Iz.'

'Yuck,' said Izzy, too loud and too quickly.

Moira looked at her. 'You didn't? Did you?'

But Izzy knew herself well enough to not fret about the made-for-TV emotions being ascribed to her. She didn't love him or fancy him; she didn't hate him either, or even particularly dislike him. She loathed his type, or at least the type he was when she met him. Charming (allegedly), good looking (so what, she didn't wet herself), at ease with himself—like he thought he was in a film, like he was in a film that anyone would want to watch. And that is why she knew Ellie and he were suited, because Ellie was like that too, except she didn't annoy Izzy as much because she was her friend, and you can't stay annoyed with friends or they stop being your friends, and then you have to hang out with people you don't really like, who are an incy bit ugly, and that would be a bad thing.

Izzy was the type of woman who tended not to like her friends very much, and Gabriel wasn't even one of her friends, so she had even less reason to feel guilty about the fact that she loathed him. She didn't want to touch his penis, and there was something a tad insulting about having to touch the penis of a man she didn't like—and who she considered to be arrogant—while he was in a coma. It was a bit like having to get someone drunk to sleep with them, but worse. However, no matter how much she didn't like the idea, this was about Ellie, and she was determined to get past her own—under the circumstances—petty little hang-ups.

'I'll do it Moira, and I'll do it on my own, thank you.' But as she said it, even Izzy wasn't entirely convinced and Ellie, who heard her from the bathroom, felt exactly the same.

'Moira?' Ellie said. 'Sorry, is there any chance you could maybe let me have a word with Izzy?'

She felt bad asking Moira to leave, but Moira smiled and said, 'I'll get some coffee.'

'Thanks. Come back soon, won't you?'

'Of course.' Moira picked up her bag and left the room.

Ellie went and stood beside the window and looked out. 'The sky over London always looks dirty. When you're young and in love with the place, it looks lived in. As you get older it just looks grimy.'

'Well, we don't come into town much these days, do we?' said Izzy. They fell into silence for a while, staring at the Post Office Tower simply because that was the way the window faced.

'Are you going to be able to do this, Izzy?'

'Yes!' said Izzy, too quickly again.

'I know you have always had ... never really liked Gabriel.'

'That's nonsense.'

'Oh, don't lie!' Ellie said. Which rather punctured the dreamy unthinking exchange that had preceded it.

'Ellie!'

'Just tell the truth. Let's get this out in the open. I am depending on you here and I need to know what is going to happen. I am only going to get one shot at this.'

'Unfortunate choice of words ... .'

'Izzy!'

'Oh don't start, Ellie, I've just had this with Moira. Christ, she thought I fancied him.'

'Did you?'

'No! What is it with women today? The slightest bit of friction between a woman and her best friend's bloke, and everyone thinks it's a sex thing. I blame Meg Ryan.'

'So what is it?'

'I don't know.'

'Izzy.'

'Well I think, and I know this sounds weird and you are not really going to like it, but I think when push comes to shove, I just don't like him very much. I mean didn't like him. I like him now.'

'What, now he's in a coma?'

'No. Now I see how good he is for you.'

'Oh don't, Izzy! You know damn well he hasn't actually been all that good for me lately.'

'No, but you love him.'

'Get to the point.'

'I think what people see, or have seen, is this good-looking, easygoing, quite funny, very loving bloke, but what I have seen is this slightly arrogant, sarcastic, grumpy, opinionated, over-dressed, flippant, not-actually-as-good-looking-as-he-thinks sort of bloke. And just because you love him doesn't mean I don't see what I see.'

'He is sarcastic and grumpy,' said Ellie.

'Yeah. I know.'

'But I do love him, and I know he's changed, it's just—inside he hasn't changed, inside he's the same. He's just a bit lost.'

'That is what love does, Ellie, and I understand that. Hell, I'm not so stupid as to think everyone else sees in Sam what I see. I know the fertility stuff has been hard, and getting older is hard, but well ... the whole "he's a bit lost" stuff, you know what I think of that, sweetie. You know what you think of that when someone we know says, "He's a bit lost" about someone they've just shagged. We think "inadequate tosser."'

'So that is what you think Gabe is, inadequate?' Ellie glanced over at Gabriel's unmoving body. She saw pale listless flesh and closed her eyes to let her Gabe in. The one that could move and talk. The one that made her laugh. The one who made her feel at home in herself when he kissed her.

'It's not what I think he is, it's how in the past he has made me feel about him.'

'Oh Izzy, you sound like a bloody therapist. Actually you sound like a revisionist. You're telling me why he is so dislikeable now, but you were mean about him from the start.'

Izzy sighed. What is it with people that they want you to like everyone they ever introduce you to? Why is it so hard to just accept that just because he likes you, and I like you, doesn't mean we are going to like each other? And what's the big deal?

If he wasn't in a coma who would have said anything? And she found herself feeling—and this almost embarrassed her—angry with Gabriel for being comatose. Bastard, she thought.

'Look, you asked me what I thought, and I'm telling you: it doesn't matter. I don't feel that stuff now; all I see is you and what you need. Honestly.'

Izzy put her arms around Ellie who sat quietly for a moment before saying, 'No.'

'What?'

'No, I don't want this, I don't want you doing this, I don't want you to touch him if you feel like that, and I'm glad you told me, Izzy, but I don't want you to do this. It's not fair, and it's no way to conceive a child.'

'Well, I agree with that.'

'Change of plan, change of plan, change of plan,' Ellie mantra'd, trying not to breathe too fast.

'Thank goodness for that, what is it?'

'I don't know yet, but it will involve your little sister.'

'Oh she'll love that.'

'No, no she won't, but she won't hate it either, and that will bring better vibes to the whole thing.'

'Vibes? What vibes? We are talking about wanking a man in a coma.'

'No, we are talking about making a baby, Izzy, you're the only one talking about the wanking—everyone else has got past that.'

'Well, everyone else doesn't actually have to do it, do they?'

'And now neither do you.'

'Fine,' said Izzy. Realising she sounded selfish and irritated, she quickly added, 'If that is what you want Ellie. You know I'll do whatever I can, or whatever you want, to help.'

Ellie just nodded. She wanted to say, 'I don't need your help' or 'No you won't' or just 'Fuck off,' but she didn't. In part because she was scared to be angry, in part because she was so confused and tired and artificially swollen that she couldn't be sure if

161

she was as right as she felt. But mostly she didn't because she felt lonely enough as it was, and if you had friends that you sometimes felt you tolerated or disliked or even hated, you had them for times like this. Just in case.

27

Christopher had found that over the years, the more information about the world he had, the less relevant the information became to what he understood. Over the course of time his view of humanity had decanted into three simple beliefs: Life isn't fair. Helping people when possible is better then not helping people. And, everyone needs a little kindness sometimes.

Sometimes when he was sitting in a group feeling a little out of time, he reminded himself of his small but perfectly formed truths, just to make sure that he could still see the wood for the trees, so to speak.

Christopher maintained that he existed to do good, but he did not do this unreflectively. He wondered about the things he had done as a guardian and he wondered what it was that made them an insufficient expression of God's will now. What was it about sitting in this room that was better than watching from the shoulders of martyrs and heroes as they went about their business? What was it that made this progress?

Did it feel as though he was doing good now, in this group? Did it bugger. He was listening. He found himself sitting there silently imploring them to tell all, waiting for them to psychically disrobe and dance about a bit, and he kept telling himself not to think, but he did think. He watched what they were doing, and he saw what they had done, and he wondered again, 'Am I doing good?' Because if an angel isn't, who is?

Kevin was talking about killing people. He wanted to rewrite his life, Christopher thought, and so he should. Therapy is probably a great opportunity to do that—how often does someone get the chance to describe themselves, their feelings, and their motives to a captive audience? What is that if not a chance to turn yourself into a hero in your story, rather than a villain, or worse, an extra in everybody else's?

'I was always a fatalist,' said Kevin. 'The people I was killing were going to die anyway. I was just part of nature's plan.'

Clemitius liked Kevin. He liked the fact that he was trying to 'do' therapy. Of course, even Clemitius knew that Kevin was working his arse off because, having killed so many people and discovered a God, he knew—no matter how modern the experiment—that hell was beckoning. But Clemitius was not convinced that Kevin was good at this process, or even interesting. Clemitius was drawn to Gabriel. Not because he saw a soul to save, but because he saw resistance to break.

Gabriel looked at Kevin as if he were speaking another language. He had learned to bite his lip, but he wriggled slightly in his chair. He looked and listened, and while Clemitius thought the currency of the group was the shared thoughts they brought, Gabriel would have told him he was wrong. He knew the currency of the group was despair.

Julie sometimes looked at Christopher. At first she would just glance at him, and if Christopher caught her eye, she looked away. Today she was holding his gaze, just for a few moments. She said, 'I don't know if it fits in or not, but I want to say something about a man I know ... or knew.'

She was looking at Christopher. This time he turned away. He had a sense that Julie had expectations of him that made him feel uncomfortable. So Julie looked at Clemitius instead. 'It's hard to get a grip on the last few days,' she said. 'It's not that I'm not trying; it's just that I feel disconnected. I want to make an effort but ...'

'But?' said Gabriel gently.

Julie smiled, knowingly and warmly. As if she were keeping part of what she knew away from everyone else—not in a teasing way, but as an act of kindness. Julie believed that sharing pain was an act of aggression. Not that she would ever say such a thing. 'It feels a bit like a dream.'

'You might be thinking of dissociation,' said Clemitius.

'Maybe it would be easier to get into this therapy business if we could see the people we left behind or something,' said Julie.

'I agree,' Gabriel followed quickly. 'I feel it would be easier to engage with this process if I could just see what it is I don't have anymore ...'

Christopher said nothing for a moment. Julie was looking at him again. She knew that he was kind, but she didn't know if he was brave. Christopher didn't even know that himself. Until now. He spoke. 'We have a viewing room; I believe I may have mentioned it before, over dinner, and I have a sense that some of you at least would benefit from using it.'

He didn't look at Clemitius, but as he spoke he felt a slight exhilaration run through him. He shuffled slightly in his seat. 'I think that you are working hard, but that there is something missing.' He looked at Julie; she was staring at him. The look on her face made him feel something about himself. Pleased? Happy? He didn't immediately know why. 'I may be wrong, but I wonder if seeing the space left behind might ... '

'You're not wrong,' said Gabriel.

'You're far from wrong,' said Julie, standing up.

'Er, where are you going?' said Clemitius, with genuine shock.

'There is no time like the present, is there? After all, you want us to move on, don't you?' said Julie. 'Well, your clearly very thoughtful colleague here is giving us a chance to do just that.'

'You're very lucky to work alongside a man, er ... angel like him,' said Gabriel. 'I'm sure he'll have you up to speed in no time.' Which was pretty much as close to a kick in the balls as you could give an angel, and Clemitius winced accordingly. Julie opened the door and Gabriel stood up to follow. Christopher looked at Clemitius, who just glared back. Christopher tried to nod reassuringly, but his head didn't move. Kevin watched, but didn't move. Neither did Yvonne, or at least not until she noticed that in the division that had taken place, she appeared to have been left sided with Kevin and Clemitius. She stood up. 'I think I'll just … '. And she followed Gabriel out of the room. Christopher stood at the door, waiting for Clemitius to speak. Christopher wanted to say something, something conciliatory, something that would at least acknowledge what Clemitius must be feeling, but he couldn't find the words. Then he felt a hand on his arm. He turned to the door. It was Julie. She was smiling, more open this time, more joyful. 'Come on.'

And so he did.

28

Michael had gone for coffee; he had been at the hospital for five hours today— not as long as yesterday or the day before. He had a vague sense that he was supposed to be writing something pointless for a glossy magazine. Something about how your favourite album is your favourite album because it reminds you of whoever you were sleeping with when you bought it. Rubbish of course, but an excuse to write about pop music for blokes and talk about sex at the same time. Not that it was getting written today.

Lynne was sitting with Julie. She had cropped hair and a large crucifix round her neck, which she would clasp every now and then while whispering some prayers under her breath. On a couple of occasions when Michael had left the room, he had returned to find her praying beside Julie. Both times he had stood silently at the door until she had either finished or become aware of him. They never spoke of God. They didn't actually speak very much at all.

Lynne had decided to like Michael from the beginning, or at least treat him as a fellow carer, whereas she had treated James like a blushing virus. She and Michael had slipped into an assumed shared mission to ensure that for the time being, at least, Julie would not be left on her own for too long, certainly not during the day or evening. Michael considered it polite not to leave as soon as Lynne arrived, as that would make the vigil seem too premeditated; anyway he didn't really want to go. He found leaving the hardest part of the day.

He felt there were things he needed to say to Julie. Important things. Unfortunately he hadn't realised that before, and now she was in no position to hear them. So he stayed nearby, because that seemed like the next best thing. Anyway he never left the hospital straight away. He found that when he left the hospital, a small cloud of self-loathing seemed to be waiting for him in the car park. He began to see his life—because he had enough task-free time to look at it perhaps—in a way that made him dislike himself. He thought of the women he had known, and when he did, he thought of the unhappiness he might have caused them. He thought of the sex he had had and how mediocre or plain messy it often was. In short, and he wasn't sure how this was happening, he found himself easier to tolerate near the comatose Julie, which was a strange reliance to cultivate but it felt a bit like, well … love.

And so he left the hospital slowly, staging his exit, looking at the silly shops at the front entrance. He had taken to stopping in the coffee area on the ground floor for a cappuccino and a shortbread biscuit, both bought from machines. The coffee area was little more than a swelling in the hallway with a handful of chairs and an assortment of vending machines. The highlight was a snack machine that spun round depending on what code you punched in, offering a selection of Kit Kats, bananas, muesli bars—no doubt as part of the government's healthy eating campaign—and some jelly beans.

It was coming up to 8:30 in the evening. He was sitting staring at his drink, trying to guess why they called it cappuccino when it was clearly very hot water with bubble bath on top, and remembering the coffee shop in Norwich where he wished he still was, caught in time with Julie. He knew he needed to muster up the energy to go back to his flat in Islington, to eat, to wash, to rest, to be able to come back tomorrow.

He looked up from his bubbly hot water to see a young woman at the coffee machine. She looked as though she had dressed in the dark, or as if a fruit stall had melted over her: banana yellow tights, a red skirt, some kind of orange paisley top. She was muttering to the machine whilst repeatedly hitting the coin return button. Finally, with neither crap drink nor money appearing, she took a step back, put her hands on her hips, and said, 'I'm not the sort of person who gets angry with machines that don't work. You are an inanimate object.' And then kicked it really hard.

'If it's any consolation, the drinks are foul,' said Michael.

'That's easy for you to say, you've got one,' said Moira. 'Have you got twenty pence?'

Michael stuck his hand in his pocket and pulled out two 20p's. 'Here you go.'

'I'll have to owe it you,' she said, walking over, taking the money and putting it along with other assorted change into the machine that she had just kicked. This time a cup of hot chocolate poured forth. 'You see? And they say violence never works.'

Moira took her drink and sat down at the only other table available. She cupped the hot chocolate in both hands and took a sip.

'Bloody hell, it's like hot sugar.'

'Told you,' smiled Michael. 'Can't be worse than this.'

'You'd think they'd have a proper café or something,' said Moira.

'Yeah,' Michael paused. He wasn't really in the mood for conversation, but then he wasn't really in the mood for going home. 'So, you visiting someone?' he asked, and smiled as he realised it was perhaps the most inane thing he'd said. Ever.

'No, I'm here for the hot chocolate.' Moira smiled.

It occurred to Michael that he didn't know the etiquette for polite conversation between hospital visitors. What can you say? 'Hope whatever brings you here isn't too serious?' Maybe a friend having a baby? Or a minor operation that has been a great success and life is going to be wonderful now? And what do you say about yourself? 'My friend is in a coma; have a nice evening.' So he muttered, 'I'm sorry, what a stupid thing to say, I'm just putting off going home.'

'Why?' said Moira.

'Because my friend is ... very ill ... and I don't like leaving her.'

'I'm sorry.' Moira paused. 'What ward? Sorry, another stupid question?'

'Cecil ward. ITU.'

'That's a coincidence, me too: well not me, obviously, but my friend. Who is also very ill.'

They sat in silence for a while, Moira trying to sip quietly, Michael trying to find the energy to stand up and leave.

'My name is Michael,' he said.

'I'm Moira, pleased to meet you .... Well, you know what I mean.'

'Yeah, I know what you mean.' Michael smiled a sad smile, and they drank their drinks in silence and in time with each other. When he had finished, he got up and nodded, and he left. So he could come back first thing tomorrow.

Moira didn't watch as he left, but quietly finished her hot chocolate, looked at her watch and decided it was time to go back upstairs.

29

Christopher, Gabriel, Julie, and Yvonne walked down the corridor much more quickly than they had walked to the therapy room. Right at the end, beside the exit from which they had left to watch Estelle the angel being banished, was a small black door.

Christopher unlocked it and ushered them in. Inside was a small cinema, with two rows of eight seats forming a semicircle around a large screen. The screen was dark; the only light in the room came from a glowing orange light that sat in the middle of the low ceiling like a broken egg. Christopher had surprised himself and was only now beginning to think about what he had done. For a co-therapist to leave a group halfway through, taking half of that group with him, was right up there with telling Jesus to stop being so pious. He felt sure there would be sanctions. But he decided not to think about that, not now.

He thought that in some ways it has already been worth it. Seeing Clemitius's face as they got up and left was priceless. The tips of his ears had turned purple. Christopher imagined him saying to Kevin, 'Well Kevin, how does everyone leaving us ... leaving you, in that way, make you feel?' To which Christopher hoped Kevin had replied, 'Actually I think it was you they were leaving, Clem.'

'How does this viewing room thing work?' asked Julie.

'Well it's like a television,' Christopher answered.

'What? Loads of channels but nothing interesting to watch?' said Gabriel.

'It can feel like that sometimes certainly, but given that we are going to look at the people you love or care about, it should hold your interest a little longer then ITV3, I think. You choose what you want to look at. On a television you see what the camera shows you. Here, you are the camera. So if for example, Michael should move beyond the area you are viewing, you can, if you so choose, follow him to see what he is doing.'

'Michael?'

'I am a blabbermouth today,' said Christopher. 'Yes, Michael, he is sitting at Julie's bedside.'

'Is he really? That's so sweet,' said Julie, flushing a little.

'Who's Michael?' asked Gabriel. 'The boyfriend you were leaving?'

'No no, that's James. Michael is a friend; he used to be in a band with James.'

'So where is James?'

'No idea,' shrugged Julie.

'He's rushing about like a mad thing trying to get that group of his back together again,' said Christopher.

'How do you know?' asked Gabriel.

'Yes,' said Yvonne, who was staring at the orange light above them 'How do you know?'

'It's what I do,' murmured the angel. 'Still.'

Gabriel could contain himself no longer. The prospect of seeing Ellie, even if it was from a distance, was too much. 'Can I go first?' he said.

'Fine by me,' said Julie.

'And me,' said Yvonne. 'I must admit I feel a bit nervous.'

The viewing screen, about six feet by four, sat in the middle of the wall opposite the door. Several small leather armchairs faced the screen.

'OK, so how do we start?' asked Gabriel.

'Just look at the screen and think of Ellie,' Christopher said.

'I haven't stopped thinking of her.' As he glanced at the screen, Gabriel saw Ellie arriving at the Assisted Conception Unit. She was getting in the lift, she was wearing black leggings with a blue dress over the top and her dark hair was scraped back.

'She's pretty,' said Julie.

'She looks so tired,' said Gabriel.

'She's going through quite a bit at the moment,' Christopher offered.

'Is that the hospital you are in?' asked Julie.

'No, that's the ACU where we were going to try to have our baby ... Is this what's happening now?'

Christopher nodded. 'I think it best you just watch.'

And Gabriel did. He curled up on his seat hugging his knees and watched his wife trying to conceive his baby.

'Good morning Ellie, how are you?' Dr Samani had never greeted her personally before; in fact she had never seen him speak to anyone outside of his office before. He looked his usual confident self though, although his presence made her feel special but anxious.

'I'm OK, bit nervous, you know.'

'Of course, but don't be nervous, this is straightforward, all the scans indicate you could have as many as 12 eggs in there, and that would be a good thing, that would give you plenty of chances at your baby, no?'

'I'm not nervous about me, I'm nervous about Gabe.'

'All in hand, if you'll excuse the pun. I told you Ellie, you just concentrate on looking after yourself. You are a brave woman, a brave woman, but we need to make sure you stay healthy. Now, if you wouldn't mind just going and getting changed—your friend, she knows the timetable we are working to, no?'

'Oh yes, she knows, she should be at the hospital by now.'

'Good, good, then we will get started, eh? We do not want the premature ejaculation, eh?' And he laughed, far too much.

'Can I see me?' asked Gabriel, who looked pale and confused.

'You can if you want to, Gabriel, but if you don't mind me saying so, you might like to wait,' Christopher said.

'How ... how do I see myself?'

'You just think of yourself.'

Gabriel closed his eyes for a moment, and when he opened them he was looking at his body, lying dead still on a bed in a small room. He was wired up to two machines and had a tube down his throat. Julie put her hands over her mouth and let out a noise that sounded like an echo.

Christopher watched as Gabriel turned away. It was why the room existed, to show them what was left, and to show them that this was real. And for Gabriel it worked. Only in our dreams do we ever see ourselves from the outside, he thought, but it didn't feel like a dream. Not now. It felt as if he had stopped being himself.

They watched together as Moira came quietly into the room, closing the door behind her and looking around for any lingering healthcare professionals. There were none. She took off her jacket and gloves and rubbed her hands together. She then took a small sterile container from her bag and put it on the bed next to Gabriel.

'Who's she?' asked Julie.

'That's Moira, a friend of Ellie's, well the little sister to Ellie's best friend. Nice woman, I always got on really well with her.'

'That's good,' said Julie as they watched Moira lift the sheets off Gabriel's prostrate body and undo the buttons on his pyjama bottoms.

'Oh shit,' said Moira. 'Oh shit oh shit oh shit.'

'She doesn't like what she sees,' said Julie.

'What is going on?' said Gabriel.

'Oh shit oh shit,' continued Moira, staring at the catheter tube that ran from the end of Gabriel's penis into a rubber pouch hanging from a stand at the foot of the bed. 'Oh shit. OK, stay calm. Think.'

She gave a little tug on the catheter. Nothing happened. She pulled a little harder: nothing. She looked around for a button or something—'What am I looking for, I don't even know,' she muttered. She picked up her mobile and began to dial before looking at the monitor that Gabriel was plugged into and the sign that said 'Do not use mobile phones.' She ran outside to the coffee area and phoned Izzy. There was no answer; the machine came on.

'Izzy if you're there, pick up the bloody phone, this is important. I'm at the hospital and Gabriel's got a catheter in and I don't know how to get it out. Izzy, Izzy. Fuck, phone me.' Next she tried Izzy's mobile but that was turned off. She left a message anyway.

Ellie would be in the clinic, she couldn't call her, and she couldn't think off the top of her head of anyone else who knew about catheters. Sarah the ward sister would certainly know, but she couldn't ask her without telling her what she was here for. She needed someone near who wasn't staff and she didn't know anyone except ... .Michael.

Moira turned and rushed back to the ward. 'Please be there, please be there ...' Moira stopped as she got to the ward. Must appear calm, she thought, and walked down the main corridor straight past Gabriel's side room to the front of the ward.

'Hello Moira,' said Sarah.

'Oh hi.'

'Anything I can do for you?'

'Yes, I borrowed some money from a man. Tall, dark, unshaven?'

'Sounds like my husband.'

'No he's a visitor, a regular, said he was likely to be around for a while; I hate owing money and I wondered if you knew if he was here today.'

Sarah looked at Moira uncertainly.

'It's a thing I have about not being in debt.'

'Wait here.'

Sarah walked down the corridor and into a side room on the opposite side of the ward from Gabriel. After a few minutes she emerged with Michael walking behind her. 'Is this the man?'

'Yes thank you, hello, sorry to bother you.'

'It was only 20p.'

'What?'

'It was only 20p, the nurse said you owed me some money.'

'Yes. No. Sorry, can I have just a quick word?'

Michael looked at Moira and at Sarah.

'Look, if it's about the accident, there really isn't anything that either of you can say that will help you or your friends,' said Sarah.

'What?' said Michael.

'The accident.'

'What accident?' said Moira

'The accident that your friends were involved in?'

'Your friend was involved in Gabriel's accident?' Moira said to Michael.

'Your friend is the man Julie hit?'

'Er, you two didn't know that then?' said Sarah.

Moira's head was spinning. This was all getting too much, she didn't know what, if anything, she was supposed to feel about this news. Was she supposed to march into this mad driver's room and tell her off, was she supposed to take comfort from the fact that she was in a coma too? She had no idea. She had a vague idea that she was supposed to do something or at least feel something, but she had no clue as to what it was, and no time to work it out.

'Look I'm sorry, I don't know what to do with that information right now. I need to ask you something in private and, while I realise that sounds bizarre, it is important to me and I wonder if you would be kind enough to give me a few moments of your time, thank you.' All in one breath.

Michael shrugged. 'Shall we get some coffee?' he asked.

'No time,' said Moira. 'Office, please.'

Sarah showed them into the office and closed the door as she left. 'Don't be long please' she said, wondering fleetingly if Moira might be a little bit mad and about to ask Michael for a date. Which would be a funny story for the next staff night out.

'So what can I do for you?' Michael was wary.

'Do you know anything about catheters?'

'What?'

'Catheters.'

'Oh Christ,' said Gabriel, who was watching from behind his knees. 'He doesn't even know what they are; I've got to do something.'

'There is nothing you can do,' Christopher said. 'Except watch.'

'Watching is going to drive me mad.'

'Tell me about it,' Christopher replied.

'Its OK,' said Julie. 'It's going to be OK.'

'How is it going to be OK?'

'He's a good man,' said Julie. 'He'll help.'

They looked at the screen. Michael was looking at Moira without wondering if she was cute. And he knew it wasn't just because of the odd assortment of colours she was wearing. It was, he assumed, because he was in a serious place. Where serious things happened. Or it might have been because of Julie. He wondered, Is this what love does? Even if you love someone who is unconscious. 'No,' he said. 'I don't know anything about catheters. Why?'

'It's a long story, and if you don't know, it won't help to tell you,' sighed Moira.

'Try me,' said Michael.

'I don't have the time,' said Moira. 'It's a matter of life and death.'

'Well, you're in as good a place as any for that.'

'I can't tell the staff.'

'What do you need to know about catheters for?'

'Because I have to take one out of Gabriel without anyone knowing.'

'Oh,' said Michael. 'Who's Gabriel'?

'Look I'm sorry to waste your time; it's just I'm desperate.'

'I don't know a damn thing about catheters,' said Michael. 'But I know someone who does. So tell me what's going on.'

'Who?' said Gabriel. 'Who knows about catheters?'

'Lynne,' said Julie. 'She knows. Look, I need to see me now alright?'

'Oh come on ... Please ...'

'No really, it will help us to see what is happening, trust me.'

Gabriel put his head into his hands. Julie stared at the viewer and thought about herself. Sure enough, up she popped—or what was left of her: heavily bandaged head, very, very pale, loads more tubes coming out of her than Gabriel had, and with old friend, former nun, and soon-to-be-qualified nurse Lynne sitting beside her.

'Jesus,' said Julie.

Gabriel looked up. 'Fuck. You poor thing,' he said.

Lynne turned as Michael came back in.

'What was all that about?'

'It's a woman who's friends with the guy that Jules hit. She needs our help.'

'It's a little early to be asking for body parts, don't you think?'

'No, not that kind of help. Look I know this is going to sound odd, but she needs help taking a catheter out of him.'

'I know they're short staffed here, but ... really?'

'The staff can't know.'

Lynne looked at Michael.

'I know, this sounds ridiculous, and it's not some kind of guilt thing, it's just ... Look. Apparently the bloke that Julie hit was in the middle of some IVF thing, his wife or girlfriend has carried on with the treatment, but the staff here won't or can't help her.'

'Well they are pretty busy saving lives,' said Lynne.

'Apparently she needs his sperm today.'

'You've come to the wrong woman, Michael. I don't do sperm.' Lynne furrowed her brow as she spoke and the lines stretched right up to where her hair would be if she had chosen to keep any.

'Moira—that's the woman I just spoke to—is here to get the sperm, but he has a catheter in and she can't get it out, I mean if she just pulls it may cause some damage.'

'Too bloody right it will. Why won't the staff help?'

'I don't know, something to do with informed consent, but Moira says he signed up for the treatment. They don't have the time to go to court to argue, his wife has taken all the drugs. Look, all she is asking is that you remove the catheter and leave her to do the rest.'

'Who's going to put the bloody thing back in again?'

'I don't know, I don't think she's thought that far ahead.'

'What if I get caught?'

'I'll keep watch.'

'Why do you care?'

Michael shrugged. 'Because it feels like a good thing to do and it would be nice to do a good thing here, while we wait ...' He looked embarrassed and Lynne stared at him.

'Christ,' she said finally. 'Julie was with the wrong bloke.'

'Amen to that,' said Julie.

'I like him,' said Gabriel, removing his knees from his chest and sitting forward for the first time since he had come into the room.

'Right,' said Lynne. 'How are we going to do this? I can't just march into this man's room.'

'Go and get some coffee,' said Michael. 'I told Moira to wait by the coffee machine, that one of us would be along soon.'

'She's all right as well,' said Gabriel.

'Used to be a nun, you know,' said Julie, looking at Christopher.

They watched as Lynne strode down to the coffee machine, raising her eyebrows at the girl wearing all the colours. Moira, on the other hand, greeted the lesbian with the giant cross round her neck like a long-lost sister.

'I'll only need a minute to get into the room and take the catheter out,' said Lynne. 'But surely you're going to need a bit longer to do what you need to do. How can you be sure nobody will come in?'

'I'll just have to take my chances,' said Moira.

'You must have liked him,' said Lynne.

'They are my friends,' said Moira softly.

The two women walked back to the ward, pausing at the doors to the corridor leading to Gabriel's room. When it was clear that there was nobody around, Moira walked quickly to his room. Inside there were two nurses preparing to give Gabriel a bed bath.

'Don't do that,' she shouted, a little too loudly.

'We have to, it's our job,' said the staff nurse, who was clearly the senior of the two. She was blonde and young and hardly turned round as she spoke.

'I know, but his wife will be along later.'

'Well I'm sure she will appreciate it if he was clean and shaven.'

'No, she likes to do it herself.'

'Well, when will she be here?'

'Later.'

'But the ward round starts in an hour.' Still the nurse didn't look at Moira.

'She'll be here before then,' lied Moira. 'Come on, it's all she has left.'

'Sorry, we need to do it now.'

'No,' said Sarah, the ward sister, from behind Moira. 'It can wait.'

Moira watched as the nurses left the room and turned the corner at the end of the corridor.

Sarah stayed until they were out of sight. 'Moira.'

'Yes?'

'I need to know just one thing and if you lie to me I will make your every waking breath a hideous nightmare.'

'Yes?' Moira stopped breathing, She felt her stomach tighten, which was perhaps just as well because without that sensation she may have forgotten she had a body, she had become so focused on Sarah.

'Is it at all possible that anyone can be harmed by what you are trying to do on my ward?'

'No. I swear. On my life, I swear.'

'Did you come here to help Ellie?'

'Yes. Look please ...'

'With the IVF?'

Moira just stared at her. Sarah held her gaze until Moira, open-mouthed and with her heart—that had returned to her with some drums and a spade—trying to tunnel out of her chest, nodded.

'OK. You'd better get on with it then.' And with that Sarah turned and marched back to the nurses' station. A moment later Lynne crept into the room.

'I wouldn't be surprised if Sarah knows something,' said Lynne.

Moira just nodded and pointed at Gabriel's crotch.

'It's in there,' she said.

'Really?' said Lynne. 'And I thought I was going to have to frisk him.'

She pulled up the covers, fiddled about with something, pulled and said: 'You see, when it goes into the bladder, you inflate a small balloon to stop it from coming out again. To take it out you deflate it. Mind you, putting it in is much harder than taking it out—took me ages to learn how to do it. There. Done. Over to you.'

'Thank you,' said Moira. 'Really, thank you.'

'Hey, it's OK. Look, you'd better get a move on. Let us know how you get on ... you know what I mean.'

Lynne poked her head round the door, looked back one more time, and whispered 'All clear.' Then she went back to her own bedside vigil.

Moira looked at Gabriel, his sallow features set like chalk on a cliff. 'Sorry mate,' she said and pulled up the sheets, picked up his penis and started to stroke it. All the viewing room could see was Moira's arm moving up and down under the sheet. Slowly at first and then faster.

'Oh my,' said Gabriel.

'Brave girl,' said Julie.

'Can you feel anything?'

'No I can't,' said Gabriel. 'Should I be able to?'

'I don't know what you should be able to feel,' Christopher said honestly. 'I mean, as you are not technically dead, there is a theoretical connection between the you that is here and the you that is there, but it would be misleading to suggest it is a meaningful link. I personally prefer to think of you as a shadow of the Gabriel on the bed. Do you know what I mean?'

'Not remotely,' said Gabriel, 'and frankly I don't think I want to … I … Christ, I think I'm coming …'

'Can you feel that?' asked Julie with interest.

'No, but I can see …'

Moira had taken an automatic step backward and was leaning toward Gabriel's penis the way you lean toward an untrustworthy garden tap. One hand continued to rub, the other carefully held the end of the sterilised container round the tip, shaking his cock into the bottle, putting the top on, and slipping the bottle into the pocket of her coat. She put her coat on and headed for the door, then stopped, turned back to Gabriel, and went over to kiss him on the forehead. 'You don't have to call, just get better,' she whispered and headed off.

'I want to see Michael, just for a moment,' said Julie.

'Go ahead,' said Gabriel. 'I need a cigarette.'

Back in Julie's room, Lynne and Michael were sitting quietly next to Julie's still body. Lynne was smiling.

'What?' said Michael

'You're funny.'

'Why?'

'Well, leaving aside the fact you persuaded me to risk my future career by helping a desperate stranger to take sperm from a bloke in a coma ...'

'How come that risks your career?'

'To nurse, I have to be on a register you know, have to be seen to be fit to serve the public and all that. I reckon the powers that be, while not having a precedent for what I just did, might not take too kindly to my aiding and abetting the phantom wanker.'

'I'm sorry, I didn't realise—I would have taken the blame of course.'

'Oh very gallant,' laughed Lynne.

Michael smiled, maybe for the first time in days. 'Well, Julie would have helped, wouldn't she?'

Lynne liked the fact that Michael thought that about Julie, but she liked even more the fact that he was asking her for confirmation. There are few comforts to anyone sitting at the side of a friend in a coma, but recognition of their right to be there is one of them. 'Yeah,' said Lynne. 'She would have.'

Meanwhile, Moira had rushed downstairs and out of the building, across the busy car park in front to the main road, where a figure on a blue Vespa scooter sat revving the small engine. As Moira approached, Knight Rider lifted its dark visor, revealing the face of a middle-aged woman set in grim determination. 'Moira?' she barked.

'Mrs Schmelling?'

'Who the fuck is Mrs Schmelling?' asked Gabriel.

'Can't be sure,' Christopher said, 'but I believe she works on the reception desk at the ACU.'

'That little lady who booked our appointments and gave us forms to fill in?'

'Apparently.'

'She rides a Vespa?'

'Apparently. Maybe Dr Samani arranged this.'

'Well, God bless Dr Samani.'

'I'll have a word, although after this I may not have much influence in that department,' said Christopher.

Mrs Schmelling unzipped the breast pocket of her leather jacket. 'Have you got it?'

'Right here,' said Moira, handing over the bottle.

'Well done,' said Mrs Schmelling. 'Must dash.'

'Right. Good luck,' said Moira, and she watched as Mrs Schmelling raced off, threading through the London traffic. A medium-paced scooter would be at the ACU in about seven minutes.

Moira sat down on the kerb, closed her eyes for a moment, and breathed out for what felt like the first time in about three-quarters of an hour. Her relief was such that she didn't notice her sister as Izzy stepped from Sam's car and headed into the hospital. Izzy, determined, purposeful Izzy, didn't notice Moira either.

30

If Wood Green were a food, it would be celery: inessential and tasteless. James took comfort from this fact as he drove toward Matthew's house. He may be rich, he thought, but what is the point of money if you don't know how to spend it?

However, Matthew and Alice lived near Wood Green in the way that the Queen lives near Penge. Rather, they lived in more of what you'd call Muswell Hill, on what was clearly one of the more exclusive roads. As James drove slowly down the wide, clean street he may have passed Kate Winslet pruning an already perfectly sculpted hedge. Landscaped front gardens, expensive cars, and no discernible traffic. Even the birds sang quietly. But perhaps it wasn't quite what he would want if he won the lottery, James thought: he would want a small castle with battlements and moat. Still, this was nice—rubbish if you are ever under attack by an army of bowmen, but nice nonetheless.

He rang the doorbell of the three-storey, red-bricked detached house. It sounded old fashioned and authentic. James half expected a butler to answer.

'James! James Buchan, good lord, what are you doing round here?' Matthew was wearing a hooped and ironed rugby shirt in black and white, and sand-coloured baggy cords. Even at the height of Dog in a Tuba's—whisper the word for fear of people laughing—fame, Matthew tended toward knitwear and a building society savings account. He was, in James's estimation, always a secondary school teacher waiting to happen. He was also pretty easygoing, so James was rather hoping for some enthusiasm about the reunion. As for Alice, it wasn't that he hadn't considered her, it was just that he couldn't really imagine her saying much. Probably because the last time he remembered seeing her she had either her mouth or her nose full.

'Wanted to see what a win on the lottery buys these days.'

'Oh, you heard about that? Bit embarrassing really. But everything happens for a purpose, eh? How are you James? It's been a very long time.'

'It has, Matt. I'm all right, mate.' The same self-conscious silence that swept in on the phone arrived quicker then either had anticipated. They stood momentarily embarrassed, quiet with each other, the way only men can be.

'So Matt, gonna invite me in or should I go round to the tradesmen's entrance?'

'Oh, sorry James, of course, come in come in.' Which bought a few more seconds and hopefully, assuming the house had wallpaper and rooms inside, would create a whole new gamut of conversational opportunity before Dog in a Tuba had to come up.

Matthew, like most people last seen in the 1980s, had swollen. In fact he was almost portly. He had held on to his healthy, thick reddish-brown hair but, seemingly because of some hair-retention pact with the devil, kept it in a style that made him look as though he had half a fox stapled to his head. He also wore a pair of John Lennon glasses.

If the house had looked big from the outside, it was palatial inside. A large oak staircase, up which you could drive a tank, failed to dominate the marble floored hallway. High ceilings gave the impression of being in a tent, or small church, and whichever way you looked there lay the promise of expensive furniture or perhaps some fields. James could see into what he would have considered a living room, if it weren't so bloody big; straight in front of him, albeit some way away, lay a half-open door into the kitchen. Before the kitchen there were three other doors off the hallway, probably a drawing room or a library or the indoor pool, he thought sulkily. He fixed his gaze on the kitchen: he could see movement and hear voices and he could smell food.

'Darling, guess who's come for dinner?' shouted Matthew, adding quietly, 'You will stay for dinner, won't you?'

'Well if it's no trouble, Matt, that would be nice, I've been living on hospital food for a while.'

'Oh dear, not been well?'

'No no, a friend had a nasty accident—I've been keeping vigil, so to speak.'

'I'm sorry to hear that, really sorry. Come in, come in, let's have a drink eh?'

James followed Matthew toward the kitchen; on the way he noticed that Matthew's cords had turn-ups. He was unlikely to notice anything else about Matthew because, as he entered the kitchen, Alice turned to see who Matthew was bringing into her home.

Alice, it occurred to James, had grown into just about the most beautiful woman he had ever seen in his life. The Alice he remembered had sniffed a lot, had blonde straggly hair attached to a blotchy teenage face, with a little too much fat round the cheeks, although she had always had a nice arse and good tits, small and perfectly formed. She may have been tall, but appeared gangly; she may have been pretty, but appeared stoned. She tended to wear ... jeans? He couldn't remember what she wore, he only noticed her when she was naked or on the way to being naked.

Now she looked as though modelling was an option, but one she considered beneath her. It was her skin he noticed first, it made everyone else look as though they were made out of cow. She looked soft, a bit Swedish, which was daft given she came from Cromer: her hair was golden, her eyes—which he hadn't ever looked at before—were green and shining. She looked like a goddess and he wanted to marry her.

'Red or white, James?' asked Matthew.

I'll have whatever she's been drinking, thought James, and said, 'Alice?'

'James Buchan?'

And, just for a moment, James thought she was going to throw her arms around him, like the long-lost love of her life he quite fancied being. Instead she said, 'My, you've aged. What have you been doing with yourself?'

'I've got older,' he stammered. 'It's what happens. You look great, really good. How have you been?'

'I'm well.' She looked him up and down, showed not the remotest sign of feeling, and turned to a small, shiny man sitting at the kitchen table.

'This is Adam Aldanack, our pastor. Adam, this is James Buchan, an old friend of Matthew's. You may have heard of Adam; if you haven't, there is every chance you will soon. He is a spiritual leader, a great man, and, we are pleased to say, our personal friend.' Said with the rolling, soulless perfection of a chat show host.

James turned to face the thin man in a grey-flecked jacket and black polo neck jumper. He had a hefty silver cross hanging around his neck, the sort of moustache that James hadn't seen outside of a porn film since the early 1970s, and thick, swept-back, dyed black hair. Adam beamed enthusiastically; he must have been around fifty. James thought that he had the look of a man who had wanted to be one of the 'Persuaders' but had settled for religion instead. He stood up and offered James his hand.

'Hello James,' he said with the over-rehearsed warmth one might expect from someone about to sell you their god.

'Hello,' said James. 'Is that an American accent?'

'Well I was born here, but spent most of my life in the States, so something of an Anglo-American I guess. But it's all just one big garden as far as I'm concerned.'

'Red or white, James?' asked Matthew again. 'James has been spending a lot of time in hospital lately, he was telling me; a friend of his is unwell, isn't that right, James?'

'Well yes, car accident, pretty bad I'm afraid. This is the first time I've been away from there in days. I thought I needed to get away, the doctors said they'd call if there was any change, but you don't like to leave just in case, you know.' Everyone looked at James and he sighed. At that moment he actually believed what he was saying himself, so he assumed everyone else was bound to.

Matthew handed James a glass of red. 'I decided for you,' he said. 'So what brings you here?'

'Well, nothing in particular,' he lied. 'I was talking to Michael, he's down with me, and he said you lived out here so I just thought I'd pop over.'

'So you don't want money then,' said Alice, smiling thinly.

James reddened.

'Alice, please,' mocked Matthew.

'That, darlin', is a little uncharitable,' said Adam.

'You're right, I'm sorry James, it was a bad joke, and you know what they can be like.' Alice stared hard at James for a moment, before adding, 'I really do apologise. But I'm sure this visit is not purely social. By the way, are you vegetarian?'

'Good God, no.'

'We are.' She turned back to a large pot and started stirring, seemingly uninterested in what was happening behind her. James sat down at the large oak table and tried not to stare at her arse.

'So, James, what have you been up to? How's Michael? I saw him on the late show a few weeks ago; hasn't he done well? I meant to give him a call to say well done,' said Matthew.

'He's fine, still writing for that magazine,' guessed James. 'What about you—teaching, I hear?'

'No, no not any more; I was, but when we won the lottery I moved on.'

'Well, who wants to work, eh?'

'Oh I don't mind working, it's just I found something else to work on.'

'What's that? Not music is it?'

'No no no, although I dabble for fun, have a studio downstairs and mess around ... but no, I work for Adam's church.'

'Oh, how nice,' said James. 'I'm a Buddhist myself.'

'Really?' said Adam earnestly. 'What does that mean for you? I mean which God do you talk to?'

'Er, the Buddhist one?' offered James, relieved when Matthew and Adam laughed. 'So are you a minister?'

'Yes sir I am, the first minister of the Church of Three.'

'Pardon me?'

'First minister of the Church of Three.'

'I don't think I know that one.'

'Well I expect you know it in your heart, you just haven't met it yet,' said the odd American. As he spoke he looked above James's eyes, staring at the centre of his forehead, and he managed to smile, really smile with all of his teeth between each sentence.

'And what do you do to help there, Matt?'

'Whatever I can,' said Matt.

'So how do you know each other?' Adam asked.

'Went to school together,' said Matthew.

'And we were in a band together, I'm sure Matt's told you: Dog in a Tuba?'

'Oh yes, Matthew has told me, his rock-and-roll phase—damn fine, I love to rock myself.' Adam drummed something out of time on the table and grinned

Really, thought James, Pat Boone or Cliff bloody Richard. 'Well funnily enough,' he said, 'that's one of the reasons that brought me here, I've been wondering about getting the band back together ... you know ... unfinished business.'

Without turning round Alice started laughing; she was annoying, James decided. Beautiful, eminently fuckable, but bloody annoying.

'I thought so.'

'I thought you thought I was here for money,' said James, trying to smile.

'Same thing,' she said reaching for her glass and holding it out to Matthew, without looking at him.

'Why on earth would you want to get the band together again?' asked Matthew, taking Alice's glass and filling it for her.

'Well I thought it would be fun, you know—see how we'd all grown up.'

'Or not,' offered Alice.

James looked away. He knew she was being hostile, but he couldn't quite decide if it was a hostility born of sexual tension, or outright contempt. Given the look on her face, the presence of her husband in the room, and the way he treated her when she was young and vulnerable, the odds favoured contempt, but you never know, right?

'But we're all in our forties. Who needs the hassle?' said Matthew, who was at least smiling.

'What hassle? Gary Guitar's up for it ...'

'I find that hard to believe,' snorted Alice.

'No, I've spoken to him. And Bernie ...'

'And Michael?'

'I haven't mentioned it to him yet ... not really.'

'I would have thought he'd have been the first you spoke to,' said Alice.

'Well my friend, the one in hospital, is a friend of his too, it didn't seem right just yet.' As James spoke, it dawned on him that he had, on some level, been aware of how upset Michael had been about Julie. This sudden realisation may have given the other people in the room the impression that James was sad.

Adam broke the silence. 'I think it's an interesting idea Jim— can I call you Jim? Yes sir. Imagine Matt, playing to a crowd again, quite a rush I'd imagine.' Alice and Matt looked at each other and then looked at the minister. It became clear to James that while what he saw when he looked at Adam Aldanack was a refugee from a 1970's detective show, they saw a man to be listened to, respected, and trusted.

'Hey, how about playing for the church?' said Adam loudly, jumping from his chair. 'A fund raiser, or congregation gatherer.'

Neither Alice nor Matt spoke.

'Well, a couple of warm-up gigs might be good,' said James enthusiastically, 'before we went on the road with ... you know, some of our peers. What kind of church is it?'

'The Church of Three? It's the church of the future son, the church of the future.' Adam Aldanack glanced upward as he spoke, as if communing with at least one of his gods, and then he closed his eyes and nodded slowly to himself. In thanks, for being the one chosen to spread the word and from being transformed from the man who once sold vacuum cleaners for his brother-in-law in Arizona to the man who turned god into a committee.

James stayed for dinner. He listened to Matt tell him about winning the lottery. 'We didn't even check the numbers, it wasn't until the Sunday when we got back from church that I happened to flick on to teletext and ... wow ...'

Matthew was perhaps one of the only people left on the planet who could say 'wow' and get away with it. What the hell Alice was doing with him was beyond James. She sniped through dinner, asking awkward questions about how James earned a living, and when he told her, she asked about the names of the bands he had produced. When he said that she wouldn't have heard of any of them, she pointed out that she was younger than him and was therefore far more likely to be aware of emerging talent.

'I never said they were talented,' said James, 'And I never said any of them got out of Norfolk.'

Adam acted like he lived there. He watched James as he ate, which would have been annoying if James hadn't been so hungry. James knew he was going to get a religious lecture at some point and he didn't even care, so long as he could eat at the same time, but when it came it is fair to say it surprised him. It surprised him so much that it made him eat more slowly.

The minister started by asking questions. Like, 'Why are you a Buddhist?' Fortunately he seemed prepared to answer them himself as James chewed. 'Because you're looking for something.' And then he whispered: 'And you, like so many others, are looking in the wrong place for the right thing, but doing it for good, good reasons.'

Adam was pretty convinced that the one true God was actually a triumvirate. Less Cliff Richard and more the Bee Gees. The holy trinity was the biggest clue to this long-hidden truth he claimed, but most importantly, according to Adam, modern life demanded three gods. They may have only needed the one god 2,000 years ago, back when things were simple, people travelled by camel, and entertainment was the occasional stoning and the odd miracle. Life was more complicated now; there were so many distractions, so many things to think about, so many things to worship. In the same way that modern shaving required two blades, it also needed the attention of three gods, to ensure we remain balanced.

How can the one true God suddenly have become three? Evolution. We have evolved, said Mr Aldanack, grown taller, stronger, more sophisticated. Are we so vain as to imagine that God doesn't evolve, too?

But credit where it's due, Adam talked and poured wine at the same time, and the more James listened, the more Adam appeared to assume he was interested. In fact, by the time James was tucking into homemade apple and blueberry pie with ice cream, it was almost as if Adam were trying to persuade James to play a benefit for the church.

'But I don't quite understand,' said James. 'It doesn't sound like your church needs the money.'

'Quite,' said Alice. 'And it's not like Dog in a Tuba will contribute to the profile of the church in anyway. I mean they were a piddly little band.'

'It's true,' said Matthew. 'We were.'

James coughed. 'Not piddly. Unfulfilled maybe, too edgy to be mainstream popular perhaps but not piddly, Matt. Never piddly.'

'Well let's not worry about that,' said Adam. 'Let's just see what it's like to promote a gig or two in our backyard, shall we?'

Alice and Matthew shrugged.

'I, er, think we might need to rehearse first,' James said.

'Never used to bother you, James,' said Alice.

'Where?' said Matthew.

'My place,' said James without thinking. 'I've got a converted barn, it'll be good. Next weekend?'

'What about your friend in hospital?' asked Alice.

'And Michael?' said Matthew.

'It would do him good,' said James. 'Take his mind off of things. We'd be doing him a favour I think.'

Alice and Matthew were silent, but Adam, who was, as far as James could see, a godsend, clapped his hands together loudly and said, 'That's settled then. Can I come? I would love to see your farm, and see you all playing together again. We could all drive up together. Alice? Matthew? What do you say?'

'OK,' said Matthew, 'be nice to see the others, and I've got a couple of songs.'

Why is it that everyone writes bloody songs these days? thought James. 'Don't worry about that too much,' he said. Alice looked at him, and James added, 'Although it would be great to hear them.'

'Don't forget to talk to Michael,' said Alice.

And even James realised she wasn't flirting. She just hated him.

31

Izzy had her faults, goodness knows she knew she did, but they did not include letting her best friend down in her hour of need. She left Sam in the short-term car park and told him that she would be as quick as she could. Sam, being Sam, asked if she had any idea how long it would take, and Izzy had snapped, 'I think you'd be a better judge of that than me.'

She made her way nervously up to the third floor, and smiled in an over-compensating kind of way at just about everyone she passed. Get a grip, she thought. People will think you're insane.

When she got to Gabriel's ward she nodded at the only nurse visible, who was talking on the phone, and pointed to Gabriel's' room mouthing 'I'm just going to visit Gabe,' just on the off chance the nurse had imagined she was popping in to give him an unprescribed hand job. Izzy was surprised to find the room empty, with just Gabriel in it. She realised that it was not simply the first time she had been alone with him since the accident, but probably the first time for about five years. Except for that time in Stoke Newington, although they weren't actually with each other then, just in the same place as each other without Ellie or Sam.

Izzy had been out with a couple of friends, they'd been to a film and for a pizza, and now were drinking wine in a Spanish bar, laughing at each other trying to salsa. Izzy remembered it well; she was pregnant, although she didn't know it. If she had known, she wouldn't have drunk as much as she did. She did have some kind of sense of something being different, a sense she liked to think had made her feel differently and thus act differently. The more they drank, the more courage they found to dance, and the more they danced—loudly, flamboyantly, and with the kind of joy that disguises a lack of poise—the more they attracted attention.

Izzy still remembered the hand landing on the small of her back. Strong, large enough to make her feel as though her waist were tiny. At first she tensed but the drink had relaxed her and so she smiled, she let herself lean back; the owner of the hand took her hand and spun her round. She couldn't remember if he was good-looking, but she could remember that he was tall and dark and Spanish, and dancing with her. Her friends clapped and laughed, which felt like it meant it was OK, and so she danced.

And the music didn't stop, her friends had found dancing partners, and it felt ... well it felt like one of those films, where the plain girl takes centre stage and shows the world that she is beautiful and dazzling, and can dance. In truth Izzy wasn't really dancing, she was jiggling about while her partner spun her round. He moved like water, and she went where he prompted. And the thing about dancing is that physical barriers get breached: it didn't seem remotely inappropriate that sometimes his hand would hold her buttocks, or that when he pulled her toward him and held her there for a moment—in perfect time of course—she could feel his cock against her stomach. That was how they danced in Spain. She only became conscious of any kind of barrier being breached when he looked her in the eye and ran his fingers down her breast. Twice. But it was OK, she looked at her friends and they were still laughing with their partners, and she looked at the dancing man and he looked, well, he looked like he was dancing. He wasn't leering, he wasn't slobbering, and so she smiled and sweated and closed her eyes as he flung her around, drew her close and grabbed her arse quite tightly.

And when she opened her eyes she saw Gabriel. Standing at the bar smiling, drinking out of a bottle and talking to someone.

Her first thought, her very first thought, was that she hoped he was talking to a woman. He wasn't, he was talking to a fat bloke, and when Izzy caught his eye he raised his bottle and smiled even more.

What kind of smile was it? Was it a 'hello, fancy seeing you' smile? Was it hell. It was a 'what a crap dancer you are' smile, or an 'Aye aye, you've pulled' smile. She remembered trying to ignore him, she remembered thinking 'I can dance if I want,' but with his eyes in the room, she began to realise she couldn't. She tried but she felt wooden, slow; the hands that had seemed so fluid a few moments earlier suddenly felt hard and intrusive. She stopped dancing. Men like Gabriel, men who looked like he did and walked like he did and expected attention the way he did, stopped women like Izzy from dancing.

They never spoke about it. Izzy didn't know to this day if he had mentioned it to Ellie. She was going to ask her but she never did. As time went on it became too hard. That was the last time they had been in the same room as each other, without either Sam or Ellie being there. Until now.

'OK, let's get on with it, but before we do, I should tell you that this is nothing personal. I don't want to rub your willy; I don't even want to touch your willy, and I certainly don't want this to count when either one of us are totting up how many people we have had sex with.'

She pulled back the sheets and, on seeing the end of the catheter that should have been inside Gabriel, muttered, 'How the bloody hell did that get out? Christ, it's been years since I've put one of these in. Still, first things first.' And she picked up Gabriel's penis, as if it were a small fish on a hook that might not be quite dead, and started to rub.

It took longer than she expected for him to get an erection, but once he had she seemed to get into her stride. In fact it did feel very functional and impersonal, except for when she looked at his face, or found herself thinking of how annoying she had found him when they were all out together. Unfortunately, the longer she massaged his penis the more she found herself thinking of her thirtieth birthday party. How he'd got off with Ellie, and how her birthday—HER birthday, nobody else's birthday—was recalled quite simply as the evening that East London's version of George Clooney and Julia Roberts got it together. The more she thought about it, the more annoyed she got, and the harder she rubbed. She realised this, fortunately, before she drew blood, and stopped.

This is silly, I need a distraction, she thought. For no reason, no reason whatsoever, she decided that she needed to sing. So she closed her eyes to the past and the penis in front of her, started to masturbate him again while humming, for no logical reason whatsoever, 'The Long and Winding Road.' And it worked, the humming distracted her, and so she got louder. But there is only so long any adult can hum without singing and so she began to sing. Which of course is when the consultant and attendant ward round came in, just as she got to that bit that goes 'Don't leave me standing here ... '

32

The group sat in silence. Christopher had entered the room feeling anxious, but seeing Clemitius sitting there looking solemn and pompous had turned that feeling into irritation. Who wouldn't want to leave a room with him sitting in it? In fact, if he could have thought of an excuse, he would have turned around and left again, but he couldn't, so he sat down. And didn't look at Clemitius. He just joined in the silence and became more aware of the discomfort of the others.

'I'm wondering how everyone feels after yesterday's little ... event?' said Clemitius. He didn't sound like a therapist. He sounded like a disgruntled teacher whose class had not come to school. Gabriel started to speak, but Clemitius held up his hand. It was shaking. 'Let me finish, please. I don't mean how do those of you feel who have been looking at your loved ones—I think to some extent you passed on your option to comment first when you left the group. My main concern right now is for those who stayed. I'm wondering how those of us ... left behind feel.'

Nobody said anything. Gabriel sighed and looked out of the window. Julie felt embarrassed but she wasn't sure why. Yvonne meanwhile screwed up her brow, pantomiming surprise. She looked at Clemitius, who avoided her gaze, and she wondered, was this man trying to tell her off?

'I have to say, I personally feel ... well, a little angry,' Clemitius continued. 'I feel something has been breached, and I feel that there is some healing to do here today.'

'I think you have to realise,' Yvonne said calmly, slipping into the demeanour that had taken control of hundreds of meetings with thousands of men she had little respect for, 'that we have been through a lot, and different people respond to difficult things in different ways.'

'Indeed,' Clemitius said. 'Kevin, you have been through difficult things as well, but you don't leave in the middle of the group, do you?'

'I wouldn't dream of it,' responded Kevin. He sat upright in his chair as he spoke. He looked neater, more ironed than when he had arrived.

'No, well, you wouldn't,' said Yvonne. 'You have such high standards of behaviour, don't you?' But she spoke evenly, with less contempt. She looked at Gabriel and Julie. Gabriel half smiled at her and she thought about her son. She thought what it would have been like to have seen him, to see him one more time, and that that possibility was somehow being challenged now. But it wasn't just self-interest that filled her. She thought about what she had seen, its messy humanity, and of Gabriel curling in his chair. And she decided that Clemitius was wrong. About everything.

'My main concern is about boundaries,' said Clemitius. 'I am worried about how safe it feels to be here now. For a group to work, everyone in it must know the space is safe, that they will not be abandoned, that they can reveal part of themselves without having that part mistreated. What is to stop another breach? And how easy does that make it for us to share our deepest feelings? You must all be feeling many things, including, I imagine, uncertainty and anger, anger with Christopher perhaps, for initiating such a rupture in what we are trying to create.'

Nobody said anything. Gabriel sighed again. He shuffled in his seat, not with embarrassment but with irritation. He opened his mouth to say 'Look,' but before any sound came out Clemitius said, 'How about you, Kevin?'

Kevin thought for a second. 'Yes, I am angry,' he offered.

'Do you know what it is about what has happened that makes you feel angry?'

'I think it's the fact that he is always so sarcastic, do you know what I mean?' Kevin nodded at Gabriel.

'Yes yes yes,' said Clemitius, a little too enthusiastically. 'I do know.' Christopher winced slightly but stayed quiet. He wasn't thinking about what Clemitius was saying. Instead he was full of what Peter might be saying if he were here.

'Well so what? That hardly ranks alongside murder, does it? Does it?' asked Yvonne.

'I think you need to try to let go of the murder thing,' said Kevin. And Clemitius nodded sagely.

'Do you? Do you really?' Yvonne turned to Clemitius. 'For goodness's sake, you should be ashamed of yourself—a man of God? You are so lost in the trees there isn't a hope in hell of you seeing any wood, is there?' she spat. 'Do you know what I'm interested in? My son being all right, nothing else. They are the same; they care about what and who they have lost. I'm not interested in working through my difficulties. It's too bloody late for one thing.'

'Not necessarily.'

'No, it's never too late,' said Kevin.

And Gabriel looked at him with new contempt. 'Oh for Christ's sake.'

'Oh but it is, Kevin, isn't it? It's too bloody late for the people you killed!' said Yvonne.

'Unless they are all sitting in some interminable group somewhere,' chipped in Gabriel.

'No no, they are all quite dead,' said Clemitius, with surprising emphasis on the word dead.

'Well it's too late for them, isn't it, like it's too late for me,' said Yvonne. 'I'm tired of all this.'

'Well of course you are, therapy is hard work and it's not actually too late for you. Heaven awaits,' Clemitius beamed.

Kevin looked pleased with this. Yvonne looked annoyed.

'Well you see, that's just wrong,' Yvonne said.

'I beg your pardon?'

'That's wrong – that young man wanted to see his wife, he clearly loves her very much and he wanted to see her, even to try to help her, and Julie, I think she felt truly awful that he was here because of the accident and I think that seeing her friends trying to help must have helped her? Those are good feelings to have, love, guilt ...'

'Oh,' laughed Clemitius. 'Guilt is a good feeling to have, is it?'

'It did help,' said Julie. 'It helped more than this does. Seeing what we do, who we love, what space we leave behind ... of course that helps ...'

'Yes,' snapped Yvonne. 'Yes I think it is a good feeling. Maybe not always, but if say, you've killed someone, I think the very least you can do is feel a bit guilty.' She looked at Kevin.

'I really feel you need to get past Kevin's previous deeds,' said Clemitius. 'You are not here to judge any more than I am.'

'Indeed,' said Christopher quietly. 'But you don't get past something without talking about it, I suppose?' Clemitius looked at Christopher and shook his head.

'Oh really, thou shalt not judge, eh?' shouted Yvonne. 'I hate that. Doing wrong is still wrong: he killed people, he took money to kill me, he did it for a living, *why* doesn't that get judged while "not fulfilling one's potential" does, whatever the hell that means?'

'I wonder why you remain so fixated on what other people have or haven't done, Yvonne. Don't you feel it's important that we get past the things people *do* and see who they are?' Clemitius spoke with a fixed grin that made him look almost maniacal. His large lips filled his face, which reddened in surprise at the show of pleasure it was so unfamiliar with.

'Yes, exactly,' said Kevin. 'I don't feel that what a man does with his life necessarily reflects who he is,' which was something he heard in a film once and had been waiting to say for about three years.

'Well I do,' said Yvonne. 'I think what we do is *exactly* who we are, and I think everything else is rubbish. Believe me, I tried to pretend otherwise for a long time, but it's just pretend. Your life is the sum of its parts, that's all. What you intend or how you explain it or what excuses you have, they're all nonsense.'

'Oh Yvonne, if only it were that simple,' said Clemitius pityingly.

'And don't patronise me, you silly little man,' she snapped. 'You may be some kind of angel thingy, but to me you're a foolish self-indulgent prick with a small-man complex.' And with that she got up and left, slamming the door behind her.

There was silence for a moment before, inevitably, Kevin spoke: 'She seems upset. Maybe it's her time of the month, if you can get that when you're dead.' He reddened. 'Can you?' he asked, looking at Julie.

'It does appear to be the case,' said Clemitius rather grandly, looking at Christopher, 'that you have set something of a precedent for leaving the group. I wonder if it might be time to start locking the door?'

33

Ellie came round from what Dr Samani had called her 'little harvest festival' to find the good doctor sitting beside her bed smiling. 'Eight!' he said. 'Eight eggs.'

'And the sperm?'

'We didn't have too much trouble finding eight good ones. Mrs Schmelling did a good job; so did your friend. Rest, then you can go home. Phone in the morning, and we will see how many embryos we have.'

'How many do you think we'll have?'

'Five, six, maybe eight ... we'll see. Rest. Like I said at the beginning, one step at a time. Soon we will see if you can grow your baby; the rest we will freeze.'

He got up to go. Ellie caught his hand. 'Thank you. Can I ask a question?' she said.

'Of course.'

'What is Mrs Schmelling's first name?'

'Hilda,' he smiled.

Ellie went home by cab. As soon as she got in, she took off her coat, lay on the sofa, and closed her eyes. She half slept, dreaming of Gabriel's hobbling sperm being pushed into her eggs. In her imagination the two cells, hers and his, hesitate. They inhale the prospect of life and they can either choke on the fumes, or live. They live. And somewhere in her atheist's head, her lost lover is cheering them on, the way he shouted at the TV when Chelsea were playing.

She woke with a start. Instantly the ball of impending panic she had been carrying around with her since the accident returned, and she thought she was going to throw up. It was the phone. Ellie reached out and picked it up without looking.

'Ellie?'

'Yes.'

'It's Sarah, from the hospital.'

And Ellie thought: He's dead. He waited until now; he held on and now he's dead. 'Yes?' she whispered.

'I wonder, when you come in today, if you could look in on me please. I need to talk with you.'

'Is he dead?'

'There's no change, Ellie. I just want a chat, OK?'

'Why ... why do you want to talk with me?'

'It can wait, Ellie. It's nothing for you to worry about. Are you doing OK? Is the IVF going ... OK?'

'What do you mean?' Ellie felt a mild panic. Did Sarah know? What could she do if she did? Could she take the sperm back?

'It's OK, you don't have to tell me. I'm just asking you: are you OK?'

'Yes, thank you.' Ellie sounded like a child. 'Under the circumstances.'

'Good, then when you come in, you and I need to have a little chat. Preferably when the consultant is seeing his private patients.'

After she put the phone down, Ellie made herself a cup of tea and ate a banana. She thought of Gabriel, or at least tried to. He seemed more distant in her memory than he had yesterday. It wasn't that she couldn't remember the way he talked or walked, it was that the place where he sat in her head, the soft chair in the middle just above the eyes but back a bit, had been shifted downward. She didn't remember that happening. She felt sad, not the same enveloping sadness she had been swallowing since the accident, but a different sad. The kind of teary, dreamy sad you felt after sex sometimes. She finished her tea, quickly changed her knickers and skirt, and went to see him.

34

Christopher thought dinner might help. He had said as much to Clemitius, but Clemitius had waved him away. Christopher had spent a long time watching people; he retained the belief that they are more likely to bond, share their feelings, and generally talk about what is important to them over good food and a nice Rioja than in any therapy group. Such a thought would be sacrilege to Clemitius. Indeed, even believing it made Christopher feel sinful but believe it he did, and his belief had been born out by the previous night's meal.

He called for Yvonne first. She answered the door quickly and immediately said, 'If you have come to discuss my leaving the group, I really do not have anything to say. That little man is a fool who needs to take his head out of his arse.'

'Er ... actually, I was thinking it would be nice if you and the others and I all had dinner together again,' said Christopher.

She looked uncertain.

'There'll be wine,' he added, smiling.

'You know the way to a woman's liver,' she said. 'Give me a minute, old habits die hard.'

She went into her bathroom, emerging a few moments later wearing lipstick and a different blouse.

'After you,' he said. They went to collect the others. Gabriel didn't seem to hear the first knock. Christopher knocked again; when Gabe finally answered he looked tired and a little pale.

'Did we wake you?'

'No.'

'What's wrong?' asked Yvonne, and immediately bit her lip. 'I'm sorry. That's a stupid question ...'

'No ... I don't know ... I feel different.'

'What kind of different?' asked Yvonne.

'I don't know.' He thought for a moment. He actually looked, Yvonne thought, as though he had aged, or at least as if he had a really bad hangover. 'I feel … like I'm going down with something? Is that possible? Here?'

Christopher shrugged nervously. 'Come and join us for dinner,' he offered, half waiting for something sarcastic about how a bowl of tagliatelle and some fresh spinach would probably not make that much difference, but instead Gabriel just nodded and picked up his jacket.

They collected Julie and finally Kevin, who Christopher thought had eyed him suspiciously when he asked him about dinner, before slipping on his jacket and bowing slightly. When he stepped from the room he smirked at Gabriel, who ignored him and walked slowly behind Christopher to the dining room. The table was set and there were two bowls of olives, some fresh bread, and two bottles of wine waiting. Yvonne poured the wine, ignoring Kevin's glass.

'So,' said Kevin as he poured himself a glass of wine. 'What did you see in this celestial cinema?'

Nobody spoke at first. Julie picked up her glass and held it just below her lips, excusing herself from talking. Finally Gabriel murmured: 'Ellie.'

'She's pretty. I imagine,' said Kevin distractedly. Gabriel ignored him. 'And you,' he looked to Julie. 'What did you see?'

'I saw my friends, Lynne and Michael, keeping what is left of me company.'

'Was that hard? Seeing your friends,' asked Yvonne.

'Yes, but I feel better for having seen them. Maybe you should think about seeing your son?'

'I'm not sure I'm up to it,' said Yvonne. And as she said it, it felt as though her heart, which she had been told had long stopped beating, went a little faster and seemed a little louder. 'Anyway old misery-guts will probably stop me.'

'Well that wouldn't be fair,' said Julie, looking at Christopher. 'I mean, if Yvonne wants to see her son, she should be able to, shouldn't she?'

'Well, by that logic so should Kevin,' Christopher said.

'There isn't anybody I want to see,' said Kevin. 'I am serious about this process.' But nobody cared.

Christopher thought for a moment. Julie was right, everyone should have the same opportunity and if the logic he applied to taking Gabriel and Julie to the viewing room was sound—that it would help them to come to terms with where they were and what they had to do—then it certainly applied to the others. 'I'd be happy to take you back to the viewing room,' Christopher said to Yvonne 'Whenever you feel ready.'

Yvonne nodded and looked at her half-empty glass.

'Thank you,' she said. 'I wonder if you would come with me?' She looked at Julie. Yvonne had never pretended to be one of the girls, but she found herself feeling something here she had not felt for a very long time, something like loneliness perhaps, not that she wanted to name it.

'I'd be happy to.'

'And you?'

'Of course,' said Gabriel. 'Whenever you want.'

'No time like the present,' she said, standing up so abruptly the chair fell over.

'I'll stay here. I am serious about this process,' repeated Kevin.

'You aren't invited to see my life,' sneered Yvonne and marched off.

By the time they got to the viewing room, her pace had slowed. Yvonne paused for a moment. Julie imagined it was because she was afraid of the emotions she might feel and reached out awkwardly to touch Yvonne's arm. Yvonne smiled. She wasn't afraid of what she would feel, but—quite bizarrely under the circumstances—she wondered if it was OK to spy on her son, like walking into his room without knocking. She shook her head and looked at the floor. Christopher opened the door for her and stood back.

It was, Gabriel thought, the quietest room he had ever been in. Yvonne sat in front of the screen and Gabriel sat behind her. Julie sat with Christopher. He told Yvonne to think of her son.

The screen shone with life. There was Yvonne's son, a tall and gangly fair-haired young man with a sallow, near-yellow complexion. His blue eyes, ringed with red, burrowed into his skull. His long thin fingers were massaging his temples. When Yvonne saw him she moaned slightly, as though someone had punched her in the stomach.

He was sitting on the same sofa that Kevin had sat on as he waited for Yvonne. She wanted to tell him, her son, to move, to sit somewhere else lest he be contaminated, and she wanted to tell him not to cry and that she loved him. She wanted to tell him not to be alone, to call his father, even though he was useless and lived in America. But mostly she wanted to hug him, to reach right into the TV screen she stared at and hold him, as she had held him when he was nine and had come home in tears because he had been told he was to play Joseph in the school nativity but had later been replaced by another child who had cancer and wasn't expected to make casting the following year. Anthony had cried with hurt but also shame and she was powerless to change the world that hurt him or to take the pain away.

Julie moved closer to Yvonne and took her hand. Together they watched Anthony staring at the faded chalk mark on the floor where his mother had lain. The doorbell rang, and Anthony looked up.

'Who can that be?' said Yvonne, in the same way she might have done if she had been cooking his tea and was expecting a quiet night in with her son. Anthony walked round the chalk outline and opened the door to a fresh-faced, tall girl with long hair. She was wearing jeans and a grey jumper and was carrying a rucksack. As soon as he opened the door she dropped the bag and put her arms round him gently, kissing him softly on the cheek and whispering, 'I was as quick as I could be.'

'It's OK,' he said. 'I think I needed a little time on my own.' He kissed her on the top of her head. 'But I'm glad you're back.'

'Who's she?' asked Gabriel.

'I don't know,' said Yvonne, transfixed.

Tash sat next to Anthony on the sofa. 'I brought some sandwiches.'

'I'm not hungry.'

'I know, that's why I didn't bring pizza,' she smiled softly. 'But you need to eat something.'

'I don't know how I am going to get through tomorrow.'

'What's tomorrow?' asked Yvonne.

Christopher looked at her and said simply 'Funeral.'

'Oh.'

'How come she's dead but we're not?' whispered Gabriel.

'Psyche profile.' Christopher said quietly. 'We had to find what would act as a more appropriate motivator, life or heaven. And anyway, what with medical technology and the "chance" factor, we cannot always guarantee a coma.'

Yvonne watched as the girl held Anthony's head to her chest.

'I wish you'd met my mum,' he said.

'So do I. Do you think she'd have liked me?'

'Oh yes,' he said, looking up. 'At first she'd have fussed a bit, nobody being good enough for her son. She may even have asked if you were after my money.'

'Too bloody right I would,' said Yvonne.

'Well, we could have put her mind to rest over that.'

'Yes, we'd have introduced her to your dad. Who knows, they might have hit it off. She was fun, my mum. People didn't give her credit for that, I don't think. Even after dad left she was fun. I loved her.'

'I know. Did you tell her?'

'Yes. I think so, every time we spoke.'

'I think that's important—if you love someone, to tell them, you know.'

'I love you, you know.'

'I know,' said the blonde girl, smiling. 'I wasn't fishing. And I love you, too.'

Which was all just a bit too Ryan O'Neil and Ali McGraw for Yvonne, and she burst into uncontrollable sobs.

Christopher watched her with something approaching pride. He was glad he had brought her here; it was important that people should get the chance to notice the lives they have lived and the people they have loved. Otherwise, he thought, how can they reflect? Or rest.

After Yvonne's sobs had quietened to gentle tears, they returned to the dining room. They expected to find it empty, but instead Kevin was still there and so was Clemitius. They both smiled as they came in.

'More TV?' said Clemitius. 'I really am going to have to put a child lock on that thing.' Kevin laughed.

'I'm glad you decided to join us,' Christopher said.

'So is Kevin, I imagine. You did read the chapter on group scapegoating didn't you? Because it seems to me that Kevin here is becoming something of a scapegoat,' said Clemitius.

'Well, it was nice of you to come and keep him company,' Christopher said. 'Will you be joining us for cheesecake?'

'No thank you,' Clemitius said. 'Good night everyone.' He paused for a moment before turning to Kevin, nodding his head, and saying, 'Good night Kevin and thank you, thank you for your help. Sleep well.'

'You are more than welcome,' smiled Kevin. 'I will.'

And he may have. Gabriel, on the other hand, didn't. After dinner he returned to his room and lay on the bed. Unable to settle, he had a shower, flicked through some magazines, and even watched a *Star Wars* video, but he could not rest.

He found himself staring at the ceiling thinking of Ellie, which was pretty much what he did with every waking moment. But tonight felt different. Usually, when he imagined Ellie he had a sense of himself watching her, as though he was floating above her, or in the same room moving round behind the sofa and out of her way to make sure she didn't bump into him. He was, in his head at least, a bit of a Hopkirk to her significantly prettier Randall, but tonight when he imagined her, he wasn't there. He could see her—on the sofa, beside the fridge, in bed—but it was like thinking of photographs that he had taken rather than a video he was in.

When he did finally sleep, it was restless and fitful. When he woke up, he felt ever so slightly further away from Ellie, and from himself, and he realised that something had changed. Deep inside he felt empty ... not distant, but absent. And he knew somehow that he would not see Ellie again, not hold her, not smell her, and not annoy her. And that if she did by some miracle manage to have his child, then he would never see him or hold him or father him because he was—he understood now—dead.

Gabriel buried his head in his pillow and sobbed like a child.

35

It was 6:30 in the evening when Ellie arrived at the hospital. Before going to Sarah's office, of course, she looked in on Gabe. There was a nurse with him, putting up an IV fluid bag. 'Any change?' Ellie asked, without feeling.

The nurse shook his head. 'I'll be back in a while to check that's going through OK,' he said. He was different to the others: older, male, with a lined and sallow face. He wasn't very friendly either, and he left the room quickly.

Ellie went over and kissed Gabe on the forehead, leaving her face near his for a moment and inhaling, looking for any trace of his scent, the smell of Gabe, the faintest of which had still been on his skin yesterday. She couldn't find it and she pulled away, but not before whispering. 'Now we wait, sweetheart.' She went to see Sarah the ward sister.

Sarah was sitting in her small office, talking quietly to her computer. 'Oh purleese, just do what you do, so I can do what I do, you stupid bloody machine.'

'Is this a bad time?'

'Are you any good with computers?'

'No, Gabe was in charge of technology. What are you trying to do?'

'Open this file?'

'Have you double-clicked?'

Sarah looked at her and smiled.

'Sorry,' said Ellie. 'That really is as far as I go.'

'Oh, it can wait. Come in, sit down please. I need to talk to you about your friend.'

'Which one?'

'Izzy.'

Ellie looked confused.

'You see, the fact that you look like you don't know what I'm talking about makes me worry.'

'I'm sorry, I don't understand.'

'Well I don't quite know how to explain this, but the ward round found Izzy with Gabriel. She said she was trying to help you, and I thought I understood ... but the doctors ...'

'Sarah, please tell me what you are talking about.'

'We found Izzy touching ... Gabriel ... we found her trying to stimulate Gabriel sexually, and humming loudly ...'

'Humming?'

'Yes, I don't remember what...it may have been something by Abba or the Beatles or something.'

'The Beatles?'

'Yes ... I don't think that is really what matters. I had assumed that, given what you were going through with the IVF, that she was trying to help you, but Moira had ... well, I happen to know that Moira had already seen to that—and all that Izzy would say was that she was trying to help—and well ... I wondered if you knew what was going on?'

'I didn't—hang on, you said you know about Moira?'

'Yes, I'm not stupid Ellie, and this is my ward, there isn't supposed to be stuff going on here that I don't know about. Like I said, in your position I think I would have done the same. I didn't mind letting that happen, I could do it without anyone finding out—but Izzy as well?'

Ellie thought for a moment. What had Izzy been doing?

'Ellie, can you please tell me what is going on, because I am going to have to manage this. I don't think either of us want the consultant making this into an issue.'

So Ellie told Sarah everything. How Izzy was going to take the sperm but couldn't go through with it, and so Moira had volunteered, and that she could only assume Izzy had changed her mind and tried to do the business solo, so to speak. 'What did the consultant say?'

'He was angry. He immediately assumed it had something to do with the IVF. He called security and he made his registrar check that Izzy didn't have any bottles of sperm on her person. He seemed quite satisfied when he found an empty pot in her bag and then he took her details, said this was a very serious matter and that he would be notifying the police and reporting an assault.'

'Oh my God. What are we going to do? Sorry, it's not your problem ...'

'Of course it is, this is my ward. Anyway, more importantly, how are you?'

'I'm OK thanks. I had the eggs harvested today.'

'Oh really? How many?'

'Eight.'

'That's good. I had six—still got three embryos in the freezer, we're planning to try again next year, when Ira starts school.'

'You ... you had IVF? And ... and you helped me ...'

Sarah smiled. 'Are you phoning in the morning? I was so nervous making that phone call.'

'Yes, they said there may be seven or eight embryos, but I keep thinking: what are the odds of that? You know, he's not at his healthiest is he, and his sperm were never exactly award winners.'

'They only need eight Ellie, they don't even have to swim.'

'I know.' But Ellie had forgotten how not to worry.

'Look, what are the chances of Izzy saying that she was simply trying to stimulate Gabe—a misguided, futile attempt to help her friend?'

'How would she explain the pot?'

'Good point. Oh hell, that's circumstantial, she may have needed a small pot to carry her ...'

' ... peanuts?' Ellie said.

'Yeah.'

Ellie looked at Sarah and giggled. She instantly felt guilty; she was in no position to laugh, certainly not here, not yet, not for a very long time. Fate—and by fate we mean luck, coincidence, an unplanned event that could have happened any time but just bumbled into being now—decided to prove it. Sarah's door opened and a nurse put her head in. She saw Ellie but looked quickly at Sarah, 'Crash, Mr Bell, crash team coming.' Sarah stood up quickly, 'You may want to stay here.'

But Ellie didn't. Sarah strode quickly to Gabriel's room and Ellie ran after her. Numb legs stumbling down the corridor, she was choking on the words, 'Not yet, not ready.' When they got to Gabriel, one nurse was leaning on his chest pushing and counting slowly and loudly, when she got to five another nurse leaned over and started to breathe into a plastic tube in his mouth. All Ellie could see was Gabe's pale lifeless body bending under the nurses.

She might have squealed, she must have, Sarah turned and took her firmly by the arms and led her from the room. Ellie wanted to struggle, to go back in and help, but she couldn't, she went where she was pointed. A few yards outside the room and Ellie was staring at the wall, the contours under the paint, the false light slightly flickering off the polished floor. She heard a trolley with two doctors and a nurse come running through the ward door toward her, turning quickly into Gabriel's room. She heard: 'For resuss?' And Sarah shouted, 'Yes.'

And whatever invisible force had been holding Ellie together through the days since the accident, and the IVF, and the lack of sleep, and the fear, and the all-consuming loneliness, left her like stale breath, and she fell on to Sarah, sobbing so hard she couldn't breathe.

36

James Buchan wasn't stupid. OK, he was stupid, but that didn't mean he was *only* stupid. He knew, for instance, that if he approached Michael at Julie's bedside and asked him if now might be a good time to leave her with the dykey woman and come back to Norfolk to play bass guitar with a band he hadn't thought about for fifteen years, that there was every chance Mikey would force-feed him a drip stand. It had finally dawned on James that Michael loved Julie, and that irritating—and given her coma, entirely pointless—state of affairs was likely to dominate Michael's every thought until the bitter end.

James wondered if the fact that Julie had until recently been his girlfriend might offer him a little leverage. Had they been having an affair? Behind his back? And if they had, would there be any mileage in trying to make Michael feel guilty about it … guilty enough to come to Norwich? It was unlikely. And if he were to try it and it didn't work, there wouldn't be a second chance. The key to persuading someone to do something they don't want to do is to wear them down, and in order to wear them down you have to avoid strategies that prevent you from going back for more.

James knew that even if he told Michael that he had managed to set Dog in a Tuba up in the X-ray department downstairs, and Matthew, Alice, Jimmy, and Bernie were there waiting for him, along with Richard bloody Branson and MTV, it would not move him away from Julie. Nothing would.

He wondered, in a detached way, what would happen if Julie died. Michael couldn't just stay there then. Not that James was wishing her dead. Far from it. But if she were going to die—and the doctors didn't seem all that hopeful—wouldn't it be better in a way if she just got on with it? Lingering wasn't going to help anyone. But there again, if Julie died, how might Michael react? Unlikely that he would turn to Dog in a Tuba and an '80s reunion tour with Curiosity Killed the Cat for solace. Not straight away, anyway.

James didn't have a plan but he did have faith. If he saw Michael for long enough to talk to him, then a plan would emerge. It always did.

Michael had taken to talking quietly to Julie. He told her the sorts of things he would be writing about if he were working. He thought that if she were awake she would smile and say something that would make the articles funnier than they would be otherwise or, better still, change the subject completely. Anyway he wanted to talk. Sometimes he told her about things he had thought about her in the past, about how she had looked or how sometimes, after an otherwise dull evening at James' cottage, he would go home and think about something she had said, leaving out the fact that he was probably having sex with someone else while he thought it. Mostly he talked because it seemed a good way of treating her as if she were alive. Because she might not be for long.

When James arrived, Michael was sitting close to Julie, murmuring something pointless and heartfelt about how his knees weren't as good at doing what knees did as they used to be, and that this was a symbol of something important. 'Yes', he imagined her whispering back, 'a lack of exercise.' Hearing someone come in, he stopped.

'Hello mate, how is she? Any change?'

'No.'

'Oh. Well, have the doctors said anything?'

'Not really. When the nurses were washing her yesterday, they told Lynne that the doctors didn't feel they could do anything more. Just wait and see.'

'Well that's a good sign, in a way,' offered James. 'I mean, if they're still washing her and stuff, there must still be a chance.'

Michael just looked at him.

'Er, anyway, I was wondering if you wanted to get a bite to eat, or a coffee—you know, get you out of here for a while?'

'I'm all right here, I don't want to leave her alone.'

'Right. Righto. Er, can I ask, Mikey, why?'

Michael thought for a moment. Why? Wasn't it obvious? Because he couldn't think of anything but her, because despite the fact they hadn't so much as kissed, he had decided that were she to wake up, he would ask her to spend the rest of her life with him. Not straight away, obviously, that would be rude, but eventually. And all this—the fact that he had fallen head over heels in love with a girl who had been funny and pretty and alive and not very far away only a few days ago—had only occurred to him since she had been in a coma. Which he thought made him a prat. 'Because it's Julie,' he said.

'Right, because it's Julie. And that's cool Mikey, it really is, it's just that I was wondering, and I'm not being, you know, funny about it or anything, I was wondering if you two were, you know, seeing each other or anything ... before. It's just, this looks to me, all a bit ... well, sudden.'

'No James, we weren't. Of course not,' said Michael, finding himself thinking Why weren't we? And then, perhaps because he was tired and loving someone in a coma, he thought: Why have I spent so much of my life waiting for my life?

'Right, I just wondered, you know. Thanks.' James paused. 'Although in a way maybe that's a shame, because, well you two were ... are ... were ... better suited to each other than she and I. I mean we were just flatmates in the end. And most of the beginning, really.'

Lynne arrived. It may have been that she had heard James, because she didn't scowl at him quite so openly as she had every other time he had been in the same room as her. She just ignored him and looked at Michael. He gave a little shake of his head, and she said: 'Do you want to get something to eat?'

'Not really.'

'Maybe you should, you could come back afterwards if you like.' She spoke softly.

'You wouldn't mind ... me coming back for a while?'

'Of course not.'

Michael smiled at Lynne and said to James, 'Come on then, let's go and grab a sandwich and a cup of coffee.'

'Cool,' said James.

37

Izzy was woken by the doorbell. It had been a fitful and short sleep. She had cried a little, after ranting about the unbearable humiliation of standing in a courtroom accused of 'tampering' with the willy of a comatose man she happened not to like very much. She would probably be struck off the nursing register and end up working in Pizza Hut. If it went to court she would find her picture in the local paper with a caption that might include the words 'meddling' and 'testicles'. Parents would not let their children play with her daughter. She would forever be known as 'That really weird woman who touches men when they are unconscious'. She would have to move to New Zealand, except they probably wouldn't have her. Not with her record.

Of course Sam hadn't understood. He even looked at one point as though he was going to smile, but Izzy threw a shoe at him and that put a stop to that. By midnight she had, helped by wine and constant reassurance from Sam, including 'We could always move to America; they'll have pretty much anyone,' calmed down enough to contemplate bed. She hadn't called Ellie. She had felt too embarrassed.

It was after two now. Izzy lay still, waiting for the doorbell to sound again, just to be sure. It did, and she kicked Sam. 'There's someone at the door. See who it is before they wake Polly,' she hissed. Sam, a man who knew how to ignore his wife, turned over and pulled the quilt over his head. 'Fine!' she hissed. 'If it's a drug-crazed killer I'll send them right through, shall I?'

Sam stirred slightly. 'It's probably Ellie, don't you think?' And he got out of bed, reached for his dressing gown, and went to the door.

Izzy stared at the ceiling. It may be that Moira had succeeded where Izzy had so spectacularly failed. But what if she hadn't? The thread of ridiculously frayed hope that Ellie had been hanging on to, the idea that somehow she could still go through with the IVF, probably snapped today. If it had been a bad day for Izzy, it had been a worse one for Ellie.

Sam opened the door and a pale, gaunt Ellie walked in. She went to speak but couldn't quite find the breath. The last thing Ellie could remember from the hospital, when the crash team had gone and all but one of the nurses had disappeared, was the look on the face of the young nurse who was taking down the drip, the one who'd burst into Sarah's office. Ellie was sitting in the chair beside the bed. The same chair that she had sat in the day before, and the day before that. Sarah was standing behind her. The nurse came over and whispered something to Sarah, who walked over and looked at the drip stand and the empty bag that hung from it. The nurse and Sarah looked at each other.

Ellie couldn't make out what Sarah said, not at first. She heard the nurse answer: 'I don't know.' And then, 'What should I do with this?'

And Sarah said, 'Take it to my office, put it in there and do not let anyone touch it.'

Now Ellie was sitting on Izzy and Sam's sofa staring at the coffee table and trying, really trying, to say 'Sorry for coming round so late.' But all that came out was, 'Sorry for ...'

'It's OK,' said Sam. 'Fancy a cup of tea? I'll go and wake Izzy.' Which was as good a cue as Izzy could expect. She had waited by the bedroom door, listening for tears or rage. The quiet had been a relief at first.

'Sweetie, I'm so sorry, I tried ... I went ... well you probably know. But they caught me in the act. Did Moira ... was Moira able to ...' Izzy walked quickly over to her friend and sat down beside her, taking her cold hand.

Ellie looked at Izzy and nodded blankly. She could see Gabriel's face. Grey and pained. And she could see Sarah, whose soft face had stiffened when the nurse had spoken to her. And she could see tomorrow like it had already happened.

'She did? Oh thank goodness, well you should be resting Ellie, shouldn't you? Shouldn't you? Have they put them together? There will be some embryos, won't there? Ellie ... sweetie?'

Ellie wanted to speak, she really did, but she had lost herself. Someone, a cruel god with a big kitchen implement, had cored her like an apple. But she found some words, from somewhere. Perhaps because she had to sleep, and she couldn't before she had spoken. 'He's dead, Izzy. He died this evening. His heart stopped working and they tried to resuscitate him. I know they did 'cos I was there. But he died. And I just didn't want to go home just yet.'

38

When they first introduced the angels to this new way of working, they showed them lots of films of different types of therapists. There was one man, a very serious American, who measured the quality of his work by how little he had to say. He could do 50 minutes—$140 worth—without making a single sound. He would shrug, furrow the odd brow, or turn his hand over and over in order to encourage the patient to say more.

Clemitius was transfixed, he considered him a genius; he said the man 'created a neutral and safe space for the kind of deep exploration and understanding that changed lives.' Christopher said he thought he was a thief. Clemitius said this illustrated that Christopher simply didn't understand the nuance of therapy. Christopher replied that the genius could have been replaced by a sedated monkey. Perhaps, Christopher realised, he had never believed. Which, given his place in the universe, was probably criminal. But what was that saying, he asked himself? 'You may as well be hanged for a sheep as for a lamb.'

Christopher knocked on Gabriel's door and waited. When Gabriel answered, he still looked ill—which Christopher understood—and somehow a little smaller, which made no sense. 'Look, I'm sorry, but I think there is something you should see.'

Gabriel just looked at him. Any capacity he had had for surprise seemed to have long since left him. 'What is it?'

Christopher didn't say anything, which was perhaps a mistake. He didn't think of himself as much of a therapist; he didn't know when to speak and when not to.

'Is it Ellie?'

'No, no, it's you, Gabe.'

Christopher turned and walked slowly down the corridor, knowing Gabriel would follow.

'Where are we going?'

'Viewing room.'

'It must be Ellie.'

'Not exactly Gabriel, I think you need to see something that has already happened.'

'Does Clemitius know we are going?'

'No.'

'I was wondering, maybe I should be trying a bit harder to follow the rules?'

Christopher stopped and turned, staring into Gabriel's eyes for the very first time. 'Why?'

'Because ... isn't that the point?'

'The point of what?'

'Why I'm here? What I need to do to get back to Ellie.' He stopped talking, and for the first time since this group business started, Christopher the angel looked someone in the eye. They stood and stared at each other, and perhaps Gabriel began to understand. He nodded, looked at the floor, and his shoulders sank down a little, the way they can on dead people. Christopher turned and carried on walking. Gabriel followed in silence.

When they got to the viewing room, they sat down in the same chairs they had had before. Christopher said: 'Actually, I have to rewind.'

'Where are you rewinding to?'

'To yesterday, while we were in the viewing room watching Yvonne's son. This is what was happening.'

They began to watch together. They saw Ellie enter Gabriel's room and put down her bag, and the back of a nurse setting up an IV. Christopher glanced across at Gabriel, who was crying, already. He was watching Ellie, and as the nurse left he hardly noticed. Because he followed Ellie the screen followed her too, into Sarah's office. He listened as they discussed Moira and Izzy, but he didn't really hear what they were saying, not all of it.

He was just looking at the woman he loved, maybe for the last time. He paid more attention when they talked about how many embryos Ellie had, and what was going to happen next: he sat forward then. But he leaned back when the nurse came in and shouted 'Crash! Mr Bell.'

Then the screen filled with Gabriel in his bed, a nurse pressing and counting on his chest, another nurse breathing through a tube into his mouth, and he saw Ellie come in and crumple a little more. He watched a crash team put two pads on his chest and shout "Clear!" He listened as a doctor said 'Again,' and an electronic voice said a number.

'Clear.'

'Nothing. Is he for resuss?'

'Yes ...'

Gabriel stared at the screen, all the activity had slowed. The crash team was putting things carefully back on to a trolley, a doctor was writing something on a chart. All the ordered energy that had surrounded his fading body had slowed and stopped. He sat in silence for a long time. Finally, he asked, 'Where's Ellie?'

'Do you need to see that?' Christopher asked, as gently as he could.

'You tell me,' Gabriel said in monotone. 'You brought me here.'

'I'm sorry.'

'Why?'

'Why what?'

'Why after a few of these groups, why? I mean all this trouble, getting me here?'

'It really isn't that much trouble.'

'It fucking was for me.'

'Quite,' agreed Christopher.

'Why now?'

And Christopher breathed in deeply and said, 'Do you know what? I'm not sure. I saw this, of course I watch, it's what I do, but it surprised me and nothing surprises me. That's why I came in here last night to look at this again, and that is why I brought you here.'

'Again?'

'Look I know it's a lot to take in, but there's more,' Christopher said.

'More? What more? I'm dead for fuck's sake that's as bloody final as it gets, I think—how can there be more ...?'

'Can we watch it again?' Christopher sounded calm, he sounded ... therapeutic.

Gabriel didn't move. Christopher nodded toward the screen. Gabriel shook his head. Christopher understood the man's reluctance. What else was there to see? But he reached and touched Gabriel's arm and whispered, 'Please.' Gabriel's volition, like so much else, had left him and he thought of himself once more.

Again he saw Ellie entering the room and again he looked at her, letting out a little groan. But this time Christopher told him: 'Look at the nurse.'

Nothing.

'Think about that nurse.'

The screen filled with the man setting up the drip. Kevin.

Kevin the Killer.

Kevin had somehow been given a reprieve to go back and finish him off.

And both Christopher and Gabriel knew by whom.

39

Michael and James had made their way to an Italian café across the road from the hospital. Just in case you didn't know it was owned by an Italian family, there were loads of pictures of Italian footballers on the walls. And a large flag. And all the waitresses looked Italian and desperately bored. And it was called "Little Italy."

They sat in a wooden booth at the back eating ciabattas, drinking coffee and, in Michael's case at least, wanting to go. Michael had already paid and James, uncertain as to when he might get the opportunity to eat this well again, was taking full advantage by wading through a side order of chips and a caramel slice, although not at the same time.

'Do you think she'll wake up?' asked Michael for no reason, other than because it was all he was thinking about.

James shrugged.

'I suppose the longer she stays unconscious, the less chance there is ...' said Michael. 'I think ... it's hard not being able to do anything ... except wait.'

'And how long can you wait?' said James, genuinely curious, 'I mean, a week? A month? A year? At some point you need to get on with your life. Anyone would have to. I don't know...' He shrugged again and stuffed some chips into his mouth. Michael stared at his coffee. James was right, at some point he would have to stop coming. Just not yet, not for a while, but when was it appropriate to stop sitting there? What if she stayed in a coma for years?

'I don't know,' Michael whispered. 'I mean it hasn't been that long yet, really, has it?'

'Do you talk to her?'

Michael nodded. 'It's silly, but you never know, do you?'

'No no, it's what you do to people in comas,' said James, as if he were an expert on stuff to try on people in comas. 'Have you tried her favourite music?'

Michael looked up. 'No, do you think that would help?'

'Dunno, but isn't that what people do? Get visits from their favourite pop stars, try familiar sounds and stuff?'

'Yeah, and smells and things. That could be worth trying. What music, do you think?' Michael paused. It occurred to him he didn't really know her favourite things, he only knew a corner of her world. In the time he had been sitting beside her, he had thought of a hundred questions he wanted to ask her. It occurred to him that maybe James knew more about her than he did. Not that he imagined James actually knew her—just things about her. 'Do you have any ideas?' he asked James sheepishly.

James thought for a moment. He didn't have any ideas, not about this anyway. But if there was anything, a song, a piece of clothing, an old teddy bear, it would be in Norfolk. 'Well she didn't have much,' he said tentatively. 'But she did seem quite attached to the things she did have. Maybe, I dunno, the smell of her favourite shirt or ... there was a stuffed toy she said she had had for a long time. We could go round to where she was staying, have a look. What do you think?'

'Stuffed toy? Julie?'

'I don't think it was hers.'

'Music is easy, I could nip down Oxford Street, buy some CDs and a portable player. Maybe I'll do that. Or I could talk to Lynne first. What do you think?'

Michael had asked James what he thought twice more in the last minute than he had in the previous 15 years. James sensed that was a good thing.

'Yeah Mikey, good idea ... but I was wondering, isn't the point to get some personal stuff, you know ... stuff that is hers? The music—good idea but, well … it's up to you.' James shrugged. He was good at this kind of game.

It did make some kind of sense, Michael thought: bringing the familiar, the reassuring, the things that meant something to Julie. And even if it was desperate, it was *something*, and if you have a choice between trying something and doing nothing, it's obvious which one you go for. 'We could go and get some stuff,' Michael murmured.

'Do you know where she was living?' James said.

'I've got a number I could call…'

'Hey, how about the weekend? I'll drive you there. No doubt Dykey Girl can be around more at the weekend right?'

'Yeah … Yes,' said Michael. 'That would be good. Thanks James. I'll call the woman Julie moved in with. Let her know we're coming.'

And James smiled sympathetically. In his head, he was turning to the crowd, hands raised aloft, milking the rapturous applause and shouting 'Result!'

40

Michael talked with Lynne about going to Norwich. He was worried that she would consider it an attempt to slip away from their shared vigil. To his surprise, she didn't. When he first mentioned the idea of getting some of Julie's things—some music, a favourite perfume, anything that might be considered a stimulus—she nodded vigorously. 'I've been wondering the same,' she said.

They found themselves sitting together with Julie, instead of taking it in turns as they had for the first couple of days. They talked, at first in whispers, but increasingly as if they were talking over coffee rather than the body of the comatose friend they both loved. As they talked, Michael began to feel comfortable with the fact that it wasn't simply Lynne's doubts he needed to address, but his own. He felt that surrounding Julie with personal mementos, playing music, or filling the room with her favourite colours would be a useful, if slightly desperate thing to do, but he didn't really know what things might make a difference. It wasn't as if he could get a recorded message from her favourite film star, or arrange for Leonard Cohen to pop in. He worried that this was further proof that he didn't actually know her, and had no right loving her, or even sitting with her. And he wondered, deep in his heart, if maybe he was going to look for Julie in order to learn more about her. But it seemed that Lynne, who had known Julie forever, knew better.

'Julie didn't collect mementos,' Lynne said. 'She found a reason to be wherever she was, and stayed there until the reason didn't seem a good one anymore.'

'So do you think this is pointless?'

'No,' Lynne shook her head. 'If there is anything we can do that might help, no matter how remote a possibility, then we should do it.'

Michael nodded. The more Lynne spoke, the softer she looked. And the more able he felt to talk. 'The thing is, I don't know what might help. What things might resonate? I suppose I don't really know her in that way.'

'Music, definitely music, but she had very specific taste; she tended to judge people throughout her twenties entirely according to what music they listened to,' she shrugged. 'Bring back her stuff, even if you haven't heard of it, and some of her clothes.'

'James said that there were still a few bits and pieces at his place.'

Lynne raised her eyebrows. 'Really? Hard to imagine Julie leaving anything behind there; she had no intention of going back. Anything he has I doubt would be of any value to her.'

They sat in silence for a while, and then Lynne said, 'When Julie leaves, she doesn't go back. In fact she doesn't even look back. She was with this guy in Mexico for a while. Not sure why, he was an old painter, in a wheelchair. She sort of pretended to play the muse and he, from what I could gather, rather liked that. She liked his art, at first she liked him too, and the age or the immobility didn't matter to her. But after a while he started acting like a prat. When he was sober he would describe his temperament as 'a stove that bakes his work' with the shallow pretensions of a man who hadn't sold anything for fifteen years. Julie said he was like a thirteen-year-old boy with borrowed hormones. She was getting bored and was planning to move on. He may have sensed it; he got angry one night after too much tequila and set fire to her curtains while she slept.'

'Did he set up a ramp as a getaway?' said Michael, disliking the stranger in the wheelchair already.

Lynne smiled 'It does conjure up a weird image, doesn't it?

They fell into a comfortable silence, Michael reluctant to go.

'I won't be away long. Up and down in five hours, I reckon.'

'It will take a bit longer than that. If anything changes, I'll call you straight away.'

'Thanks.' He still didn't move.

'Look, it's none of my business, but about that mate of yours.'

Michael looked puzzled. He couldn't think of a mate ...

'The one who comes in here, the bloke that Julie tolerated for a while.'

'Oh right, James—yes.'

'Don't trust him.'

'No, well, what's to trust?'

'I mean I don't think you should trust him, hope you don't mind me mentioning it. I wouldn't if I didn't think I should, but I think I should. He has something about him.'

'He's a shallow, self-serving opportunist, if that's what you mean,' Michael smiled.

'Well, that obviously, but—and I'm good at this stuff—I'd like to say, ask Julie, but I can't. So watch yourself, OK?'

'OK,' said Michael, who thought of James as benign, like a fading boil, and as incapable of doing anything to touch him beyond be annoying and cadge sandwiches and coffee. But then boils can flare up again, if you don't lance them when you have the chance.

41

Ellie was lying in a darkened room with her legs in the air, and an unflattering, old but soft cotton nightie with bluebells and daisies on it pulled up round her hips. Izzy was beside her; Moira and Sam were in the waiting room. High in the corner of the room was a TV monitor, on which Ellie would be shown her embryos before they were placed inside her. She was having two implanted, which left her three more frozen as insurance or as, in a place far beyond her wildest dreams, a sibling. Dr Samani had said that statistically he was surprised that they had only managed five embryos, but given the fact that the sperm provider had been in a coma at the time of retrieval, and little research had been done on sperm from the comatose, it perhaps wasn't that unusual. He also added, softly, that Ellie's own health may not have helped, but under the circumstances he felt she was doing remarkably well.

And so she was. Yesterday she watched her partner die; today she was trying to get pregnant. Life goes on. It seems.

Dr Samani himself was doing the implantation, and he was being helped by his senior nurse, who should have been on a day off. Ellie was touched that these strangers should try so hard to help her, and as she lay on her back with her feet in stirrups, staring at the ceiling, and holding Izzy's hand, she realised that since Gabriel had been run over, nobody—with the notable but now irrelevant exception of his consultant—had shown her anything but kindness and generosity. Even down to the strangers who helped Moira, despite the fact that they had their own grief: they had taken a risk, ultimately, to help her. She'd give her legs for the chance to say sarcastically to Gabe, 'See, you grumpy old sod, people are OK,' and her eyes burned.

Dr Samani came in smiling. He took her hand and asked, 'How are you?'

Ellie shrugged, and he nodded. 'OK, this is what we do. In a few moments, if you look up there on that monitor, you will see your embryos, two of them, then they will be brought in here, and I will put them into you. Simple. Afterwards you stay here a few minutes, and then go home and take it easy ... as easy as you can. Remember Ellie, you cannot change the past, but you can shape the future, yes. This is Claire. She will be scanning your uterus, so I can see where they go.'

Ellie nodded. And in a festival of nodding, Dr Samani nodded at Claire, who nodded right back and covered the end of her scanner—which looked like a smooth-ended electric razor—in jelly, and started to rub it over Ellie's belly. Beside Ellie was a trolley with a monitor on it, turned so both Dr Samani and Ellie could see it. It began to flicker into life, and what looked like static appeared.

'Good,' said Dr Samani. 'Good lining, under the circumstances, I am not sure how you got it, but your womb looks as ready as it could be for your embryos; it will keep them warm.'

A voice from next door called, 'Ready.'

'OK, OK,' said Dr Samani. 'If you look up at that screen in the corner Ellie, you will see your embryos.' The TV in the corner flicked into life and there—in the best traditions of a library-science picture were two baby planets, one smooth like a near perfect sphere, one coarse and uneven, more asteroid than moon.

'Is that one OK?'

'They are both fine. If they weren't we wouldn't be using them.'

Then they vanished from the screen, sucked into what looked like a giant straw. Moments later a bustling embryologist walked into the room saying, 'Ellie Saines, two embryos, numbers 32643 and 32646.' Like a messenger in a hotel lobby.

'Yes,' said Dr Samani.

'What happened to 32644 and 5?' asked Izzy.

'They're in the fridge. We chose these because they had grown more quickly. The others will be fine ... for another time. Right, Ellie: lay still and try to relax. Claire, I'm ready.'

And everyone got serious. Ellie could feel the room darken, although it may have been the concentration of those around her keeping the light out. Claire rubbed the scanner over Ellie's belly looking for the picture Dr Samani wanted. She found it almost effortlessly.

'Good,' he said. 'OK Ellie we're going in now ...'

And Ellie breathed deeply, closed her eyes, and took something like comfort from the fact that he had said 'we.'

Seventy minutes later, Ellie was sitting in the front seat of the car next to Sam, who was driving at exactly thirty miles an hour and thus inviting a stunningly wide array of abuse from London's road users. Ellie was staring in front and trying to picture her embryos Lola and Luca snuggling into the deep cotton wall glued to her uterus. The names had been a running joke for about five years. Luca after someone to do with Chelsea, and because Ellie liked it even though the Chelsea Luca had long since left. Lola because Ellie came up with it one night when she and Gabe were playing the Name Game in bed. Where once post-coital activity had been a fag or pizza and a gentle reminiscence, or the soft, safe sleep lovers share sometimes, now it was a game where they came up with a name they liked for each letter of the alphabet. Ever since that time, whenever Gabe or Ellie referred to their imagined child, he or she was Luca or Lola. And so they were.

Izzy and Moira sat in the back of the car in pretty much the way they had when they were kids. 'You OK, pet? Sam's not driving too fast is he?'

'I'm fine.'

'I can't drive much slower.'

'I know. Could you imagine if Gabe were driving behind you, the names he'd be calling you?' She needed to hear his name in the car right then; she needed the thought of him as she cradled their maybe-babies home. Then returned her mind to the tasks that lay ahead of her, tasks that would somehow keep her breathing.

She'd get home and rest because she had to, and then she would phone the hospital. She had things to sort out: the funeral, and his mother was finally flying in tomorrow, and Ellie had to tell her that she didn't want her staying in the flat, as nicely as she could. And then she had to rest more and talk to work about how long she would be off. And sort out money … how? Why hadn't Gabriel's work been in touch? She'd left a message the day after the accident, but had heard nothing. Not even a card.

'There is so much to do,' she murmured.

'When we get to yours, you need to rest for a while, we'll have a cup of tea and work out the things we need to do, OK sweetie?'

'Yes.'

Silence as everyone bar Ellie held their breath for a sleeping policeman.

'Do you think there's a God?' asked Ellie.

'I don't know, sweetie … do you?' Izzy was in full-on psychiatric nurse mode.

'No, but it's times like this, you realise why we invented him.'

'Why?' asked Moira.

'Because there is nobody else to blame.'

'Well,' said Sam feeling Izzy's eyes burning into the back of his head. 'There is another way of looking at that.'

'Oh, shut up Sam,' said Izzy.

'How do you mean?' asked Ellie.

'Maybe we invented him because without him, who would we all be praying to for Lola and Luca tonight?'

And Ellie remembered again why she liked Sam so much.

42

Michael and James were in very different moods. Indeed, the further they got from London and the nearer to Norwich, the more distinct their mental states became.

Michael was tense from the beginning. He had grown accustomed to his daily rituals that had formed over the last week and the further he got from Julie's room, the thinner the air felt. A couple of times he nearly asked James to turn the car around to go back, but he didn't. He had decided upon this mission of sorts, and as he clung to the armrest and stared out of the window, he convinced himself that this was the only thing he could possibly do that might make the slightest difference to Julie. To not act, to stay and stare at her almost-lifeless body, was selfish and passive. At least this way, he reasoned, he was not simply waiting for her to die. It had occurred to him, in the way it can to the overtired or overwrought, that he had already spent too long taking the easy option.

James, meanwhile, was tuned in to Magic FM, and currently bouncing around to something that Michael considered wholly unnecessary by The Alarm. James was happy to be away from London, particularly pleased to be away from the hospital, and really looking forward to playing the Apollo. Any Apollo. He hadn't given much thought to what exactly might happen between the point where he arrived in Norfolk and the Apollo part, but detail was never his strong point.

His plan was to get to the barn before the others and tidy up a bit, make it look like a working studio. Of course the others may have expected him to have one or two songs to play them, Christ knows Gary Guitar would have a couple of dozen ready, but how hard could it be to ignore those for the first rehearsal? James reckoned that mostly they would all just want to reacquaint themselves with their instruments, jam a bit, play 'Stand By Me' a lot. Maybe run over some of the old stuff. The old magic would start coming back when they were all there together. And there would be plenty of time to write some material in the next few days.

Bernie was picking Gary up around three. They may stop for a bite to eat, but should be at the cottage by six-thirty. Matthew and Alice were leaving early but stopping off in Cambridge to pick up the mad religious bloke. They were aiming for seven or seven-thirty. James was on schedule to get home by three and there was no way he could keep Michael there for four hours. But he had a plan.

'So Mikey, how about I drop you at my place, you pick up your car and go over to her new place. I'll have a really good rummage around, up in the attic, over in the barn. I'll go through the music collection and see if I can find anything? Then you come back to mine and pick up the stuff. Maybe stay over? You don't want to go back down tonight, do you?'

'Er cheers, yeah OK, but I will go back tonight. The traffic will be better than in the morning. But I'll drop by after I've been to Brenda's.'

'Brenda?'

'Yeah, the woman Julie was staying with. I phoned her earlier. She was really lovely. She said Julie was special.'

'Well she was, mate.'

'*Is* Jim—she's not dead yet.'

43

Ellie was supposed to be resting. She lay on the bed for a while staring at the ceiling, and then got up and started walking around the flat pretending to tidy things up, even though she had already watched Moira and Izzy have a tidying-Ellie's-flat competition.

'Lie down,' Izzy said.

'Why?' said Ellie.

'I don't bloody know, it feels like you should.'

The doorbell rang. 'Shall I?' said Moira. Ellie nodded distractedly. At the door was a large man, breathing heavily and looking nervous.

'Hello,' said Moira.

'Hello ... Ellie?'

'No.'

'Oh. Is she in?'

'Who are you?'

'Ah, my name's Dave, I'm a mate of Gabe's.'

'Dave?' said Ellie, 'Gabe's talked about you—come in, I've been trying to get through to your place for ages but nobody answers the phone.'

'My place?'

'Work.'

'Oh right,' Dave looked embarrassed. 'Where's Gabe?'

Ellie stared at him.

'There was an accident; Gabriel died yesterday,' said Moira.

'Why haven't you been in touch?' asked Izzy.

'What?'

'He hasn't been at work for eight days and nobody has called. Aren't you supposed to be his friend?'

'Dead?'

'Yes,' said Ellie. 'He was hit by a car over a week ago in Shoreditch, on his way home.'

'Shoreditch?'

'I don't know what he was doing there; he told me he was covering something ... but ... I don't know why he was covering it in Shoreditch. He had bagels with him, my favourite. I think he felt guilty about working late. He was working late, right?' Her eyes began to burn.

'He had been with me,' said Dave. He sat down. He had turned white. He looked up at Ellie and then back down at the carpet. 'And he was trying to work. I'm so sorry, so so sorry.'

'What do you mean he was "trying to work"?'

'Look,' said Dave 'The last thing he said to me ... . Dead? Oh fuck. I'm so sorry, and you ... with the IVF ...' And big Dave started to cry. Ellie sat down beside him, put her arms round him and cried too. The two strangers leaned on each other, sobbing.

'Anyone want a cup of tea?' said Sam, emerging from the kitchen.

Dave looked up. 'Sam! Sam knew.'

Everyone looked at Sam.

'Knew what?' snapped Izzy.

'Gabe asked me not to say anything. It wasn't an unreasonable request in the circumstances.' He looked at Ellie. 'And he was trying to do what seemed to be the right thing, despite the fact that he didn't want to do it.'

'What thing?' said Ellie.

'And when were you planning on saying something ... and why didn't you say anything to me at least, anyway?' snapped Izzy.

'Oh, shut up,' said Sam, who had decided in the face of dithering uncertainty simply to keep his word to his mate and hope that he would wake up.

Dave sighed. 'Look, the last thing he said to me was that he was going to come home and tell you the truth. When he didn't come into the new place I thought ... well ... "Spartacus." '

'What truth? Gabe never lied to me, never.'

'Yeah I know,' said Dave softly. 'That's why he said he had to tell you the truth.' And so Dave told Ellie everything about the redundancy, the desperate attempt to get work, and even slipped in that he had lost his second 'job' in a fortnight for lamping the editor, finishing by saying sheepishly 'He, Gabe I mean, didn't want to do it, but he ... you know ... loved yer.'

44

Gabriel was in his room, sitting on the edge of his bed, staring at the floor. Even the angels couldn't do much about the feeling in his chest, the one that ran down to his stomach and made him feel riddled with the pain that exists only to remind people that they had the very thing he had lost.

He may in time, who knows how long, get to the multitude of conflicts screaming at him from the last stage of his life. How he was promised a 'chance' by the kind of folk who one would expect to keep their promises, yet didn't really get that chance. How the very thing he longed for, a chance to go back and see Ellie, was given to a murdering scumbag. A murdering scumbag, incidentally, who not only killed him but was actually in the same room as Ellie, near her, spoke to her, and didn't even give her a message.

How did that happen? How on earth did *he* get time off? Was this ground leave only available to professional killers? Doesn't the life you lead matter, even if there is a God in heaven?

These thoughts swirled around the middle of Gabriel's mind, struggling like drowning cats to get to the surface. But they couldn't get past Ellie. He would never see Ellie again, or touch her, or smell her, and he would never make a baby with her. And if there were any advantages to being dead, surely they should be that he couldn't feel this burning pain, but he did.

In fact, from Gabriel's perspective, and he saw it clearly as he sat on a motel bed under heaven, it was clear that this wasn't a bus stop on the way to eternity. It wasn't part of God's modernisation programme and it wasn't a chance to turn himself into a better man. He was in hell, and there was nothing he could do about it. And it wasn't just any old hell either, he wasn't just getting prodded with hot sticks or performing sexual favours for the evil dead. This was a very specific hell, personal and perfectly constructed in every detail. He stood up and kicked the foot of the bed. It really bloody hurt. All this, and bruising too? Hell.

Two or three years ago, he and Ellie went to Brighton for the day. They had, even then, joked occasionally about one day moving down there—with the rest of London—and raising a family. They spent the day ambling around the Lanes and sitting on the beach. They went on the pier and had a go on the ghost train and the roller coaster. He threw bean bags at tin cans (5 times, £2 a throw) to win her a scraggly-looking stuffed toy worth 70 pence. They drank wine on the beach and watched the sun go down, and walked back through the town the long way so they didn't lose sight of the sea until the very last minute.

It was one of those days that felt as natural as breathing. It didn't feel 'get out the camcorder' special, you didn't run around like a puppy on amphetamines, you didn't dribble nonsense about happiness or life or love. You hardly noticed you were living; you just lived. But when he looked back, that day became a touchstone. It may have been one of the last carefree days he had had before the infertility and all it brought with it became overwhelming. It may have been the landscape: sunset, sea, lots of smiling, relaxed people strolling around in linen, and the balmy evening air that smelt of sea salt and sweet crepes from the pier. Or it may have been the togetherness. No greater than any other day but clearer to see, and in retrospect so easy.

They got to the station just in time to see their train leave. They smiled and bought coffee. There are few occasions in anyone's life when missing a train doesn't matter—this was one of theirs. They drank coffee and chatted about what it would take to live by the sea. Jobs obviously, a house they could afford, but there is nothing to be gained from worrying about the realities of modern life when you want to bathe in the luxury of choice, so they shrugged about work and vaguely talked about commuting, or starting a business, or stumbling into well-paid undemanding work that nobody else wanted.

Two youngish men were singing and laughing in the middle of the station. Drunk enough to stand out but not so drunk that they were about to fall over. Their sense of abandon grew alongside the delusion that they were entertaining. They shouted half-heartedly at a couple of women as they passed, edging perhaps toward the point where they would feel offended that the rest of Brighton had not drunk a litre of cheap sherry at the railway station.

Gabriel half watched the men, aware of their presence and the irritating unpredictability it offered. He saw the thin, short young man skip-walking across the concourse. Tight cream top, pale jeans; pristine, pretty, and camp. As he drew nearer the drunks, one of them wolf-whistled, the other laughed and started to mince around like John Humphries.

'Oh, do fuck off,' said the young man without even pausing, and they should have laughed—in fact the mincing drunk nearly did—but his friend had instead gone in a different direction. 'What did you say?'

'I said fuck off. What are you deaf, stupid, *and* fucking ugly?'

'Come here, you cunt!' the drunk shouted: loud, unbridled anger from out of nowhere. He started to walk toward the gay man, who of course should have carried on walking, not even looked back. But he stopped and turned.

'Oh dear,' said Gabriel.

The drunks walked forward and, without thinking, Gabriel got up and walked toward them. Ellie followed. Gabriel managed to get between the drunks and the thin man, who was by now shaking. Gabriel smiled. 'Let it go fellers, eh?'

They both slowed. 'What has it got to do with you?'

'Nothing, except I don't want to watch a couple of blokes hit another bloke. I've had a lovely day and I don't want to see him get hurt or you two arrested.' All the time Gabriel was smiling, almost shrugging.

Everyone paused. And then the angry drunk laughed, and so did his friend. Stepping back from angry to amiable the way only a drunk can. 'Fair enough, have a nice evening, young fella,' aimed at the gay man standing with Ellie. 'And you too mate,' he nodded at Gabriel. And they walked toward the exit, and the nearest off licence. Gabriel turned and smiled at Ellie.

'Fecking homophobes,' said the slightly shaking man, younger than he had previously looked. Gabriel shrugged, still smiling. 'I'd go a different way to them, if I were you.'

'I'm not scared,' he said, sounding scared.

Ellie kissed Gabriel on the cheek, put her arm through his, and guided them both toward the coffee shop. 'My hero,' she whispered in as mocking a way as she could muster.

There were times when Gabriel had done the right thing but toward the end, when he looked at his life, he couldn't see them.

Now he was thinking about what had got him here. They had never been specific about his failings, but he had long been full of them anyway. His misanthropy, his disengagement, his cowardice. He had become a fearful man. Of course, what he should have been punished for was not loving Ellie well enough. For having at the heart of his life a woman he adored and who loved him right back. But life is never that simple. It should be, he had told himself many times that it should be, but it isn't. He had thought of the infertility as a test, but the test became a punishment and finally some kind of symbol, and how useful are those these days? He had railed against his lack of power, but in truth before now he had never known what it was to be powerless.

Well, he thought, there is always something you can do. It may be pointless, it may not affect anything, but you can always do something, if only to prove you are still there. Or at least had been once. So he went to the bathroom, opened the adequately stocked cabinet and took out the spray-on deodorant. I've never liked these, he thought. Murder on the ozone layer.

45

When James finally arrived at home, Michael had jumped out of the car and straight into his own. As Michael pulled away, James was standing in the drive, waving like an overcaffeinated holiday rep. 'You come on back after you've got the stuff and I'll have anything of Julie's I can find all ready for you!'

Bizarrely, when Michael pulled up at her cottage, Brenda was waiting at the open front door. She walked down the garden path to the gate and was smiling warmly at Michael before he got out of the car. Brenda was a short, stout woman in a lemon dress and a black cardigan; she looked as though she might once have been in the military, her short, permed ash-grey hair was moulded to her head and she stood erect and alert as Michael got out of the car.

'Hello, Michael,' she said softly. 'Come inside and have a cup of tea. I expect you want to get back to London quite quickly.' Which could have sounded as if she'd like him out of her house as fast as he could manage, but didn't. Instead it felt to him as though she understood.

'A cup of tea would be lovely, thank you.' Michael had to duck through the front door. Inside, the hallway was narrow and dark. He followed Brenda into an immaculate small living room. It wasn't overly furnished: a two-seater sofa that looked like nobody had sat on it since the '50s, a matching chair, a small desk, and two bookcases on either side of an old-fashioned, still-working fireplace. Above the bookcases were two paintings. Michael stared at them: they were both of Julie.

They weren't bad; hell, he could tell they were Julie. He wondered if she posed for them before going to London. He looked more closely. Brenda was quite good: one of them in particular captured something about Julie. She had her head turned slightly sideways, and the beginnings of a smile were on her lips. Julie's eyes were closed. Like she was having a pleasant dream.

Brenda came back in with tea and a plate of assorted biscuits.

'Good likeness,' Michael said.

'It's hard, but one must persevere,' said Brenda.

'Quite,' said Michael. 'I was rubbish at art at school.' They both carried on looking at the pictures. 'Was Julie a good teacher?'

'She was lovely,' said Brenda, without answering the question. 'We all loved her instantly. She was very respectful of our own varying abilities, and that to me is what a teacher of people of my generation should be.'

They sipped their tea, still staring at the wall. There was a ticking clock on the mantelpiece that served to slow down time and made Michael too self-conscious to have a custard cream.

'Would you like to see some more?'

'Oh yes, of course,' said Michael.

'Follow me,' said Brenda.

They left the living room and went next door to what might once have been the dining room. Light streamed in through the French doors that almost filled the back wall. In the centre of the room was an easel, beside it an old two-leafed dining table covered in newspaper. On the easel was another picture of Julie. On the table, lying beside a box with paint and some brushes, were three, four ... six more pictures of Julie. All with her eyes closed. Michael scanned the room. There was a small armchair in the corner with a cat asleep on the back and two, maybe three more pictures of Julie on it. On the floor beside the table there were two more. Michael thought he had strayed into 'The Wicker Man.'

'None of them are quite right,' offered Brenda. She seemed perplexed by this.

'Well full marks for trying,' said Michael. 'Er, did she pose for these?'

'Good lord no, I did them after I heard about the accident.'

'Right.'

'The police found this address in her bag; they came round that night. I was so upset. I sat up all night. In the morning I went into her room. I didn't like to, I respected her privacy and she came here for—well, sanctuary, in a way, and I wanted to respect that, but I decided that I couldn't help her if I didn't go into her room.'

'Help her?' Michael felt a little anxiety creep into him. He walked over to one of the pictures and lightly touched the corner of the thick dry paper.

'Yes. I needed to get a sense of how she was feeling before the accident, where she was in her life. So I sat in her room all morning, looked at her things, tried to soak up the atmosphere. She hadn't been here long, only about two hours, but I have known her for a while.' Brenda paused and looked into Michael's eyes. 'It feels like I've known her for a very long time indeed.'

Michael thought about how he might change the subject, but before he could Brenda had followed him across the room to the painting and was standing so close it made him step sideways and bump his leg on a small coffee table.

'Do you think she was happy the last time you saw her?' she said. She spoke with a clipped authority, as if she was used to giving orders and used to having her questions answered. But she retained enough gentleness, or so Michael felt, to stop anyone from commenting on her tone. She sounded, he thought, like a policewoman.

'Yes, yes I do.'

'Do you think that maybe that was because of you? At least in part.'

'I'd like to think so.' He had not articulated to himself what Julie might have thought or felt about him. He had been rather overwhelmed by the fact that he had found himself feeling so full of her. But he did suppose she was moved in some way by him. He felt it in the café; if he had been honest or at least attentive, he had felt it when he had been at James's house on lots of occasions. He had dismissed the flirting and the directness of their conversation as being playful but somewhere he 'knew' it was more than that.

'So would I. Shall we paint?' And Brenda started to take paints out of the paint box and line them up on the table. Michael looked nervous. Not just about the threatened art lesson, but also about the mad woman who kept painting Julie.

'Er, I'm not really much for painting.'

Brenda turned and looked at him. 'When did you last try?'

'I don't know.'

'Quite.'

Michael watched as Brenda took her painting from the easel and placed it on the ever-growing Julie pile. She put a fresh piece of paper up, picked up a brush, and handed it to him.

'Brenda, I don't want to paint.' He put the brush down firmly on the coffee table he had just bumped into.

'Oh, but you must.'

'Why.'

'Because it will help.'

'Help what?'

'Help Julie.'

'How? How will me, painting badly in Norfolk, help Julie?' Michael was exasperated now. More, he was frightened. He didn't know how this little old lady with the mad ideas and the houseful of portraits could do him harm, although it was possible she had drugged the tea. But he was anxious anyway and he wanted to leave. In fact he wanted to run, but that would not help Julie either, not unless he ran via her bedroom upstairs.

Brenda looked at him. She didn't say anything at first, just invited him to look into her eyes, pale grey and watery, challenging him to find some lunacy, inviting him in. She put the brush down on the table and said softly, 'I'm sorry, this must seem like madness to you.' Which is a disarming thing to hear from a mad person. 'Look,' said Brenda. 'How can Julie live, if we can't imagine her living?'

Michael stared at her. Her voice, which had been nearly severe in its efficiency a few moments ago, was soft; her eyes moist. 'I think of Julie all the time. I remember her here, and the spring in her step after she came back from seeing you, and I think of her in that hospital bed all wired up ...'

'There aren't really all that many wires ...' offered Michael.

'But I can't see her with her eyes open. And I thought, well, I can pray. And I do believe. But if I can't imagine her being awake, then being awake must be a long way away. Do you see?'

Michael didn't understand remotely what the old woman was saying, but he could see that she meant it, whatever it was. Instinctively he took her hand, and said, quietly, 'How about we go through Julie's things? Do you know, I have never been in any room that has just been hers. I'd really like, with your help, to see where she was going to sleep, maybe choose a few things to take back to London, and then we could sit together while you paint, and just talk?'

Brenda stared at him blankly, then nodded. 'OK, let's do that,' she whispered. 'But remember that while the odds are I am quite insane,' she opened her eyes widely and shook her head, 'quite, quite insane, you, young man, don't actually believe in anything right now. Nothing. And if there is a one in a million, even one in a billion chance that humouring a tweedy old girl in the country might help the woman you were meant to meet in this lifetime to live again, then it's you who would be completely mad to turn that chance down, wouldn't you?'

46

Bernie and Gary Guitar had spent two and a half hours approaching the Dartford Tunnel the way a lion approaches a gazelle: slowly, very slowly. They were in Bernie's VW Golf. Gary had been planning to buy a car, something big and German probably, but as he never had anywhere to go, he hadn't got round to it. He wasn't comfortable in the Golf and he wasn't comfortable in the traffic jam.

When Dog in a Tuba were a proper band, Bernie quite liked Gary, albeit mainly because he didn't cause him too many problems. As long as he had some cough linctus and his plectrums and, for a while, Alice, he was happy. Gary on the other hand came to resent the fact that Bernie gave James so much more attention than him, reasoning the way the average ten-year-old does that bad behaviour really shouldn't be so readily rewarded. Gary kept his resentment to himself, although when Bernie called after Gary made it big in America he was slow to call back. He didn't want Bernie asking for any work or anything.

But all that was in the past, now they were just two middle-aged blokes going to meet old friends in the country. Should they ever escape the M25.

'Where the fuck are all these people going?' asked Gary again.

'Where the fuck have they come from, you mean?' said Bernie. 'It's only a little country, overpopulated by people with cars.'

'Yeah, people with cars who want to go to Norwich.'

'Exactly, you are not going to tell me that everyone wants to go to Norwich. Nobody wants to go to fucking Norwich, or Chelmsford or whatever the hell else is up the M11. I tell you this is probably small fry. Just imagine what the traffic is like on the way to places that lots of people actually do want to go to.'

'Well, lots of people want to go to Norwich, Bern, I think.' Gary was tapping out a rhythm on his legs; he got louder whenever Bernie talked.

'Nah, it may feel busy Gary, but this won't even make it on to the traffic bulletins. This is normal. That's what I'm saying.'

'Right. What are you saying, Bern?' Gary tapped and as Bernie began talking, Gary hummed quietly.

'I'm saying that if you could see right round the country now you'd probably find this kind of tailback on the M6, the M1, the lead-up to the Blackwell Tunnel, the M62. All probably chocka.'

'Is that up near Liverpool?'

'Yeah.'

'Fuck off, won't even be a queue coming out of Liverpool.'

'Why not?'

'Everyone would have had their cars nicked.' Gary laughed at his own joke and played his thighs with a flourish.

'Nah I'm serious, Gary, this queue here is probably nothing compared to the rest of the country. Our little island is too full.'

'Maybe, or maybe it's just too full of people with cars.'

'Same thing.'

'It isn't.'

And so it continued for two and a half hours. By the time Bernie and Gary were on the M11, they pretty much hated everything on the planet, including each other.

Meanwhile Alice, Matthew and the Reverend Adam Aldanack were at a service station near Cambridge, trying far too hard to make a dull journey interesting.

'Have you ever stolen anything?' asked Adam smiling. He was usually smiling. It made him feel serene.

'Er no, I don't think I have,' said Matthew. Matthew had driven the BMW X5 and had insisted on stopping. They were in a Costa Coffee sipping lattes.

'Maybe we should,' said Alice excitedly.

'Why would we do that? We're rich.'

'For the thrill,' Alice whispered loudly. Alice, it was fair to say, had embraced the Church of Three Gods and its message to live life as fully as possible with the enthusiasm she once reserved for cocaine. Matthew looked around. They were in a motorway service area. The most soulless place in England. The magazine shop sold some stuffed toys, some coloured mugs with names on them, and a lot of sweets.

'Do we need any coloured mugs, I wonder?'

'Oh Matthew stop being so ... so...'

'Frightened?' suggested Adam.

'It isn't fear so much as ... well, it's a silly thing to do. Pointless.'

'Oh honey ...' purred Alice. 'There's a mug over there with my name on it.'

47

Michael didn't believe in a lot of things. God, astrology, performance art, crystal healing, the impartiality of the BBC, reflexology and aqua-aerobics, for a start. He was a polite sceptic. He was too mellow a man to make a big song-and-dance about not believing in things that others might love (God) or enjoy (aqua-aerobics), and so he kept his beliefs to himself unless of course he was stuck for something to write about for a magazine that didn't care how it filled the spaces round the adverts as long as it filled them. Then he'd wheel out disdain and call it wit as willingly as the next man.

However, he was at heart a man who believed mainly in what he saw. And what he had seen at Brenda's house was a woman who believed in a whole realm of possibilities that he had never remotely entertained. A pile of mumbo-jumbo rubbish. At its heart was the belief that they—together—could paint Julie awake. It was, he thought, like straying into someone's dreams. But while that was what he thought, it wasn't what he felt. Brenda had said quite clearly that he might consider her mad and that he might be right, but in a world like this one, where so much that passed as knowing was just guessing or hoping, what difference could it make to humour her? And she said it with a gentle smile on her face and held his gaze as she spoke.

He didn't know what to do. Part of him—the part that thought she was two tokens short of a pop-up toaster—thought it best if he played along. He did, after all, need Julie's stuff. But there was a tiny part of him slightly mesmerised by the idea of sitting in that tiny cottage painting Julie as though she were awake. Therapy, he decided; he needed it as therapy. He wasn't proud of the fact that he had needs when he wasn't the one in the coma, but that didn't mean he didn't have them. Sitting with Brenda and painting quietly whilst she talked about the Julie she knew made him feel better, and so did the paintings he now had sitting in the back of the car. Anyway, given that he had got through the last few years by sleeping with people without knowing their second name, this might even constitute progress.

Brenda had talked about Julie as they painted. She told him that the Julie she knew was quite reserved when she first started teaching at the day centre. When they had asked her questions about herself she had avoided them and they had experienced this as shyness bordering on coldness. But after a few weeks one of the older men told them about the cancer in his liver, as he painted a carefully constructed pile of books. He said that he wasn't afraid of dying, but he was worried about his wife who he felt needed looking after. He talked about her maybe finding someone else after he had gone and he seemed sad as he did it.

Julie asked him how old his wife was and he said 'Seventy-nine. Eighty next month.' And Julie laughed. Brenda said that to her credit, even though everyone looked at her she didn't seem embarrassed to be laughing.

'How long have you been married?' she asked. Fifty-eight years he said. And Julie said that she didn't imagine his wife would look for someone else because she wouldn't need to, and she explained that she was in her mid-thirties and living with a man she didn't remotely like and wondering if she would ever meet someone that she wanted to be with for ten years, let alone sixty. And Brenda said that Julie smiled at the old man and said with an unusual honesty, 'I would give twenty years of life—and I believe in life—to be able to die knowing the sort of love you have.'

And after that, she seemed far more relaxed. It turned out that she had been told not to talk too much about herself, as it would be considered 'unprofessional.' As Julie later joked, 'they don't actually pay me enough to be able to call me a professional.'

He did feel calmer. When he had left James's house, all he could think was that he needed to get to Brenda's, be polite, pick up Julie's stuff, back to James's, grab anything James had found, and get back to London. But he'd stayed at Brenda's for more than four hours. He had picked up a few clothes: a green cardigan that smelt so much of Julie he insisted on putting it on the seat beside him; some pictures from when she was travelling, and a lot of her music. Some Nick Cave and Paul Quinn and the Independent Group, which was in her CD player, so she must have been listening to it before she left. And some old compilation tapes that, because they were tapes, made him think they might remind her of someone or something from a long time ago. From when she was conscious.

As he drove toward James's house, he tried to imagine anything that might exist in the world that could appeal to whatever senses were currently available to Julie. What might James have found? And then he reminded himself that this was James he was thinking about. Lynne had said that 'when Julie leaves, she leaves.' She probably wouldn't have left anything at James's house.

Michael asked himself how he would feel if he didn't go back. Guiltlessly relieved was the answer. Although he had spent more time up here than he had planned, he had got what he had come for, and more besides. He could phone James from London. He lightly touched the green cardigan, put the Paul Quinn CD on, and headed for the A11. James would be fine.

And at that point James was. He'd unthinkingly rolled a fat joint as soon as he had got home and put his head round the door to what had been Julie's room to confirm his impression that there was nothing left. He ambled downstairs smoking and went to the CDs. There were three or four that must have been Julie's.

Belle and Sebastian, Mazzy Star, Tompaulin. Ridiculous names; no wonder they didn't have any hits. He would give these to Mikey, he wouldn't miss them.

His joint had gone out. He grabbed some matches as he went through the kitchen and into the barn. It was a mess, the big rusty metal barrels took up more space then he'd noticed, and they smelled. The smell made his eyes water.

No matter, he thought. Soon everyone would be here and it wouldn't look or feel like a barn. It would become a studio. James lit his joint and inhaled deeply. The smoke ran up behind his eyes, made the inside of his head foggy. When everyone was here, it would all be OK; it would all fall nicely into place.

48

Ellie stared at the ceiling, her hand on her stomach. She could smell something, a staleness. Unwashed clothes maybe, dirty air perhaps. She hadn't opened the windows for days. But the smell suited her; she didn't want it to go away.

The thing about love, one of the things about love, is that it arms you against your failures. There are those who think that the cloud-stopping, breath-catching, blood-freezing love that charges every cell of your body fades in time, into something like companionship or, worse, forgetful surrender. Ellie didn't believe that was true. She knew the clouds started moving again and her blood thawed; she knew that if it hadn't, nothing would ever happen. But that didn't mean it wasn't the same love. The feeling she found herself with after that first weekend with Gabe, which was still messing around with her ability to function properly when they first went on holiday and when they first moved in together—that feeling was still there. There had been times when she wished it wasn't, and she thought about them now. But she knew those times would do her no good: they didn't before, why would they now? After all, what kind of person wishes away love?

He had gone away for a weekend a few months ago. Ostensibly to see his mum in Spain, but it felt to her like he was offering her some time. A chance to see if she missed him. She thought it was a reasonable thing to do and she accepted it with grace. She felt quite clinical about it. She arranged to go out for a drink with Izzy and Moira, but she didn't fill the whole weekend. She wanted to rattle around in the flat, listen to her own music, watch her own trash on TV without either having to compromise or listen to Gabe commentate on the inanity of 'Strictly Come Dancing.'

The first evening was nice: she stayed in and watched a film, went to bed late and read. The next morning was fine: she messed around at home, tidying and playing old Smiths CDs and listening to Radio 4. The afternoon was good too: a film, a wander round the shops, home for a bath, and out to meet the girls.

That was when his absence began to unnerve her, and then slowly make her feel incomplete. Izzy was talking rubbish, Moira was encouraging her by arguing, and Ellie's soul began to itch. When she lay in bed that night, she thought about what she was missing. The familiarity? Someone to dissect the day with? Surely not the sarcasm or the irritability. It might, she thought, have been the 'old' Gabe who she was missing, even though that Gabe hadn't been around for a while. She wondered if maybe the possibility of him—the man she had fallen in love with—was closer when the shell he had formerly occupied, but lent to the grumpy bastard currently calling himself her boyfriend, was in the house? But even as she thought, and even as she grew annoyed at the bloke not occupying the empty space beside her, she knew that it was Gabriel she missed. In all his misery.

Sometimes, if you are lucky, you find yourself with someone—and they may be an annoying sod—who simply fits. Gabe and Ellie fitted. And if she thought about how life without that might be now that he was dead, she would want to die too, so she didn't. Her instincts told her to think about Gabriel the liar, to think that the tie that bound them had been broken before he died, and that somehow she had less to mourn. But what kind of lie was it? A simple 'I want to make it OK' lie, more despairing than deceitful. A lie that lasted only minutes, before he knew he would have to tell the truth. If he had come home, she'd have shouted at him, complained about feeling patronised, chided him with the 'we are doing this together aren't we Gabe' line that she had said before he'd gone out. But she wouldn't have loved him less. She didn't love him less now either. Damn, she probably loved him more. Death can do that.

She rested her hands on her stomach, closed her eyes, and thought about Lola and Luca. She breathed deeply. In a way, she thought, Gabriel isn't quite dead yet. She thought it the way people think things they aren't convinced by: like trying on a dress that someone else says will suit you, but you think looks like a curtain wrapped around a wriggling pig. You are hopeful but disbelieving. But this dress looked OK. As long as the embryos were living inside her, he wasn't quite dead; not completely.

She knew, vaguely, what she was doing: lying, tricking her head into concentrating on her body. And it might have been a kind of madness, but it seemed to help her breathe. The way the strangest things can when your life is collapsing around you. And so she patted her stomach and imagined Gabriel willing her on. Her and the small collection of cells that might find a way to live. Ellie fell asleep like that. She didn't dream.

49

Gabriel came in last. He didn't look at Christopher or Clemitius. He didn't look at anyone; he just sat down and stared at the floor in the middle of the circle.

Clemitius waited for a moment. 'I want to say something.'

Gabriel carried on staring at the floor. Yvonne looked at Julie and then at the wall behind her. Julie looked at Christopher, then Yvonne, then Gabriel, and last at her feet. Only Christopher and Kevin looked at the puffy-lipped angel.

Clemitius continued. 'I'd like to say that I think we can still work here. I didn't before, or at least I wasn't convinced. But I've thought about it, about the way some of you … well, most of you, have behaved, and I think that what you have done is not disconnected from why you are here. Impulsive perhaps, distracted, ill-disciplined some might say.' He paused. Nobody was arguing; perhaps nobody was even listening. Mostly they were gazing into space. Except Kevin, who stared attentively at Clemitius like a zealous PA. Or a puppy.

'It is all work for us to commit to. It is all symptomatic of whatever brought you here—the lack of focus, perhaps. The inability to establish a perspective, or a worldview if you like, that would enable you to have lived as you could have. I'd like to suggest something if I may. I'd like to suggest that you are trying to distract yourselves from the work that deep down you know you have to do. That you, Gabriel, your concern about Ellie masks your deeper concern about yourself. Julie, that your guilt about running Gabriel over masks your guilt over a life that has been unfulfilled, and you, Yvonne, your denial—well, your denial is perhaps symptomatic of the denial you have lived with for years.' Clemitius nodded sagely, his dry lips folded inward, proudly nestling against his teeth.

Yvonne smiled to herself but didn't say anything. Julie looked at Christopher again and, as he turned to face her, she quietly shook her head.

Kevin hadn't taken his eyes off Clemitius. When he was sure Clemitius had finished, he spoke. 'I've said from the beginning that I am here to work.'

'Why?' Gabriel asked immediately. 'Why are you willing to work?'

'Because,' Kevin was half laughing, he seemed happier than he had been before. 'A power greater then me says I should.'

'Who? What? God? Or that psychotic angel over there?'

'I can assure you I am not psychotic,' Clemitius smiled.

'Well if you are, you'd be the last to know, wouldn't you? Anyway I'm asking Kevin the Killer a question, so if you don't mind ...'

Kevin looked at Clemitius. Clemitius nodded.

'That's the spirit, let him off the leash,' sneered Gabriel.

'You seem even more aggressive than usual this morning, Gabriel. I wonder if there is anything we can do to help you with that?' said Clemitius.

Gabriel lowered his head and raised his hand to his face as though he were sheltering his eyes from the sun. He slipped his other hand into his jacket and seemed to be almost hugging himself, his shoulders hunched, curled up slightly like a child afraid of being hit. For a moment Christopher, ever the watcher, ever the protector, thought he might be crying. Christopher felt something. Disappointment? Embarrassment? He looked at Julie, who was sitting upright and staring enquiringly at Gabriel.

Gabriel raised his head and smiled; no tears. There did appear to be something in his hand. He stood up.

'Oh for goodness sake, Gabriel, leaving so soon? This really is a habit you need to address,' said Clemitius.

Gabriel took two steps into the middle of the room; a thin can was in his right hand, behind his back. He turned to Clemitius. He may have been shaking. 'I'm not going anywhere, as you well know.' Gabriel pointed the deodorant at Kevin and sprayed him in the eyes.

It was only an anti-perspirant, Christopher was guessing, something icy-fresh. It wasn't some kind of nerve gas. Kevin was never going to roll around screaming that his face was melting. At best it left his head smelling nicer and an annoying taste in his mouth. Perhaps because it made his eyes sting a little, it stopped him from standing up quickly and breaking Gabriel's head, but the delay would only be about four seconds. Hardly worth it, one might think, yet it was time enough for Gabriel to take a two-step run-up to land a right uppercut to Kevin's jaw that sent him tumbling backwards in the chair.

Clemitius went to speak but didn't, perhaps assuming that Gabriel was finished and a natural pause would occur after this unprecedented brutality.

But Gabriel hadn't finished. He walked quickly past the tipped-over chair to the stunned and flailing Kevin and kicked him in the ribs. Twice. Kevin was unbalanced, but the pain in his ribs didn't compare with the pain in his jaw; Gabriel seemed to realise this, because as Kevin rolled backward from the kicks to the ribs, Gabriel landed an almighty kick to the side of his head.

Yvonne let out a little scream; Julie gripped her chair but didn't make a noise. Kevin's head jerked backward and his arms, which had been trying to lever him upward, collapsed under him. He lay on the floor groaning and bleeding.

Clemitius went to speak again but Gabriel turned to him and raised his finger. He then kicked Kevin in the head seven or eight, maybe nine times. He was never going to kill him— not here—but that had to hurt like hell. Then he turned to Christopher and said quietly. 'Tell them. Please. Tell them.'

So Christopher did.

50

It had occurred to James that he should not look too eager when the rest of the band started to arrive. However, when Gary and Bernie pulled up, he was standing outside the barn with his second joint of the day in his hand, grinning like a daytime TV host.

'Guys, glad you could make it,' he drawled, grinning in a way that suggested he might hug someone. Nobody likes to be greeted by a drooling, middle-aged dopehead, particularly when they have just taken nearly five hours to drive 87 miles.

'Call this a farm?' muttered Gary, uncoiling himself from the car.

'Good trip, Gary?' James was too stoned to be sarcastic.

'I've been trapped in a small car with a Christian fundamentalist for half a fucking day. Of course it wasn't a good trip.'

'Didn't hear you complaining when I was paying for the petrol, you mid-Atlantic plonker,' said Bernie.

'Well, you're here now,' nodded James inanely. A long silence followed. 'Wanna come into the house, drop your bags and have a drink? The others will be here soon.'

The three men went into the house. Gary went straight over to the fireplace and stared up at James's blue poster. 'Cool, isn't it,' smiled James.

'It's a poster, you ponce,' sneered Gary. 'What are you, fifteen?'

A car pulled up in the drive.

'Could be Mikey,' mumbled the grinning James, who was beginning to resemble Keith Chegwin.

Outside, Alice and Adam the minister were getting out of their Mercedes. 'Hey hey hey,' said James. 'Great to see you! But where—where's Matthew?'

'He, er ... got arrested at the Happy Eater,' said Alice.

'What for?' asked Bernie.

'Shoplifting,' said Adam, smiling.

'Shoplifting? I thought you lot were rich?' said Gary.

'He was doing it for the thrill,' said Alice, looking embarrassed.

'What was he stealing?'

'A mug. A mug with my name on it.'

James had stopped grinning. 'Well, we can't have a reunion without Matthew.'

'He'll be along later, I expect. I mean, how long do they hold people for shoplifting?'

Everyone stood in the courtyard, trying not to look at each other. Finally Adam said, 'Well is anyone going to introduce me to ... hey, you're Gary Guitar, you're in Karma. I love your stuff man. Can I ask you, are you religious?'

Gary shuffled his feet, pleased to be recognised. He was about to say something but James spoke first. 'Come on, let's all have a drink and I'll show you the studio ... well, rehearsal room really, but we can use it as a studio too.'

Inside, James made drinks for everyone. Bernie had orange juice; everyone else had something with vodka in it. Large ones. James rolled another joint and to his surprise Adam smoked most of it before passing it on to Alice. Adam was telling everyone how many times he had seen Gary and Karma play. And Gary was telling behind-the-scenes stories from each of the gigs Adam mentioned. None of the stories were very interesting so James made more drinks, this time with more vodka, and rolled another joint. It did cross his mind that he was using up a lot of grass but he decided it was an investment. This time he passed it to Gary first, which prompted Adam to take a bag from his inside pocket, open it out on the table in front of him, and say, 'Anyone want one of these?'

'What are they?' asked Gary.

'E's are good,' grinned Adam.

Gary thought for a moment. 'Not got any cough medicine in them, have they?'

Two hours later Alice's phone rang. It was Matthew. The good news was they had let him off with a warning. She passed on the news as if reporting the relief of Mafeking. Everyone was very happy that he was free: Gary and Bernie hugged in celebration; Adam said a little prayer and had a big swig of vodka. The bad news was that Matthew was in Newmarket with no car. Bernie cried. Gary comforted him. James made more drinks. Matthew said not to worry, he'd get a train. Everyone cheered on re-discovering the existence of a rail network and their gallant friend's ability to problem-solve. He said he might be some time. Bernie got a bit a teary again. James rolled another joint and found himself staring at Alice's denim-clad crotch. There is nothing like recreational drugs for rekindling old friendships.

It was dark by the time they staggered toward the barn. Michael's absence had been noted but lost in the fumes and happiness the drugs had proffered. 'He'll be along later,' said James confidently.

The barn was cold and damp. It smelled of manure and something like almonds, which made Gary's eyes water. 'What's that smell?' asked Bernie.

'Rock 'n' roll!' shouted James.

'Nah, it's not,' said Gary, tapping one of the barrels that were stacked against the longest wall. 'What's in here?'

'Dunno,' said James, who was looking at Alice's arse. 'I just store some stuff for a mate; well, neighbour, really. He ran out of storage.' He wandered over to Alice. 'So, how long did Matthew say he'd be?'

Alice giggled. 'He didn't,' she smiled, and picked up his hand, taking the matches he was carrying from him, and putting them on one of the barrels. 'I'll tell you what though '—eyes wide, so close he could taste her breath.

'What?'

She ran his hand down to the zipper on her jeans, held it there for a moment and then pushed it away. 'Doesn't matter how long he is, you ain't getting in there,' she said, and laughed.

'Right,' said James. 'That's for religious persons only, is it?'

But Alice had already turned away. James picked up his matches to light another joint. Bernie was looking at the equipment. 'It doesn't look like any of this stuff has been used for a while,' he noted.

'Who's surprised?' said Gary.

'Is this what studios always look like?' asked Adam.

'Is it, fuck!' said Gary. 'This is a barn with a tape recorder in it.'

'Bit more than that, Gary,' said James, whose joint had gone out again. He struck another match.

'Oh yeah, some amplifiers, a desk that looks like it was last used by Sigue Sigue Sputnik, and a drum. Oh no sorry, that isn't a drum is it? It's a barrel full of shit.'

'There's a bloody big puddle over here,' said Bernie. 'Right where the mike is. That can't be safe.'

'Where's the keyboard?' said Alice, for whom the drugs were wearing off.

'Where's the power?' said Gary.

'Is there any heating?' asked Bernie.

Adam had wandered over to the microphone and picked it up. He started singing into it. James couldn't hear what it was, but Alice was laughing. James drew on his joint. Dead again. He could hear Adam now; he was singing 'Every Breath You Take.' In tune, too, in so far as it had a tune. James inhaled. This was going to require a calm head, he thought, and patience. He couldn't rise to every little comment, he had got this far, and in a moment they'd set up. Adam was still singing, Gary and Alice were clapping along in time; Gary was even warbling some kind of harmony. Adam was swaying in Sting-like fashion, the bloody karaoke queen.

James nodded to himself. 'You see,' he thought. 'They've got the music in them'—before thinking, 'Hang on, I'm the fucking singer.'

He looked at his joint. Out again. He struck another match, lit the joint, and inhaled: instant calm. He flicked the match into the air and wondered, momentarily, if the puddle beside the barrel in which it was about to land was flammable.

It was.

51

Christopher was sitting in the watching room staring at the screen, trying not to wonder too much. On the screen was a tired-looking Ellie buttering toast. He heard the door open behind him, and he knew who it would be.

Peter sat down beside him quietly and looked at the screen. 'Her name is Ellie. She is the partner of Gabriel, the man in our group who ...' Christopher paused.

'Who beat up a fellow group member?' Christopher nodded. 'She is a lucky woman.'

Peter wasn't a cruel angel. Christopher had always trusted him, respected him, revered him. He believed that Peter had a serene even-handedness that one should be able to expect from someone in his position, yet seemed rare. He was tall and straight and perpetually calm. And he retained an ability to make Christopher nervous, had done for centuries. Christopher had never questioned his judgment about anything. But he had watched Ellie and seen Gabriel. And neither of them seemed to him to have been lucky. 'I don't think so,' Christopher said, looking ahead.

Peter sighed. 'There is no excuse for violence.'

'No.'

'And I understand that you have been less than...boundaried in your dealings with Gabriel. In fact, you have been unclear in communicating your role with just about all the members of this group.'

'I can see how you might think that.'

Peter turned to Christopher. His hooded eyes stretched as his eyebrows rose: more animation than the half-hearted therapist had ever seen from him.

'These boundaries,' Christopher said. 'They don't always help.'

'Without them things get confusing.'

'Sometimes things just are confusing. Boundaries don't stop them being confusing; they just make us feel in control.'

'That is naïve. The important thing is, and you know this is the case, you broke the rules.'

'I wasn't the only one.'

Peter looked disappointed and that made Christopher almost flinch with shame. He put his hand on Christopher's shoulder gently and whispered, 'I'm sorry.' He stood up. 'There is a meeting for everyone in the courtyard in an hour.' He stared down at his old friend, waiting for him to speak, but Christopher didn't think he had anything to say.

He could see that from a certain perspective it was all his fault. Not believing enough. Not simply doing his job. Therapists mediate; that is all he had to do, just let the process run through him and not burden it with whatever he felt. He had failed to do that. He knew that he had become involved in ordinary lives and worse, had been drawn into some kind of conflict with Clemitius at the expense of those ordinary lives.

If I had done nothing, if I had seen what Clemitius called the bigger picture, he thought, then Gabriel would probably still be clinging to life and Ellie could be clinging to Gabriel. Clemitius would not have strayed from the room he owned as therapist, if Christopher had not given him reason.

Christopher nodded slowly. It was his fault, or at least his responsibility.

Peter turned and walked slowly toward the door.

'Peter,' he said quietly. 'I'm sorry.'

'Are you?'

Christopher turned and looked at the old man waiting to leave. He had set off a chain of events by straying from the path—the last thing any angel should do. But there was no need to lie as well. He shook his head. 'Not really, no.'

273

Christopher looked back at the screen and thought of Gabriel, Gabriel as he had been in his hospital bed, with Ellie at the door and Kevin dressed as a nurse.

'How do we know,' he asked tentatively, staring at Gabriel on the screen in front of him and willing Peter not to open the door, 'that we are still doing good?'

52

Kevin hadn't needed an incentive, but Clemitius had given him one anyway.

'The Lord works in mysterious ways' mantra'd Clemitius. 'There are times when only someone with special skills can serve him.'

Gabriel was not engaging with the group in an appropriate way, Clemitius had reasoned, and whilst he seemed to have persuaded Christopher that the best way to help him with that was to show him the life he was no longer living, Clemitius knew better.

'I would like you to help him to die,' Clemitius said matter-of-factly, when Kevin was left alone at the dinner table. 'Could you do that? If you were back on Earth?'

'Of course,' Kevin had said, biting his lip and not saying 'It would be my pleasure.' But it was his pleasure.

'Just go to bed this evening and you will wake up in the hospital. The rest is up to you,' Clemitius had said.

Returning to life did not feel strange; Kevin had never had a firm enough grip on whatever reality he inhabited for a radical change to feel strange. He walked the corridors of the hospital and wondered if this killing might be more than a simple task, if it might prove to be his redemption. Perhaps some time tidying up bits of life that the angels were unhappy with would not just keep him out of hell, but would eventually lead him to heaven?

He didn't think about it too much of course, in case an all-knowing God noticed. And anyway, he didn't think too much generally.

He knew that if the regular staff found him on the ward they would ask him what he was doing, and so he waited. In the middle of the day—the time he had suggested to Clemitius when he had been asked when would be the appropriate time for him to 'do his thing'—all of the staff ending their shift met with the staff starting theirs for a handover. The ward was all but empty apart from a support worker and a student nurse. Kevin waited for them both to take someone to the toilet and slipped into Gabriel's room.

He felt nothing, looking at the man in the bed. The sallow, empty face. Gabriel's skin gleamed as if, unable to do anything else with him, the nurses had polished him like an apple. Kevin thought about smothering him with a pillow. He liked the idea because he wanted to feel whatever life was left in Gabriel leave through his hands. But he was, he reminded himself—despite being dead—still a professional.

There were two transparent tubes leading into Gabriel. One from a bag on a stand into his arm, the other from a machine into his chest. The one leading to his arm had a steady drip from the bag with a purple wheel at the point where the tube met the bag. Kevin turned the wheel and the drip accelerated. He turned it some more and it became a stream. He squeezed the bag hard and the stream became a steady flow.

He looked hard at Gabriel. He saw yellow skin wrapped around a man he had come to dislike. A man who kept reminding him not only why he did what he did for a living, but why he had spent his life on the outside of almost everything, even what people called human. Well, maybe now he was in the right place. Maybe now he was seeing what people meant when they talked about a 'grand plan'. He was part of something he had never imagined. And it even played to his strengths.

As he stared, he played with the purple wheel on the drip bag absentmindedly, turning it on and off and then full on again. He looked up and stared out of the window. London was grey; it looked like a painting and he hated paintings, and he might even have said something to the city if he had not heard Ellie come in.

She was pretty, he thought. Puffy round the face, especially the cheekbones, and she could use some make up, but quite pretty. 'I'll be back to check that in a while,' he said and turned away as he made for the door. It occurred to him that that was a clever thing to say. Authentic. And he wondered if he only ever said the right thing when he was killing people or if this was something that had happened to him since he had joined the angels.

Because in his mind, at that moment, that was what he had done: joined the angels.

53

It was nearly eight pm. when Michael finally got into central London. He had decided to go home rather than to see Julie, but when the time came to steer away from the hospital, he couldn't quite bring himself to do it. Instead he drove into the West End, parked up in Bloomsbury and found himself sitting in the car, listening to the end of a Nick Cave CD. He ejected it, put it in its case, and slipped it into the bag with the other stuff he had decided would constitute the first wave of nostalgia. As he did so the radio came on, and he distractedly listened to something on the news about an explosion in Norfolk: several people dead and the surrounding area being evacuated because of an ugly green toxic cloud that was making the sheep cough. Fire officers said the explosion could be seen as far away as Cambridge.

It didn't really register as significant; Michael's mind was elsewhere. Later he might shiver at the thought of what might have been, more likely still he might get drunk with Matthew and listen to his old friend curse fate, James Buchan and Adam Aldanack. But Michael would never be so dishonest as to imagine that any grief felt would belong to him. And these things, if they came, would come later.

He grabbed his bag and walked quickly toward the hospital. Of course, visiting hours were over, but the staff had been flexible and he was pretty sure that Lynne would be there. Anyway, he wanted to see Julie again, maybe play her some songs, tell her about Brenda. Probably just look at her for a while.

He was right: Lynne was there; she smiled when he came in. He raised his eyebrows, which was enough to ask if there had been any change. She shrugged and shook her head. He looked at Julie—the bruising around her face was healing and, without the expressions of life or the trauma that had shrouded her immediately after the accident, she looked younger. And thinner. In fact her body seemed to be retreating into the mattress. And she looked peaceful, which made Michael look away. He didn't want to think of her as being at peace.

'I didn't get anything from James's place in the end. I thought about what you said, and I spent more time at Brenda's than I expected.'

Lynne was looking through the CDs, nodding. She took the green cardigan out of the bag. 'I bought her this years ago,' she whispered.

'Really smells of her,' said Michael.

Lynne put the cardigan beside Julie and smiled. 'Now, what music shall we play first?'

54

Christopher did as he had done before. He called on the group members and asked them to come with him. He imagined that Julie, Gabriel, and Yvonne sensed his sadness, his fear. He walked between the bruised and embittered Kevin and Gabriel to ensure no further violence could occur. Not that Kevin was in any sort of position to do anything. His head and hands were heavily bandaged and he was limping slowly. People left the physical pain of life—and in Kevin's case, death—behind them when they came there, but they got to keep whatever they experienced with the angels.

As Clemitius said, 'We don't want to encourage any of that dissociation nonsense.' So Kevin was going to be aching for quite a while.

The rest of the group couldn't have cared less. They didn't say very much. Julie caught Christopher's arm as they walked down the corridor, heading for the same door that he had led them to on their first day.

'Are you OK?' she whispered.

His mouth was too dry to say anything so he smiled, touched by her concern.

Outside the light was beautiful. Full of freshness and the promise of new beginnings. Christopher took a deep breath. He never tired of light, even when it was incongruous. As before, other groups and other angels were gathered in a semi-circle, and it struck Christopher that he would feel embarrassed when Peter called him. He smiled to himself, and thought, It's funny, you can live for a thousand years or more, you can be taught to look for meaning in the lives of others and to develop insight into yourself and your own feelings about the world, but it can still come as a surprise to remember that you are at heart, quite shy.

Peter emerged from the quiet but attentive crowd. Dead strangers watching with a dulled curiosity. They were all now in therapy and aware of the limitations that faced them. They were less capable of surprise. Peter looked around him. Everything went quiet. Clemitius came and stood beside Christopher and Kevin, staring straight at Peter. He looked the way he looked in the group, smug and unsympathetic. As Peter began to speak, Christopher took a small step forward.

'Hello again,' Peter said softly. 'I seem to recall saying recently that this kind of gathering was not normal, and yet here we are once more.' He looked around. 'This ... experiment ... in helping has not always run smoothly. Like many projects, it has brought out the best and the worst in many of us.' His eyes rested for a moment on Gabriel and Christopher.

'Sometimes when we look at the world we see ...' he paused. 'No, let's not blame the world. People and angels have more in common than perhaps we realise. All of us, after all, are looking for meaning. People look for it on earth; we look for it in the tasks we are given by God. But I think that maybe the best of us are the ones who can live well without answers. Living with not knowing what is true, or what is going to happen to us, is the test we all face. Inventing answers, resolving conflict ...'

And then his voice grew quieter. 'It is a type of retreat, a retreat from the glorious uncertainty that is life. And when we do it badly, poor therapists who want to write people's lives like children's stories, or false gods who send stupid rules to earth for people to do bad things with ... then it is a wrong ... nearly wicked. Life is precious, beautiful and precious and chaotic. It should never be crushed.'

'I think Peter has been drinking,' whispered Clemitius. 'This is embarrassing.'

It's true that it wasn't like Peter: he looked uncomfortable. Christopher didn't want that to be the last thing he saw. He took a step toward Peter, hoping to remind him why they were there. Trying to help him. Peter turned and faced Christopher, raising his hand to stop him. He stared into his eyes and smiled. Christopher stood still.

'Not yet,' he said quietly. 'I'm sorry, I don't want to burden you all with my rambling and no doubt unhelpful thoughts, although ... I believe we should ask ourselves more questions than we are accustomed to, about whether what we do is good or bad.' He sighed. 'Let us return to the task at hand. We are here again for a banishment.'

He turned to Christopher and the group. 'You really should know who you are.'

Christopher took a step forward. Behind him Gabriel and Julie both stepped forward, too. 'Hang on,' said Julie.

'No Christopher, not you,' said Peter. 'Clemitius, step forward. And bring that murderer with you, please.' Clemitius didn't move. He just stood there staring. Then he slowly turned to Christopher and Gabriel, his fat lips dry and trembling.

Gabriel said, 'That nice man up there just called your name.'

Clemitius edged forward. Kevin stood still.

The silence was broken by Yvonne half-shouting, 'Excuse me, when you said, "Bring that murderer with you please," did you mean this murderer here? The one who in fact murdered me, or are there others present? Because if there are others, you need to be more specific; if not, well this one's name is Kevin. We call him Kevin the Killer.' And she shoved him hard in the back.

Clemitius and Kevin walked slowly forward. Kevin limped even more heavily; Clemitius, head bowed, looking for some confidence, some understanding. They made their way to Peter, who looked past them toward the rest of the group.

'Surely there has been a mistake,' said Clemitius.

'There have been thousands, I suspect,' said Peter. 'But yours is the one I'm interested in today. You sent this, this—man—

back to earth to kill another man out of spite. I don't know what you think you are, but whatever it is, you are wrong.'

'It wasn't me,' whispered Clemitius.

'Really?'

'It was them ...'

'You are an arrogant fool.' Peter turned to Kevin. 'And you, you don't belong here. You belong elsewhere.' And Kevin vanished into nothingness, leaving nothing, nothing at all. 'Do you have anything to say?' Peter asked tightly.

'I think ... I think you seem angry, Peter, and I am wondering if maybe you are putting that anger somewhere it doesn't belong. Christopher ... . It was Christopher who took the group away from what they should have been doing, and it was me who tried to bring them back to the project. I did what I did—and let's face it, I only moved us a step nearer the inevitable—in order to focus the group's attention on the important matters. That is what we are doing here, that is our project, a project to cleanse and help them. I think this process throws up a lot of feelings, but we need to be clear about where they belong before we act upon them ... .'

'I am deeply disappointed in you, and angry, and sickened. I believe those to be appropriate and healthy responses in the face of what you have done. And it seems to me that you are failing to reflect on your actions, your responsibilities, and your moral obligations. Now, one of the benefits of banishment, for you, will be an eternity to reflect. And for us? We just won't have to listen to this overly refined, bloodless, and soulless twaddle ever again. You are banished.'

Peter looked at the lake. After a moment's pause, Clemitius started to walk slowly toward the black flat water. As he got the edge he hesitated.

'What will happen to him?' whispered Julie.

'Nobody knows for sure,' Christopher said. 'He will live on earth, although not as he is now.'

'Might he go back as a cow?' asked Yvonne. They looked at her.

'I was just wondering,' she said. 'To me there was always something cow-like about him.'

Clemitius put his foot in the water and the skies grew cloudy. He waded in until he disappeared. He didn't look back—hardly caused a ripple. After a few moments the crowd began to disperse. Gabriel and the remnants of the group stood quietly until they were the last ones left outdoors.

Peter walked over.

'I thought it would be me,' Christopher said.

'What happens now?' asked Yvonne.

'Nothing,' said Peter. 'You are, I'm afraid, dead.' Gabriel stared at the lake, Yvonne at the ground.

'Julie isn't,' Christopher said.

Julie blushed. 'I'm sure it's just a matter of time.'

'Why? Why is it?' said Gabriel. 'You just said life is precious and shouldn't be crushed.'

Michael and Lynne had tried three CDs and a compilation tape with David Bowie, The Clash, and some very old soul on it. Lynne had told Michael that Julie made tapes for people she liked, but didn't always give them to them. 'Why not?'

'Because she liked listening to them, of course.'

'Of course.'

'What is this Paul Quinn CD?'

'Ahh she loved that, bought it for everybody she knew.'

'Didn't bloody buy it for me,' muttered Michael.

'She would have.'

Michael put it on. A deep, rich voice sang 'Will I ever be inside of you?' and Michael listened. The song went on forever: six, seven, eight minutes. It sounded clean and dark; a chopping guitar, some kind of weird opera bridge. Some harmonies. More guitar. What a beautiful voice. 'Meanwhile, back on earth,' the singer crooned.

Michael had listened to it in the car; it had suited the night skyline over the city more than it suited this little dusky room. He imagined being outdoors again, cool air on his face. He imagined a park, lying on his back, looking at the stars, listening to this music with Julie, and her telling him how she came across it, and why it was important that everyone she knew should own it. It was a good song. Michael was tapping his foot.

And then he heard what sounded like a child coughing, and he looked at Julie, who was looking back.

The ever-diminishing group stood staring at the black lake in silence, watching the clouds slip away and the bright early autumnal light return. There was no breeze. It was neither warm nor cold. It was as it had been the first time, but without that thin, deluding hope.

'I'm sorry.' Peter said softly. 'There is nothing we can do. In the scheme of things, a death is merely a death. They happen every day. It is hard for us to experience it as...well, as you do. As something bad.'

Gabriel stared at him. Tears were running down his cheeks.

'I am truly sorry.' And he was. It was just a death, and it wasn't the death of a happy man, which somehow matters to the angels in a way that might not make sense down there. They have a sense of life as being temporary, a sense that too many people appear to have lost. The angels expect it to shine and they expect people to enjoy it if they can. Of course, they are aware that many can't: the hungry or the pained for example. But mostly it can be done, and if you don't—well, the view from where the angels stand is that it's your own damn fault.

But Christopher had journeyed with Gabriel and had watched Ellie. It was hard not to feel for what they were, and what they wanted to be.

'It was too brutal,' whispered Gabriel. 'Too sudden—not complete.'

'Nothing is complete,' said Peter.

'I mean I didn't just die. I lingered, I saw. And I was powerless ... always powerless.' Peter didn't say anything. Christopher did. 'The flowers.'

'Pardon?'

'The flowers: before the accident you sent some flowers to Ellie. I've, er ... I've sort of been holding them back.'

'Holding them back?' said Peter. 'Your level of interventionism is really something we are going to have to talk about. How exactly?'

'I just helped the order get a little misplaced.'

'And the card?' asked Gabriel.

'Yes, the card as well. You could rewrite the card here. You will have to be relatively circumspect of course, it will have to be checked, but ... what do you think, Peter?'

Peter grimaced a little and he pursed his lips. He nodded once. 'But Christopher? This kind of thing has to stop now.'

'Yes.'

'I mean it.'

'I promise.'

'What do I say?' Gabriel stammered. '"I know that I haven't seemed myself ..." No, it's not about me. "Please don't ever doubt how much I have loved you ..." No, too Whitney.' He closed his eyes and thought of Ellie. 'I want to say ... to tell you ... I want you to know that the thing that will define my life as well-lived, is you. That every day I spent before I met you was spent waiting, and every day afterward was spent wondering what on earth I had done to be so lucky. You were the first thing I thought of when I woke up in the mornings. I want you to know that I am sorry for any moment of any day that I let you feel less than the only triumph in my life ...'

'Oh bollocks' he said out loud. 'I've got a better idea.'

'What?'

'Could I skip the goodbye in exchange for a small miracle?'

And now Christopher was sitting staring at the lake. Everyone had gone and he was expecting to have incoming, of course. A ready-made group from the explosion in Norfolk. The angels weren't finished with this project yet, and with James and Alice, Adam, Bernie and Gary Guitar, there would be some work to do. But for now it was quiet, and Christopher still didn't know if he had done good or bad. He believed it would have been hard, at any point, to have done anything differently. And he thought that the thing about people is they always want more: you give them a hairdryer and they want a trouser press; you give them satellite and they want Internet access. Show them the viewing room and they want editing rights.

Christopher saw Julie after she woke up. He watched after the crying had stopped. There is a point when the celebration ends, when people stop hugging and dancing around, and they draw breath. It happens when a child is born, a life is saved, or a crisis averted. In that moment you see for the first time what your life looks like, what it feels like when you get what you have wanted.

Sometimes, more often than Christopher would have liked to believe, they find they still want more. That dreams coming true just isn't enough. They want a trouser press, too. When Michael stopped hugging everybody—Lynne, Sarah, the nurses, a cleaner—he stopped and stared at Julie.

She stared, wide-eyed, back. 'You been here all the time?'

'Yes, well no, I went to get some of your things. Lynne, Lynne has been here all the time.'

'He's been here,' said Lynne. 'I like him.'

'Good,' said Julie. 'Did I miss our date?'

Michael nodded.

'Got any more?'

'Yeah,' he said. 'Although I should tell you something.'

'Have you got back with that Teletubby?'

Michael laughed. 'Never mention that again, anyway she wasn't a ...'

'So what?'

'Well it occurs to me that … well. Fuck it. I love you. Didn't think I'd get to tell you, what with the coma and all, but you're awake and it's true. Thought I'd better own up. I love you.'

And Julie just smiled and said, 'Good.'

55

Ellie was sitting on the sofa, half-heartedly going through a box full of papers. Bank statements, mortgage letters, car insurance. She was vaguely hoping to find something about Gabriel having taken out a pension without telling her. She didn't expect to find anything; he wasn't really the type.

She put the papers down and looked behind her. The emptiness was different now: it is a different kind of silence when you know the person who is out is not coming back. Not that she could bear any noise. No music, no radio. The quiet made sense, in as much as anything did.

When she was small, Ellie would walk to school and try not to tread on the cracks. Stepping on twenty cracks meant she was an elephant. When she got a little older, not stepping on the cracks meant more: it brought small rewards. It meant the boy she liked in the class next door would like her too, or she wouldn't get into trouble for not knowing how to do long division. She made deals with a universe she hadn't even met, just like she had been doing for the last year or two.

'I won't want anything again. Just please let me have a baby.'

Gabriel used to whisper, at the beginning at least, that people didn't really understand just how special making a life was, until they were told they couldn't do it. He believed it too, but he realised it made him sound bitter rather than profound. And anyway he realised that he was saying it on the off chance that some God he had never believed in might mark him down as a man who has learned the intended lesson, and send him some more sperm as a reward.

For the past few years, when they made love it was tender and despairing. Afterward they would hold each other and talk softly about miracles. Sometimes they would giggle at the idea of a confused and lonely tadpole paddling its way toward an egg. 'Swim, swim for your life, little fella,' Gabriel would say. 'And you,' he teased Ellie. 'Put your legs in the air! It's hard enough as it is without gravity crushing down on the little chap.'

Later, as Gabriel turned inward, he would mock himself by ranting at a world that took so much for granted. 'The problem with modern life is there is too much bric-a-brac. Every other shop, in every other town, sells rubbish. Shiny stones, crystals, porcelain cats, painted boxes, crystals with porcelain cats in them, decorated mirrors, maps to places that don't really exist, bracelets made out of soot. It's all rubbish. We have too much money and we don't know how to value anything anymore. That is why so many people are unhappy.'

Although Ellie knew that was not why he was unhappy.

When he retreated, so did she. And they both became fearful. Ellie wouldn't step on the cracks. Gabriel wouldn't do very much of anything.

'What would I give?' he would ask himself. 'You could have my dreams and my liver and even the sunrise, if that helps. I'll stop being sarcastic; I'll stop being angry. I'll be small, so small nobody can see me. I'll be pretty much whatever you want me to be; I'll surrender, if you let me be the father of Ellie's child.' Like anyone was listening. And sometimes, when they lay together in the dark, still, barely touching but awake, Ellie offered up the same.

She put away the papers; there was nothing there. She went to the kitchen for more toast. Later Moira would come round with organic pasta and an expensive yet disgusting fruit drink with added goodness. They might go for a walk in the park. Ellie didn't want to go to the shops in case she found herself looking absentmindedly at baby clothes. Too many cracks. She couldn't drink coffee, so she made tea. She didn't want the television and she didn't want to read. She ate a rice cake, thought about tidying the bedroom, but preferred it in a mess. She looked out of the window: it was cloudy, a little grey. She touched her stomach, she imagined Gabriel kneeling down beside her and whispering to Lola and Luca, 'Hold on tight, and grow.' Because he would have, had they got this far before he died.

The doorbell rang. She carried on looking out of the window. There was some blue sky under that grime, she thought, and some light.

The bell rang again. She wasn't expecting anyone, so she walked to the door slowly. When she opened it, there was nobody there. Resting against the door was a mixed bouquet with two small sunflowers. Not the sort of flowers you send when someone has died. There was a scribbled note on top that read, 'Sorry for the delay in delivery.' Ellie closed the door. She put them down and went to get a vase, thinking, Delay?

There was a card attached—damp, crumpled, but clear. Her eyes caught fire and the words blurred.

She looked at the bouquet. The sunflowers were not ready to open yet, but they would be. And when they did they were going to be quite, quite beautiful.